The Queen's Lady

Ladies of Justice, Volume 1

Laura Henning

Published by Laura Henning, 2024.

This is a work of fiction. Similarities to real people, places, or events are entirely coincidental.

THE QUEEN'S LADY

First edition. November 10, 2024.

Copyright © 2024 Laura Henning.

ISBN: 979-8227150530

Written by Laura Henning.

This book is for my husband. The love of my life, my best friend, and the one I get to annoy most forever.

Prologue

Lady Sariah Fortham headed to the Queen's chambers. She had specifically requested that Sariah attend her this morning. Usually that meant one of two things: Sariah did something to make her angry, or the Queen had an assignment for her. She looked around as she walked down the hallway. The castle she called home was nothing to look at in terms of luxury, but was instead more functional. The hallway ended in a sturdy wooden door that was flanked by guards.

She approached the guards and curtseyed, as was expected of a Queen's Lady. The guards bowed to her and opened the door to the Queen's room. Sariah was a bit apprehensive, but as a Queen's Lady, it was nothing unusual to be asked to attend Her Majesty. She walked into the room, and took a seat on one of the plushly cushioned sofas that Queen Elliana was wont to keep for guests. Crossing her legs at the ankle and tucking them underneath her, Sariah got ready to wait. Queen Elliana wasn't known for keeping guests waiting, but it was early enough in the morning that she might not be ready to receive yet.

As Sariah was smoothing down the skirt on her ruby red dress, Elliana walked in with a smile. "Good morning, Lady Sariah. Thank you for coming to me so early." Lady Sariah nodded her head in acknowledgement of her thanks.

"As always, it is my pleasure, Your Majesty." Queen Elliana sat down across from Sariah, and leaned a bit forward in her chair. Sariah could tell that she had something important to tell her, and that from her posture, it was something she was not exactly excited to share.

"Lady Sariah, I have a mission for you. As a Queen's Lady, you are particularly trained in espionage." Sariah nodded her ascent. "Lord Darian Thomas has long been in the trading game. He is a dangerous man. He controls a vast army, and is not opposed to hiring mercenaries to help him get his way." Queen Elliana paused to collect her thoughts. "I am seeking an alliance of some type with him. A trade alliance with a power such as his would be quite beneficial to our people, and our country. I'm not sure what kind of man he is, and am afraid that he might jump straight to a marriage alliance between the two of us." Queen Elliana appeared quite concerned about this thought.

Lady Sariah nodded to Queen Elliana. She had an idea where this was going, but she wanted Queen Elliana to fully get her thoughts out before she decided how to respond. Taking a breath, Elliana continued, "I need you to go to his kingdom, and get some information about him. He is known as somewhat of a womanizer, so, if you're not opposed to seducing him, it would potentially give me an out of his proposal if he insists on it."

Lady Sariah considered what Elliana had said. She was not opposed to using sex for information if she needed to. She was not a particularly prudish person, but she also didn't just have sex with anyone anytime she wanted. Seeing how much it could help Queen Elliana though, she thought in this case, it could be needed. "How long would you like me to stay there?" Sariah looked up at Elliana with a determined look on her face. She had decided.

"I would need you to go there, become known to him, and gather as much information on him and his workings as you can, in any way that you can." Queen Elliana took Sariah's hands in her own. "Please be careful. There are some stories out there about Lord Darian, and they are not pleasant."

Sariah had been trained in hand-to-hand combat, as well as with various weapons. Her body, albeit curvy, was muscled and honed.

She was a fighting machine when she needed to be. "I'll be careful, Your Majesty, I promise." She bent down and kissed Queen Elliana's hand. "I will leave tomorrow morning, and will send word once my work has been completed." Sariah stood up, and then curtseyed, waiting for the Queen to pardon her.

"Thank you, Lady Sariah. I shall look forward to any reports you are able to send." Queen Elliana motioned with her hand, and Sariah left the room, already packing her trunk in her head. She knew that Queen Elliana would have to send a letter of introduction since Sariah was not invited to Lord Darian's court. Sariah walked down the hall, hoping that this mission would not take too horribly long, and she'd be able to return home soon.

Chapter One

A man climbed up a small mountain face to a cave that he knew was just up ahead. He had a woman slung over his shoulder, her wrists and ankles bound together so that she would not fall as he climbed. The cave was a secluded place, in the middle of a forest, on the border of two lands. A major road ran through these forests, a trading road.

He reached the landing where the mouth of the cave was. It was a natural landing, one that only someone who knew where the cave was would be able to find. It had been used in the past by lovers for trysts, and by bandits for a hideout. Today it would be used for a different purpose. Setting the woman down near the ledge, he scoped out the cave.

He stood silhouetted against the entrance of the cave. He was speaking to himself. "I'm not sure where to go from here. My world is shattered." He began pacing a bit as he spoke. "My love is gone. She didn't die, oh no. She decided to leave me. Betray me. She was bound to another. Another man, another woman, I don't know. I don't care." He paused his pacing, and looked towards the back of the cave. "I would have given my life for you. Died for you. Killed for you. And yet, what do you do? You leave." He looked back out of the cave.

"There's only one thing left to do. If I can't have you, no one can." He turned away from the view; the sun was just coming up over the forest, and he looked towards the back of the cave again. She lay there, unconscious. "I'll wait. I want to see your face when you realize what is coming. You need to pay. You need to feel the pain that I feel, knowing that we'll be apart." He put his hand on his chest over his heart. "You tore my heart out, and ripped it to pieces. You'll learn. And you'll die."

Sariah clenched her fist and winced in pain. She was laying on a cold stone floor. She couldn't remember how she got here, why, or even where she was. She laid still, taking stock. She could tell she'd been in a fight. Her head was sore; someone got a good blow in there. Her ribs too. She'd be surprised if she didn't have a cracked rib. Her hair was loose around her head- someone had ripped out the bindings, leaving her long, raven black hair to create a halo around her head. She was lying on her stomach, and she closed her eyes against the lit sky. Even though she was in a cave she was pretty sure the day was dawning. She could tell that much from the smell of the air, and the way the light permeated it.

She heard movement from the direction of what she assumed was the mouth of the cave, and she immediately froze. She was not alone. She did not know what her situation was, or if she was with friend or foe. Assuming her company is the one who brought her here, either they rescued her from an unfortunate situation, or they were the one who gave her the aches and pains, and put her in her current predicament. She shifted a little, trying to feel if any of her weapons were still there. Her belt was missing, which meant that her short sword and at least one of her daggers had been stripped from her. She flexed her calves a bit, trying to make it look like she was just stretching. Dammit. They took her boot knives too. She could tell her leather bracers were off her wrists, so they also got her throwing knives. Whomever was in the cave with her did not want her to wake up armed.

Her situation still did not tell her if she was with friend or foe. Since she was moving around, she assumed that they knew she was awake, or at least waking up. She was sore enough that moving very quickly would be painful, but since she didn't think anything was broken, she thought she could manage it. The one question was whether or not she had a concussion. If she had a concussion, all bets were off.

Whomever it was, they were waiting patiently. Whether it was not to startle her into action, or for some other purpose she wasn't sure. But she knew she'd have to act soon. She was stiffening up on the floor, and moving quickly would soon not be an option. She tilted her head up a little so that she could observe her watcher through the curtain of her hair. All she could see clearly was that he wore soft, grey riding boots, those of the wealthy, and that he was definitely a man. No crests or signs that could tell her who was with her.

"M'lord!" The call came from a long way off, and the person calling was clearly shouting. "Dammit all to hell." The blood in Sariah's veins turned to ice. She knew that voice, intimately. "What is it?!" he yelled down to whomever was calling to him. He clearly did not know that she had awoken, and for that she was grateful. She knew that when she faced him, she would have to have her wits about her, or she would fail.

If looks could kill, Darian would have the head of the page riding towards him. "I told all of you that I was not to be disturbed. My business with Sariah is of the utmost importance." He yelled down to the page. He started mumbling to himself again. "I need to see her. See the truth in her eyes, hear it in her voice... right before I run her through with my sword. Or, maybe, I'll embrace her, almost as if to kiss her. Start to tell her everything is alright before stabbing her in the back with one of her own daggers." He turned to look at Sariah's unconscious form again. "You came fully armed, and I have to admire the amount of steel, as well as the quality of the steel that you carry."

He rubbed his hand over his mouth. "Is it any wonder I fell for you? The idea of your betrayal makes me see red, literally. I want to bathe in your blood as it sprays from your body. Maybe that could wash away this hurt; the pain I feel when thinking of my woman... *MY* woman." He was so angry that he was almost panting at this point. He was also pacing again. Sariah was still holding as still as possible. She could not believe what she was hearing from his lips. He sounded like a madman.

"You belong to me. You know you belong to me. Why would you ever try to leave?" He paused for a moment, and looked at her before continuing with his tirade. "Your blood, covering me, is the only thing I believe that could cleanse me of your love. Your enchantment. I know that there is no way that I could be this obsessed with any woman without magic being involved. I am such a great man, and have so many people that I worry about other than myself- why would I focus on this... this... scrap of a girl? One who was oh so far below me."

Sariah was angry and worried by the words she heard. She thought that she could take him in a fight if they were on even ground, with equal weapons, or hell, if she was armed at all, but now? With him having the advantage of her? She honestly wasn't sure. She focused on her breathing, making sure to breathe steady, even breaths so he would think she was still out.

"M'Lord!" the page shouted again. Darian snarled, showing his teeth at the boy. "I'll be down shortly. Leave me be." He began to turn away from the boy, but another voice called out. "Lord Darian! Your King commands your presence, immediately!" Darian froze, his head still turned towards Sariah, clearly thinking his options over. Sariah held her breath, while the man before her considered his options. She heard his footsteps come nearer, and knew it was not going to end well for her... If only she knew what to do or say to him, if she could remind him of their love... but words failed her.

He stopped right next to her. He made no move, no sound. Finally, he tapped his fingers on his leg, as he was wont to do when we was contemplating something. In one swift move, he reached down and grabbed Sariah's hair, exposing her neck. He slipped one of the daggers he took from her into his palm. "Your bracers are quite ingenious," he admitted. "I will have to replicate their design." Sariah was struggling against him, but in order to hold her still, he put one of his boots in the small of her back. He looked into her grey eyes- icy as the ocean waters in a winter storm, and without saying anything, slit the knife along her throat, spilling her blood on the ground below her. He smiled and wiped the blood off the blade with a kerchief, slid the blade back into the bracer, and walked towards the entrance of the cave.

Sariah tried to gasp- she couldn't get enough air. When he had dropped her back to the stone, her face landed in the hot pool of her own blood. She looked towards the mouth of the cave, watching him walk away. The small smile that he gave her right before he slit her throat was pure evil. It was a smile that he had given her many times before, but usually it was reserved for the bedroom, before he did wicked things that made her gasp and writhe in pleasure. As the cold set in, Sariah couldn't believe that this was the end. She felt she had barely lived. She had so much left that she wanted to accomplish. Her vision began to go dark. She reached one hand out towards the mouth of the cave, beseeching. Not to him, oh no. She knew she'd get no mercy from him. Whom she was reaching out to, she wasn't sure, but she knew she needed someone, and that no one was going to come for her. As the last breath shuddered out of her body, Darian had made it to the mouth of the cave, looked back once, and walked away.

Chapter Two

Slowly, light and sound came back. The aches and pains that Sariah had felt before were multiplied substantially. Her head felt like it was going to explode. She breathed slowly, checking for additional damage. What had happened? She remembered waking up in the cave, remembered someone with her, and then.... Nothing. She heard a strange scratching near her head, and gingerly tilted it up so she could see what it was.

A small black crow hopped towards her, its claws making the scratching noise she heard. Its glossy black feathers reflected what little light there was of the day. When it was a few inches away from her face, it tilted its head at her, looking at her with one eye, and then the other. It opened its mouth to let out a caw, but no sound came out. Sariah shut her eyes, and just focused on breathing. If the carrion crows had come for her, she knew she was done for. When she turned her head back, she realized that the stone under her cheek was sticky. She grimaced, and made to wipe her face, but stopped. She was laying in a pool of a viscous substance. It looked black, and had an odd smell to it.

Slowly, since her body still ached so badly- it felt like she'd been run over by a herd of horses- she sat up. She looked over to where she had last seen the crow, and it was still sitting there, this time completely still, with all of its attention focused on her. She made a shooing motion with her hand. Since she was obviously still alive, this crow was going to be deprived of its dinner.

Rather than flee, the crow merely cocked its head at her again, as if to say, "Really?" Sariah sighed, and turned away from the crow. It was clearly no threat to her. She surveyed her surroundings, but they looked the same as she remembered- a stone cave, fairly small, with one end open to the darkening sky. Sariah frowned. When she woke up before, day had just been breaking. Now, it seemed the sun was setting. How long had she been out? She looked herself over best she could in the gloom, using her hands to assist her search when something felt particularly tender.

She realized as she took inventory that the stuff she was lying in was all over her front. She sighed again. It wouldn't be the first time she'd gone home covered in some unknown goo. At least this should come off fairly easily as long as she didn't leave it too long. She moved to get up, when she realized that she still didn't have her weapons. She felt around on the floor, getting herself out of the sticky substance, but to no avail. Whomever had been with her before must have taken them. That stung. She usually carried a small arsenal with her, all of which was quality steel. It would cost her dear to replace her blades. She also had a small emotional hitch, and frowned at the cave. While she didn't love her blades per se, she was attached to them. And learning a new blade took some time. So, to her? This was a blow.

Sariah stood up, feeling a bit unsteady, closed her eyes and just held still for a moment, hoping for her vision to stop spinning. All of a sudden, she had a flash of memory, like a dream, but she was still awake. It was Darian, giving her that wicked smile she loved so much. But this time, rather than giving her pleasant tingles, she felt dread. She got chills and felt sick to her stomach. She grabbed her stomach with both hands and doubled-over some, feeling like she'd just taken a fist to her belly.

She heard that small scratching again, and cracked one eye open, seeing the crow hopping towards her. "You're still here, hm?" The sound of her own voice shocked her into standing up straight. She instantly regretted that decision, and stumbled over to one of the cave walls. She used the wall to hold herself up, and looked over at the crow. It cocked its head at her again, and opened its mouth with that silent caw. Sariah's voice, which had once been called smooth as warmed whiskey by some, was raspy and gravelly. It reminded her, honestly, of the sound of a crow's caw.

Pursing her lips and looking down at the cave of the floor, Sariah shakingly reached a hand up to her throat. Not sure what she was expecting to find, but needing to explore it anyways, all she felt was the black stuff from the cave floor, and her own smooth skin. Well, almost. She also felt a line across her skin, like she had fallen asleep with a blanket under her. Again, she had that feeling of dread in the pit of her stomach, but she couldn't figure out what was causing it. Looking up from the floor, Sariah cast her eyes to the mouth of the cave. She was not looking forward to figuring out how to get home from here. She was not even sure where "here" was. She had a feeling that she had a long walk ahead of her.

Sariah let out a deep, rattling sigh. Jumping a little at the sound, she looked at the crow again. "Well, that's going to take some getting used to." She paused and cleared her throat before continuing. "What do you think? Wanna come for a walk?" The crow cocked its head at her again before spreading its wings and taking off out of the cave. Great. Now she was alone again. Even though the crow couldn't talk back, having something there with her was a small comfort. "Guess not. Okay, no worries. I've got this."

Sariah slowly and shakily stepped towards the mouth of the cave, using the cave walls to help make sure that she wouldn't fall and injure herself further. Eventually, she made it out, and into the night air. For she had indeed been right, night had fallen, and the last of the sun's rays could just be seen on the horizon. She took a deep breath, and felt a little tickle in her throat, which made her bend over in a coughing fit. She was glad she still had been holding on to the side of the cave wall, otherwise, she might have tumbled over the edge.

Looking around, Sariah realized that she was in a cave that was on a rocky mountain face. She wasn't too far up, and would be able to make it to the ground, even in her injured state, but if she had fallen, it would most definitely have hurt. She took in her surroundings, trying to see any landmarks or signs of humanity that could help guide her. She sat down at the edge of the cave, deciding to wait a few minutes to see if smoke from any fires would become visible as people began needing the light.

A very patient woman, Sariah took a few more breaths, starting shallow, and then deepening them each time she breathed in. By slowly expanding her lungs, she found she was able to breathe easier, and avoid further coughing fits. She had her legs crossed, and her hands were on her knees. She looked out again over the trees, and closed her eyes, trying to get her equilibrium back. Something big had happened, she felt, and it left her uneasy that she couldn't remember it.

Sariah heard a rustle in the air, and opened her eyes. She looked around for a moment before she spotted her little feathered friend. The small crow landed next to her on the stone. "You're going to need to find a place to rest, friend. Crows are day birds- you'll have trouble seeing soon." The crow ruffled the feathers on its head and blinked at Sariah. Sariah thought the little bird odd, but then again, she wasn't about to turn it away. She had been hoping that maybe her voice would return fairly quickly. It sounded almost like she'd been yelling too much. Since it hadn't happened so far, she thought maybe if she could find something to drink, it would help.

Sariah sat by the entrance to the cave for a while, looking for signs of life. She eventually spotted the smoke from a fire not too far away. Must be a hunting camp, she thought. She made the decision to head that direction, hoping that she could at least gain some insight as to her location from whoever was bedding down in the forest. She stood up, and made to reach down for the crow. It made a short flight to her shoulder, however, seeming not to want to be alone, either. Well, at least she had a traveling companion, even if it was a silent one. The crows' claws dug gently into Sariah's shoulder, not enough to cause pain, but enough that she wouldn't forget that they were there. She stood up straight, and made one last look around the cave. Not seeing anything of hers in the cave, or anything useful, she got down on her hands and knees, turned towards the cave, and started to climb down to the ground.

Sariah slowly climbed her way down the rock face. She wasn't up very high, thank goodness, but without leather gloves, and with her sore body, the climb took longer than she'd usually have liked. She also picked up several scrapes and bruises from the rocks, since she was climbing barehanded. Her crow friend occasionally flew off her shoulder and back as she climbed. She wasn't sure if it was getting upset at being jostled, or just wanting to look around. Either way, it didn't stray far, and always came back to her.

When Sariah's feet touched solid ground, she let out a breath she didn't know she'd been holding. She found herself ensconced in trees, the base of the hill or mountain- she wasn't sure which, having been covered in growth. Sariah paused for a moment to take in her surroundings. While she didn't feel like she was being pursued, she was always cautious. And with her current memory lapse, she wanted to be extra cautious.

When she detected no unusual noises for a forest at dusk, she picked the direction she thought most likely to lead her to the hunting camp, and set off. She had little trouble seeing- full dark hadn't set in yet, and she had seen a waxing moon cresting the night sky as she climbed down. Having grown up near the forest, she was no stranger to nighttime among the trees. She was carefully stepping so that she wouldn't trip over any tree roots or fallen branches. The toes of her boots would be shiny, having rubbed so many rocks by the time she was out of the forest.

Her crow friend ruffled its feathers again as it huddled down on her shoulder, closer to her neck. Crows don't have the best night vision as a rule, and they were a particular favorite prey for owls, so, it was not a surprise that the crow wanted to be as close to her as possible. As far as crows go, it was on the small side. She reached her hand up towards the crow, and the crow gave her a small nip. It wasn't painful, and seemed almost playful. Sariah knew that she'd have to figure out what was going on with this crow at some point, but for now, she was happy enough for the company.

After walking for a while in the same direction, Sariah began to see a glow a little off to the right of the path she was forging. She slowed her pace to help hinder any excess noise that she was making. Soon, she also smelled smoke from a fire. She paused to consider the situation. She knew she was almost upon the camp, but, not knowing who or what she would find, she didn't want to stumble into something that she couldn't handle. While she was unarmed, as a member of the Queen's Ladies, Sariah was trained from her adolescence in hand-to-hand combat. While many thought that the Queen's Ladies were merely pretty handmaidens that helped the queen, in reality, they were her additional bodyguards. Why send a Queen into a ladies only area with no one to guard her? The Queen's Ladies fixed this problem.

Even though Sariah was good without a weapon, she was still a young lady, and was smaller than most men. She knew that she had physical limitations in terms of hand-to-hand combat, and would hate to find herself among a large group of burly men who showed intent to harm- or worse. Part of Sariah's training was subterfuge, so she had very little trouble switching over to a slower and quieter walk. She took her time, measuring each step carefully so as to not break any sticks, or rustle any leaves and give her position away.

As she neared the clearing that the camp had made, Sariah crouched lower to the ground to survey the scene. Her feathery friend held utterly still as she creeped towards a tree that would shield her while she took stock. She heard some soft nickering not far off, and a couple of large bodies shifting. Horses, and they knew she was there. There was very little noise in the clearing which was a bit unusual for a camp, unless, like their horses, they too knew she was there. Senses on high alert, Sariah inched closer to the tree. She wasn't expecting the scene that unfolded before her eyes. She stopped, and considered what she had found.

A single man sat on a fallen log that he had dragged near his fire. His head was bowed, his long hair swung forward over his shoulders. He was wearing a cream colored linen tunic shirt, and grey leather pants. His boots were black leather, and appeared well-made. She couldn't see his face, but his shoulders were broad, and his pants were tight enough that she saw he had very muscular legs. He held a stoneware mug in his hands, light grey with a seemingly random blue decorative design on it. His hands looked rough, with dirt on his knuckles and around his nails. He appeared to be dozing, or maybe drunk. However, Sariah would not leave her life to chance. She would proceed as if he were awake, aware, and ready to fight. There was no food currently on the fire, but she saw the remnants of a hastily-made spit with the remainder of dinner on it set off to the side.

Sariah's stomach rumbled, but she pushed her hunger down. She couldn't afford to steal food right now- not with the man so close, and her not knowing what he was doing there. She wasn't starving, just hungry, so she must have eaten within the last twenty-four hours. She saw the horses that she had heard on her approach on the far side of the man, tied together with a lead, and then the lead tied to a tree. They had packs on the ground near them, and while their blankets were still on their backs, they were currently unsaddled. Seeing the packs, Sariah realized that this was a traveling vendor, or a merchant who was moving wares. He was likely to be armed to protect his goods. She looked back at the man, and found his bright green eyes staring at her. She froze immediately, not even breathing. She felt the prick of a blade at her throat at the same moment.

Chapter Three

Sariah slowly held her hands up to show she wasn't armed. "Stand up. Slowly." The voice was male, and tense. Sariah stood up, trying not to move as much as possible. The man clearly knew what he was doing with his blade, and while the point was still on her skin, he did not cut her. She moved to turn around, and he pressed the blade a bit more firmly. "No. Don't turn around. Walk forward. Towards the fire." Something nudged her a bit in the small of her back.

Sariah didn't have much choice, with that blade at her throat, and so she walked forward. The crow shifted a bit, but also held very still on her shoulder. As she walked into the clearing, and came somewhat into view, the man by the fire looked her over, but said nothing. "I'm going to frisk you for weapons." Sariah nodded slightly so that the man behind her knew that she had heard him, without making enough movement to startle him, or make the blade pierce her skin. Seeing her acceptance, his hands made a businesslike but thorough perusal of her body and clothing for any weapons she might be carrying. Finding none, he stepped back, removing the blade from her throat. "You may turn now."

Turning slowly, and keeping her hands raised, she saw the man who had managed to take her by surprise. He was dressed in all black leather, and had a balaclava style mask on, so that all she could see were his eyes. And what eyes they were. Rich velvety brown with flecks of amber like warmed whiskey. His skin was tan, and that's all that she could tell. He was dressed for night stalking, and he looked every inch the predator he was embodying. He wore a black leather vest that had convenient straps, loops, and pockets on it so that he could store weapons or items. His pants were tight but she could tell would allow easy movement. While she was looking him over, he did his own perusal, a frown appearing on his face, and getting darker by the second.

The crow ruffled its feathers, and let out its silent caw at the dark man. He scowled at the crow and Sariah both. "You're a lot younger than I expected. And unarmed. Are you a vagrant?" He seemed genuinely confused by Sariah's appearance. Well, that made two of them. If she could answer him as to why she was unarmed, she'd be happy to. Sariah put her hands down slowly, since he had seen for himself that she had no weapons to reach for.

She had to clear her throat twice before she could reply confidently. "Sir, I mean neither you nor your companion harm." She paused a moment, and cocked her head a bit, deciding what to say. "I am unsure of my direct location, and seem to have lost my way." When you're not sure of whom you're facing, or what they might already know of you, try to stick as close to the truth as possible. Sariah didn't feel any threat from these men, but she had no idea how she had arrived in that cave or where her weapons had gone, so she knew she needed to be cautious.

The dark man looked a moment at his companion before considering the slight girl before him. He rubbed his hand over his mouth, and then remembered that he still had his balaclava on. He slipped the hood off, revealing his face. His look was still stern as he took her in.

Sariah looked his face over after he removed his hood. He had long black hair, braided down his back. Dark eyebrows over his eyes, with a scar just below his left eye. Strong cheekbones, and a long straight nose. Full lips that were over a squared chin. He was not handsome in a conventional way, but he had a roguish look about him- although his outfit could be giving him that air. However, Sariah remembered the way he handled his blade, which she now saw was a dagger he still held in his hand. He also had a longsword that she saw now at his side, and thought better of the outfit. This man knew what he was about. And roguish seemed to be the right word for him. She shifted a bit from foot to foot as the men scrutinized her.

He considered her again before looking behind her at his companion. "Well, my lord, what do you want to do?" Sariah's mouth opened a bit in surprise at the question. She had pegged the situation completely wrong. Sariah turned slowly to the man behind her, giving a slight curtsey. He gave her a regal nod of his head before pulling his hair back into a ponytail at the base of his skull. His hair was the color of honey- not quite brown, but not blond either. He had sat his mug down, and was looking Sariah over carefully.

"What's your name, girl?" He didn't say girl with any sort of inflection, just using it as a moniker since he did not have a name for her. She could tell he meant no offense.

Sariah dipped into a courtly curtsey as she responded, "Lady Sariah Fortham, m'lord. Member of the Queen's Ladies to her majesty Queen Elliana Grace of Blackmore." She stayed in her curtsey as was the custom. Since the man was above her rank, she needed to wait for him to make the first move. The silence in the clearing was deafening. She was not the only one who had misjudged the situation. She raised her eyes a bit to the man by the fire. His jaw was slack in shock, before he quickly recovered.

He shook his head slightly, as if to clear the fog from his mind. "Forgive us, m'lady. We had no idea that you were of the nobility. There are bandits about, and with our goods, we must be cautious." He motioned to the horses as he spoke, and he was contrite in his response. Sariah stood from her courtesy and gave his apology a nod of her head. "I am Lord Heath Sandram, and this is my friend and guard, Sir Javier Rahul." She turned to glance again at the man at her back. He put an arm across his midsection, and bowed to her in a very gentlemanly way. His scowl had disappeared, but he still frowned at her slightly. Behind her, Lord Heath spoke again, "Please, tell us how you came to be here with no escort and no belongings but the clothes on your back, and what we can do to assist you."

Sariah turned back to Lord Heath, and placed her hands together demurely in front of her. She knew the reputation that the Queen's Ladies had, and she knew how to play her part. "My lord, I am honestly not sure how I came to be here. I woke up not far from here with no escort and no horse. I am clearly in riding clothes, so, as far as I can discern, I was out riding, and perhaps was thrown by my horse. I do not seem to be injured badly, although I am a bit sore. I saw the smoke from your fire from where I woke up, and decided to see if I could find help." She lowered her eyes, and stood still, waiting for a response. She was still mostly in the shadows, having only stepped into the clearing far enough for the men to have made out that she was no threat to them.

"Come closer to the fire my lady. It sounds like you have had quite the ordeal." Lord Heath motioned to the log he sat on, and made for her to sit near him. She assumed that he meant for her to join him to ascertain more of her story. She was weary, and hungry, and the company would be welcome, although she would stay on her guard. Something about this situation didn't quite seem real, although as far as she was able to tell, everything was above board.

As Sariah walked further into the clearing, and came closer to the fire, the men saw her more clearly, and she quickly found the blade pressed against her throat again. Startled by their response, she froze, putting her hands back up. The crow on her shoulder took flight at her sudden stop and the men's movement, and settled on a branch above the group. Sariah wondered what had caused them to react this way. She really was a Queen's Lady, so that could not be in question. "What are you playing at?" Sir Javier snarled at her from behind. The look on Lord Heath's face had likewise turned dark.

Sariah stammered a bit, as she really wasn't sure what to say, since she didn't know what had startled them. "M'Lord, Good Sir, I know not what you refer to. I am just looking to find out where I am, and how I can get back to my Queen." She was unable to turn, since Javier had the blade pressed against her throat tighter than before, almost to the point of drawing blood. She took shallow breaths, worried that breathing too deep might cause the blade to pierce.

The men shared a look. Sir Javier moved the blade just enough back that she could move her head a bit, but still kept it close, letting her know where she stood. "Well miss," Sariah started a bit at the demotion in title, but let Lord Heath continue... "your appearance does not exactly match your story." He motioned to her, and was clearly looking at her attire. Sariah had not had a chance to clean up yet, it was true, but she didn't think a little mud or dirt would cause such concern. She looked down at her clothes, and gasped. All down the front of her clothes, over her hands, she was covered in blood. Sariah started shaking before her legs gave out. Neither man attempted to stop her fall, and she slid bonelessly to the ground. The crow flew back to her immediately, and landed on her shoulder, angrily but silently cawing at the two men.

Sariah held her hands before her, her mouth open in shock and awe. She had no memory of where this blood could have come from. She remembered waking up in the sticky substance on the floor of the cave, and suddenly, her awakening took on a whole new light. However, for that much blood to have been on the floor, someone must have died there. Sariah's face became deathly pale. While Sariah had killed before in the line of duty, she was no murderer. And there was no dead body around her when she woke up. This must be some kind of trick. Animal blood poured on her by whomever left her in the cave, to frighten her when she awoke. Well, it was certainly working.

Sariah looked up at the two men from her position on the ground. While she was technically in a vulnerable position compared to the two men, she was not helpless. She could easily take Javier down with a swipe of her legs, and charge for Heath. The Lord appeared to be unarmed. But other than showing her some hostility at the sight of her being covered in blood (and she really couldn't blame them for that), they had shown no signs of harming her until that point. She considered the situation, looking from one man to the other. Javier had moved the blade quickly when Sariah fell to the ground so that he did not accidentally cut her. Sariah looked down at the hands in her lap. She had to say something. She held her hands up towards them, and opened her mouth to speak. Her world suddenly went black.

Chapter Four

Sariah woke slowly, blinking her eyes. She was getting very tired of these new sudden naps. She shivered a bit, and realized she was laying on her back outside. She opened her eyes fully to see white above her. She felt damp, and realized she was in a mist.

She sat up slowly, but realized all her aches and pains were gone. Looking around her, she realized that she was in a field of some kind. The men were nowhere to be found, and there was no sign of the camp or the fire. There was grass and purple flowers all around her, although she could not see very far due to the mist. Thinking of the men she just left and the name of the lord, she realized it was heather. She was in a misty field of heather.

She heard the sound of large wings approaching, and the biggest crow she'd ever seen in her life landed a few feet in front of her. It was almost the same size as Sariah when she was sitting down. Sariah reached out to touch the crow, but it opened its beak and let out a low, rattling caw. The caw was not a normal one, but sounded instead like the rattling of bones. Its silky black feathers had a sheen to them, like oil on water- almost like a rainbow.

Sariah pulled her hand back, but the crow made a little hop towards her, and cocked its head at her, blinking the one eye she could see. It ruffled the feathers around its neck and leaned towards her. Sariah reached out and gently pet the crow. The feathered body shuddered and closed its eyes in bliss, and she scratched its neck a little, allowing it to turn this way and that so that she could get all the itchy spots. After a moment the crow opened its eyes back up and hopped a little away from her. Sariah watched the crow closely, but she never saw the change.

All of a sudden, Sariah was looking into the stormy grey eyes of a woman swathed in black layers of a gauzy material. Her hair was black and long, but it was very unkempt. There were bits of twigs and leaves woven throughout it. Sariah even thought she saw some small bones. But there was something about her black hair. It was very fine, almost feathery. And that's when Sariah realized that the hair closest to the lady's scalp was indeed a fine down, rather than normal hair. She opened and closed her mouth a few times, wondering if she was dreaming. People did not turn into crows, and vice versa. She thought of her new crow companion.

"Have you ever wondered what happens when you die?" The woman's voice sounded like it came from everywhere, even though her lips never moved. Sariah was startled by the loudness of the sound, and the woman's lips quirked up into a slight smile.

Sariah realized what the woman had asked, and pondered for a moment. Before Sariah was able to formulate a complete answer, the lady cocked her head at Sariah, much like the crow had. "Well, child, now you'll never have to."

Sariah's mouth opened in disbelief as what the woman had said finally sunk in. "I'm dead?" She asked, her voice shaking some. She felt a tugging at her memory, like a moth beating against the glass of a lantern. Something was there, but she could not bring it forth.

The woman looked at her intently, before her voice came again. "Not anymore. I brought you back from the brink. You are one of mine now."

Sariah stared at the woman before asking angrily. "What happened? How did I die?" She figured Javier must have run her through with his sword, and silently cursed him.

"Sir Javier is an honourable man. He'd never kill an innocent." Sariah figured she must have spoken that part out loud, until the woman continued. "I am The Morrigan. Also called the Great Battle Crow, or just The Crow. You do not need to speak for me to hear your call." The woman paused to let that sink in for a moment before continuing. "I have need of you, Sariah Fortham. Your innocent blood was spilled in rage. This cannot stand. My link to the mortal world took her last breath some time ago. I am in need of a new one." She paused, and looked around, frowning, as if she lost something. She shook her head a little and focused back on Sariah.

"She who becomes mine will mete justice upon those who prey on the weak. She will be the voice of those who cannot speak for themselves. She will be judge, jury, and executioner. You have had a hard life, and yet your heart remains pure. Even in the face of evil you did not falter. You will be mine." The woman spoke with such a surety.

Sariah moved to speak but paused, waiting. The Crow nodded her head, giving permission for her to speak. "Do I have a choice?" The Crow pondered Sariah a moment, cocking her head from one side to the next. Though the movements should look strange, since she was still in her human form, they looked right on her. Normal.

"Yes. There is always choice. But with choice comes... *consequences.*" The Crow's last word had such a sense of finality to it that Sariah instantly knew what she meant. If Sariah didn't accept The Crow, she would no longer walk among the living. The Crow would return her to her rightful place among the dead. Sariah swallowed in fear, and then again in anger. She clenched her fists, but rather than anger a goddess with words of spite, Sariah waited, and thought things through.

Slowly, Sariah's anger cooled as she thought. While it seemed unfair at first, she realized that rather than trapping her in some form of servitude, The Crow was giving her a second chance at life. To be able to make a difference in her world. "How long would I be yours?" Sariah had a feeling that there had to be a catch to it all, and she dreaded whatever that catch would be.

"As long as you wish it, and as long as your heart remains pure. If you choose to no longer be mine, you will cease to be. If your heart becomes tainted, I will exact vengeance upon you." This was not said with malice, but was stated as a fact. The Crow cocked her head again at Sariah, waiting for her to work through what she had said.

Sariah knew that she really had no choice. If she wanted to remain alive, she would have to accept what The Battle Crow was offering. "If I became your arm of justice, does this mean that I would be killing people? I'm not opposed to killing when it's needed, but I do not want to become an assassin." Sariah, with her training as a Queen's Lady, would be a fitting arm of justice. Her training, both in hand-to-hand combat as well as with weapons would allow her to exact justice with violence if that is what The Crow meant. She also believed strongly in right versus wrong, and felt that right should always prevail- which she knew was not always the case. She was torn over the idea of taking lives needlessly.

"My dear child. Your moral goodness is what allowed me to pull you back from death's grasp. I would never ask you to do something that would taint those beliefs. No, with the exception of the one who sent you to your death- which, I leave to you to decide his fate, you will not be making those decisions, or carrying out the sentence."

The Crow seemed to be contradicting herself. Sariah was utterly confused, and bowed her head to tactfully ask, "My Lady, you just said that the one who is your arm of justice becomes judge, jury, and executioner. If I am to do that, how am I to avoid bloodshed?"

The Crow smiled at Sariah, and it was not all together a sweet smile. It made Sariah a bit uncomfortable to see, in fact, since it seemed a smile that promised blood. "Child, I also said that you would become *mine*. I mean this in the literal sense. I would be able to embody you upon your missions for me. You would still be there, and would still remember everything, but we would be a shared consciousness in that time and space. My... avenger, let's call her...

allows me to walk among mortals, albeit for a brief time only." Her smile was almost wicked by the end of her speech.

Sariah was a bit worried about that smile, but she didn't feel any malice from her. More than anything, Sariah was still confused by The Crow. Sariah was mostly a normal woman. Why was she chosen? The Crow said she was pure of heart, but she had her faults... The corner of The Crow's mouth quirked up at that. Sariah remembered that she could hear Sariah's thoughts. Sariah ignored that fact, and continued to think. Saying it all out loud would be weirder than The Crow just being able to hear it. "I don't remember my death. Will I know who did it if I meet them?"

The Crow's face turned grave at this. "I have the means to provide you with the memory if you wish. It is not a happy one. And it would most likely take you a long time to recover. If you choose not to take it now, it will come back to you when you see the person who took your life. Regardless of what you choose, you will remember it at some point." The Crow steepled her fingers, and set her chin upon them, contemplative.

Sariah was quiet, thinking again. She was not sure what she wanted to do. She had decided to take The Crow up on her offer, but she wanted to stay here a bit in case she had more questions. However, the sky started to darken. The Crow turned her eyes upward and frowned. "Since I know you've decided to become mine, it seems we are out of time. Your small crow companion is also mine. She cannot speak, but she is a great listener. If you have need of me, let her know, and I'll come to you that night when you sleep. If the matter is urgent, I will come immediately, and take you as I have now, or I will join you in your quest. Until then..." The Crow leaned forward quickly, and laid a gentle kiss on Sariah's brow, before Sariah's world went dark once again.

Chapter Five

Sariah came back to herself very quickly this time. She found she had some very large, warm arms around her. But that was only to steady her. She was riding on a horse, and from the color of the hands and sleeves around her, Javier was the one steering the horse. She looked down and saw that her hands were loosely bound by some rope to the horn of the saddle. She could easily escape them, and realized they were just another way to help steady her through the gait of the horse. "Come back to us, have you?" Javier asked with a slightly amused tone.

Sariah cleared her throat a couple of times before replying. Her voice was still very raspy. It was at that moment that she realized that when she had been with The Crow, her voice had been back to normal. "What happened?"

Javier got silent for a moment, as if deciding what to tell her. She saw Lord Heath ahead of them on the road they were traveling. The fact that they seemed to be on a main road was somewhat reassuring. Had they planned on killing her, she assumed they either would have already, or at least would not be traveling where they could be seen with her. "You collapsed. We both kind of stood there a moment trying to decide if you were pretending to get out of answering our questions. When we realized you were not, we cleaned you up best we could with some water and a rag before deciding to move on. Since you claim to be a Queen's Lady of Queen Elliana Grace, we decided to head back to Blackmore Castle to take you to her. You've shown no violence towards us so far, even though I believe you had plenty of time if you had chosen to, so, I volunteered to take you on my horse. Besides that, I'm his Lord's guard as he mentioned. I have been for many years. I was not about to take a chance with his life now."

Sariah tried sitting forward a bit to get some space between them, but her body ached once again, and she found she was extremely tired. She sighed and leaned back into Javier's solid chest. He was very warm, which felt good in the cool evening air. "Sleep if you can, Lady Sariah. I won't let you fall." Sariah believed what he said, partly because he sounded earnest, and partly because The Crow had given him a good reputation. While she leaned back into him and tried her best to not bother him, she was not able to sleep. She rode for a while in silence.

"Do you have some water, Sir Javier?" Sariah was parched, and she thought maybe the water would help soothe her throat. She was still confused at the sound of her voice. She had no pain in her throat, and other than feeling a little dry, she had no discomfort with it. She reached up with her bound hands, and rubbed her throat. As soon as her fingers touched her throat though, her whole body stilled. There was a rough line across her throat. She had thought before that it was just a crease of her skin. She began feeling it with her fingers. It went across her whole throat. She felt Sir Javier become still behind her then as well, when he realized what she was doing.

"I do have some water, yes. We were going to ask about that mark on your throat. It's certainly an interesting scar. It almost looks like your throat has been cut. Must not have been too deep since you are still alive... or must have been something else all together. When did it happen?" She felt him reaching towards his belt, presumably to grab a flask or a water skein. His stiff posture belied his innocently curious tone. He was wondering if she were a criminal of some type who had escaped execution, she was sure. Or something just as damning.

"I honestly don't remember it." Sariah left it at that. She did not have this scar before today. She was sure of it. And with its location, her new raspy voice suddenly made sense. A flash of a memory hit her suddenly- the feel of a knife on her throat. It was not when Javier took her by surprise. This was across her throat, and was her own blade. Remembering what The Crow had told her, she quickly pushed the memory down, knowing that she needed to stay in the present and alert at the moment. While The Crow had given Javier a good reputation, Sariah still did not completely trust him, especially since she was unsure of what was going on with herself. All of a sudden, she felt small claws land on her shoulder, and a beak nuzzle at her hair and ear before it took off again.

"Your little crow companion has been doing that every so often since we left the camp. Do you have it trained to your shoulder? It's dark, but we've kept to the road where it's mostly clear. It has had little trouble keeping up with us." Javier sounded amused rather than annoyed by the small corvid.

"I'm not sure how I managed it, really. She just kind of showed up one day, and has never left. She seems quite attached to me, and I don't mind her company, so, I guess she is mine. I haven't named her yet though." Once again, Sariah was sticking as close to the truth as possible. She smiled at the thought of her small crow friend traveling with them. She was still not alone, even here with these strangers. Again, she remembered a snippet of the conversation with The Crow, and how if she was needed, Sariah just needed to tell her feathered friend.

Sariah saw Javier reach one arm forward, holding a water skein. She leaned forward a bit, and fixed her mouth on the spout. Javier tipped it up for a moment, and then quickly back down, making sure he did not give her too much water. A moment later, at her nod, he did it again. She pulled her mouth away from the skein, and cleared her voice again, realizing now upon hearing the sound, that nothing of this world would be able to return her voice to what it once was.

"Thank you. I needed that." She felt Javier nod behind her as he took the water skein back to affix to the horse.

"Are you hungry? We had finished dinner when you showed up, but I do have some bread and jerky I could get for you." Javier seemed totally at ease with Sariah, although she had a feeling if she tried anything untoward, he could and would take any means necessary to disable her.

"Thank you, but no. I was just a bit thirsty." While that was a lie, Sariah was not about to have him hand feed her while she remained bound, and she knew that there was no way he was going to loose her hands before they made it to Blackmore.

Javier chuckled behind her. "You're a horrible liar."

Sariah scoffed at that.

"Your stomach gives you away, my lady. Please, let me help you get some food." He chuckled again as she felt him moving around behind her, presumably to reach his rations.

Sariah was truly offended at him calling her a terrible liar. Clearly she was a great liar, or she never would have made it in the Queen's Ladies. But, just like the general public, Javier would have no knowledge of what the Queen's Ladies really were. He probably thought she was a silly little palace girl, or, at worst, a lying thief, and perhaps murderer, based on all of the blood she still wore. She thought of what Javier had said, how they cleaned some of the blood off of her. While she was not a modest person in general, the idea of strange men being in control while she was helpless made her eye twitch. However, since her clothes were still on and covered in blood, and it just seemed that her hands and neck had really been cleaned, she wasn't too concerned.

A moment later, Sariah felt Javier's arms come around her again. He pressed a roll into her bound hands. "I figured starting with some bread would be easier on your stomach. When you're ready for the jerky, let me know, and I'll get you some of that."

Sariah was grateful that he did not try to feed her. That felt like an intimate thing, not something she wanted to share with someone she had just met, and who held her all but captive. Intimacy was a strange thing for Sariah. Being raised with a group of women from a young age, small things with men felt intimate. Sex was just sex. She understood sex. It was a biological imperative.

Sariah thought as she ate, and as they rode along the road. Growing up with royals, she learned about sex early. And being in the Queen's confidence, and among her personal guards, she had seen sex and lovemaking on more than one occasion. She was able to tell the difference between coupling and passion. And don't get her wrong, being a woman herself, she had taken part in her fair share of sexual encounters. But she'd never thought of them as anything more than scratching an itch, or satisfying curiosity. She was not immune to the feeling of Javier's arms around her, nor his warm musky scent that seemed to surround her. But as he'd shown no inclination, and the situation hardly warranted it, she was able to focus on more important things- like staying alive, and getting herself back to Blackmore.

When the thought of staying alive came to her, she remembered what The Morrigan had said about wondering what happened when she would die. "You'll never have to." Sariah wondered what exactly that meant. She did not mean to test the limits of her new benefactress, but she wondered if she'd be harder to kill, or if it would even be possible to kill her while she was working for and with The Battle Crow. She looked around a bit, trying to gauge her surroundings.

"Where exactly are we? When I woke up before I came to you, I couldn't see far enough away to see any settlements." Sariah needed to get her bearings so that she'd know where to run if she needed to escape. She did not believe that Lord Heath or Sir Javier meant her any harm at this time, but they were not the only threats out there. If they were set upon by bandits, for example, she did not plan on being helpless.

"Blackmore Castle is about half a day's journey down this road. We plan on going without stopping. Lord Heath is very concerned for you. While we at first thought maybe you had killed someone, after seeing the scar on your neck, he's more worried that maybe you were attacked and do not remember it. Especially if you really are a Queen's Lady." Javier was very factual, and did not spare her feelings at all. It was clear that he doubted who she was, and what she was doing so far away from her "home." However, it seemed he was willing to follow his Lord's lead to a point. Javier was clearly dangerous, and able to take care of threats. If the situation were a little less dire, she'd be inclined to like him. As it was, she was reserving judgement.

"Your doubts are interesting, Sir Javier." Sariah adopted her upper class tone for this and straightened her spine, as a Queen's Lady would, since she meant to put him in his place. "Especially since I'm apparently such a horrible liar..." He again chuckled in amusement behind her.

"Well, my *lady*," he paused, making sure she heard the emphasis on her title, "your story has some obvious holes in it. And as you came to us covered in blood, without an escort, we were duty bound to assist, even if we were unsure of your true motives." She heard him get serious when he was talking about her state when she came into the camp, but he was amused again by the end. He would be fun to cross swords with, if he was as talented with a blade as he was with his banter.

Sariah tilted her head back, being careful not to hit Javier, but trying to spot the moon. Since they were heading into Blackmore, she knew they would be on one of two main roads. And if Javier was telling her the truth about how far away they were, she wanted to know what time it was.

Javier bumped her forward a bit with his shoulder. "It's around midnight. We should get to Blackmore about sunrise." Sariah sighed again. Nothing for her to do for the next few hours then. She once again leaned back into Javier's chest, and closed her eyes. She trusted him to get her home safe. Soon, she was dozing.

Chapter Six

Sariah opened her eyes just as the sky started to lighten. While she hadn't been able to sleep, she dozed off and on, enjoying the feeling of the horse moving under her, the man at her back, and the knowledge that just for a little bit, she didn't have to remain on high alert. She looked around a bit, but saw nothing to either side of her to tell her quite where they were. Up ahead she saw some fenced pastures, so she knew they were getting close to civilization at least.

Since she had sat forward, alerting Javier that she was awake, he said, "We're on the outskirts of Blackmore. We'll be in the village proper soon." Javier didn't sound tired at all. He had not faltered all night, never once letting his charge slip from his arms. Sariah wondered at his strength. The man must have trained like a gladiator to become so strong and resilient. She wondered how his training compared to her own.

"I don't think I've ever come into the village this way. Nothing looks familiar. What direction is the lake from here?" Blackmore Lake was a large lake that took its name from the village and castle nearby. Its waters were dark, so the name was fitting. Parents often liked to tell their children stories of monsters in the deeper parts of the Lake, and that naughty children were what kept it fed. Sariah looked around to see if she could see the lake, or the mountains, or anything that would help her figure out where she was.

"The Lake is to the North East of here. The village is directly East down this road. We'll be there shortly." The trees were giving way to more farmland. Sariah preferred the Eastern side of Blackmore. It was not yet cleared, so the forest gave it a dark and wild feel. And from that direction, the moment you cleared the trees you could see the Lake. It was truly a sight to behold. Since it would be a while before they would reach the village or the castle, Sariah realized that she should find out more about her companions.

"Does your Lord do business with Blackmore and Queen Elliana, or will I need to broker an introduction?" Sariah was uncertain what the welcome would be for the two men if they showed up with her tied to the horse. In the growing light, she could see that her clothes were still crusted with blood, and she was sure that her appearance would startle and frighten anyone they would come across. She was not looking forward to facing the Queen's Guards this way. Alas, there was nothing that could be done about it. Had they gone the way of the lake, she could have persuaded the men to let her freshen up a bit before they approached. As it was, she was just going to have to figure it out as she went.

Javier spoke up behind her, "He does not often do business with Blackmore, no. However, he is not unknown to Queen Elliana or her court." Sariah started a bit at this. She'd been with the queen for over half of her life now, and had never heard of Lord Heath's name, nor did she ever remember seeing him in court before. "His Father and Queen Elliana's father were arranging a marriage of his Lordship and Queen Elliana's sister before the elder Lord Sandram's untimely death. Lady Sandram decided that Princess Ariana would not suit her son's lifestyle, however, and broke off the engagement. Neither side was overly upset, I'm told."

Lady Sariah smiled at the last words. "Princess Ariana has been married for many years now, and happily. I'm sure there is no bad blood remaining with Queen Elliana. She dotes upon her sister as well as her niece and nephews." Sariah smiled wider, thinking of the young children. They often came to visit the castle, and trouble seemed to follow them wherever they went. "Regardless, you're returning one of her Ladies, so that should garner you some good will." Sariah smirked a bit at the thought of her being a damsel in distress. She could play it up if she needed to, but she was no damsel.

She had to admit though, that currently, she was in a bit of distress. Once she was armed, and was able to change her clothes though, she would feel much more like herself.

Javier did not respond. Sariah assumed she had answered any doubts he had about their welcome at Blackmore, and that he was not one prone to conversation without cause. This suited her quite well, as she also was not one for small talk. Sariah shifted forward a bit in the saddle, trying to stretch out her back. Being a fair horsewoman, her bottom wasn't sore from the saddle, but riding in front of someone, slightly hunched over all night had given Sariah an ache in the small of her back. Javier must have realized what she was doing, for he grabbed the reins in one hand before placing the other on the small of her back. "Please, m'lady, allow me to get this knot for you." Sariah nodded, and Javier quickly and efficiently worked out the knot. Since they were already sitting so close together, the act did not seem like something overly intimate, and was rather a kindness. Or he was just annoyed that she was shifting so much trying to get comfortable.

The rest of the journey was spent mostly in silence, as the whole party was starting to feel the exhaustion of not having slept all night. Sariah had gone longer before, but it was never easy when she had to be on high alert and she was sleep deprived. In the village proper, she had slumped forward. She kept her breathing easy and steady so as not to startle Javier, hoping that he would just figure she had fallen asleep. Her hair had swung forward, which covered most of her from view. This was her intention so as to not scare anyone in the village as they rode past. She was not unknown in the village, and if word of her state got to the castle before she did, she was afraid of their reception.

As they approached the open castle gates, she saw movement on the walls, as well as near the gates themselves. The guards were mobilizing. It was an odd hour for someone to be showing up unannounced, she knew. And with her looking fairly helpless like she was, the guards were bound to take notice.

Sariah looked around through the curtain of her hair. Thankfully it hid more of the gruesome aspects of her appearance, so that they did not startle any of the villagers, as she intended. The guards were thicker than usual at the gate, suspecting trouble from the unannounced trio, she assumed. There were several guards she recognized. She did not want to excite them by revealing who she was, so, she said under her breath to Javier, "Lift your right hand as if you're signaling to someone. Then call out that you're a party seeking shelter, and you have a message from me." She barely moved her lips, and kept it as quiet as she could, while making sure he still could hear her. He did as he was bid, and Sariah saw some of the guards relax a bit. That changed when Luc recognized her, and the predicament she was in.

A particular favorite of the guards, Sariah had befriended a few by giving them gifts. Luc was a mountain of a man. Married to one of the other Ladies, he was allowed in on the secret of the Ladies, and he had become Sariah's regular training partner. He treated her like a little sister, and seeing her tied to a horse, apparently injured, and at the mercy of two other men had fire in his eyes. He moved his hand to the hilt of his sword when he saw her make a cutting motion with her right hand. At her signal to stand down, he moved no more, but he left his hand where it was. Luc knew Sariah, and knew what she was capable of. Hell, he had taught her much of her subterfuge and moves in her adult life. Damsel in distress she was not, but she could tell he was unnerved seeing her like this.

Putting a friendly smile on his face, and raising his left hand in greeting, Luc left his right hand on the hilt of his sword. He approached the trio as they came closer. "Good morning gentlemen. Miss." Sariah could tell that pretending he didn't recognize her when he saw all of the blood down her front took everything in Luc's being. She knew that he was ready to rip these men off of their horses and behead them on the spot for having touched her. Whomever caused this atrocity would pay the price with their life.

Sariah felt Javier stiffen behind her at Luc's approach. She knew he wasn't buying the gold ole' boy act. She was going to have to diffuse the situation and quickly, or someone was going to die. She cleared her throat a couple of times before speaking. "Luc, I'm okay. I need you to stand down." Luc's shocked look at the sound of her voice had him gripping the hilt of his sword tighter. Javier tightened his hold on Sariah, she assumed reflexively. Either that, or he was about to do something really stupid. "Luc, I promise, I'm alright. Let us through, and follow us so that nothing bad happens, and I'll explain all."

"FUCK." Luc nodded his head in ascent before shouting a command to let the party through. His language let her know that he didn't like it, but knew that if they weren't going to shed blood here at the gates, he really didn't have a choice. Once they were through the gates, they were in a large open courtyard, where off to the side was a set of small stables and hitching post for mounts that would only be there a short while. The larger stables were beyond the castle walls. Luc followed Javier's horse closely. She could tell that he was not about to let her out of his sight. She hoped that she could come up with a good explanation for all of this, or there would indeed be blood spilled over these cobblestones.

Javier did not relax at all as they moved into the courtyard. She figured he saw the archers on the walls, some leveling crossbows in their direction. There were soldiers everywhere, armored up, and fully armed. Few seemed to be paying attention to the small party that made its way towards the stables, but all who were in the courtyard were eagerly and discreetly watching and listening. "Is he someone to you?" Javier asked Sariah.

Not knowing exactly what he was getting at, Sariah said confusedly, "What?"

Javier tried again. "This Luc. Is he your lover or your husband?"

Sariah snorted. "He is the husband of one of the other Ladies. He is like a brother to me." Sariah's voice sounded weary. After the trip, she knew she was in for a long day, so she was trying to conserve all of the energy possible for explanations. All of a sudden, her crow friend landed on her shoulder. Startled, as she didn't realize it was still following them, Sariah stiffened, and Luc made a noise. "It's all right Luc. This is sort of a pet of mine now." Luc saw the crow, and scowled a bit.

Javier sounded surprised as he murmured to Sariah, "The way he reacted, and as familiar as you were with each other, I suspected some type of romance. A brother-like relationship makes sense though as well." Javier had relaxed a bit. Luc, on the other hand, anyone could tell, was unnerved. It was understandable, seeing a woman he thought of as his sister showing up covered in blood. Sariah knew that the rage Luc was exhibiting was held in check only by her words. She wondered if Luc thought that he and Lord Heath were the cause of the blood. If that was truly the case, she was surprised that Luc had held on this long.

Once they reached the stables, Lord Heath dismounted, as did Javier. Steadying Sariah in the saddle from the ground, he untied her hands, before helping her off of the horse. While she could dismount by herself, she wanted to keep close to Javier. She was the only one who could absolve them of any wrongdoing. Luc moved towards Sariah with his hand held out. "Lady Sariah, please step over here. I will escort you to your rooms where you can clean up and change before meeting with Her Majesty." Luc clearly wanted Sariah away from the men, but whether it was to question her on what happened, or to have the men detained for questioning, she was not sure. Javier put a hand on her shoulder. Rather than fighting him, Sariah leaned into his touch, and looked up at him. He seemed a little surprised, and looked down at her with a frown.

Luc watched this interplay intently. Sariah could tell that he was bursting with curiosity, but she would not let anyone know anything until she was ready. Showing that she did not seem frightened of the men, and they did not seem harsh with her, he relaxed a fraction. "Lady Sariah, please let me escort you." he tried again. She knew he wasn't going to give up on getting her away from the men, but if she really was against it, he would at least go with the group to make sure she was not there under duress. She smiled at Luc in gratitude, thankful to have such a man watching over her.

"Sir Luc, may I introduce Sir Javier Rahul, and Lord Heath Sandram. I came across them when I was in need, and they were so *kind* as to escort me back to Blackmore." Sariah put emphasis on the word kind, but other than that, she sounded tired. She knew she needed to get cleaned up, and word of her arrival would have already reached Queen Elliana. However, she did not feel that she could let Lord Heath or Sir Javier on their own right now. With how she looked, she was genuinely worried for their safety. "Sir Luc, I would be eternally grateful if you could escort them to guest chambers. I can make my way to my chambers on my own. Thank you." She gave Luc a look that he recognized well. She had made up her mind, and no one was going to change it.

She turned towards Sir Javier. "Sir Javier, I appreciate your assistance in bringing me back to Blackmore. I need to clean up and change, but I will meet you gentlemen in the main hall later, where you will be presented to Her Majesty." under her breath, so that only he and Luc would hear her, "I promise, you will not come to any harm. Luc is a man of honour, and I trust him with my own life. I know he will take me at my word when I say you are not to be harmed." She looked over her shoulder at Luc, making sure he had heard. He nodded his head at her almost imperceptibly. She knew that he trusted her judgement, and that he would hold his own until he knew more. Sariah curtseyed to Sir Javier, then to Lord Heath before turning towards the main doors of the castle, and walking stiffly through them.

    She stood just inside the doors where no one in the courtyard could see her. As much as she trusted Luc, she knew that this was an extraordinary circumstance. Sir Luc looked between the two men. "M'Lord, Sir Javier, if you would please follow me." He waved a hand to motion to someone behind them. "Our stable boys will see to your horses, and make sure they are comfortably settled for the duration of your stay." His words were curt, but not unkind, and he bowed a bit, directing the men towards the castle doors with an outstretched hand. Javier and Heath looked at each other for a moment. Javier twitched his shoulder a bit, but began to follow Luc. Lord Heath followed Javier. They didn't seem overly happy, but they didn't really have much choice at this point. Seeing that things were well in hand, Sariah turned and walked towards her room.

Chapter Seven

Sariah had an awkward moment when she found her room locked, and realized that she didn't have the key. She was able to hunt down a maid, who was able to get her into her room. Once there, and alone, Sariah took a good look at herself in her looking glass. She sure wasn't much to look at right now. Her grey riding outfit was most likely ruined by the blood. She walked over to her bath, and pulled the cord for warm water. Sariah loved the fact that Queen Elliana had spent the money once she was Queen to get running water indoors.

Sariah sat on the lip of the tub, running her fingers through the clean, warm water that was filling her tub. She stood up, and started removing her clothes, taking stock of her body as she did so. She found numerous new bruises under her clothes from having fought her unknown assailant. Her ribs were tender, but not cracked, she thought. She felt each rib with her fingers, moving them from her waist up her belly to just below her breasts. Nope, just bruised, she decided. Fully undressed, she moved back in front of her mirror, turning this way and that, trying to see just how badly she was injured. From what she could see though, she just had bumps and bruises.

She turned back to the tub, keeping an eye on the water level, and went over to her trunk. She took a dagger out, and carried it over to the bath with her. Once the tub was filled to her satisfaction, she stepped in, pausing a moment as she adjusted to the heat. She set the dagger down within reach but out of sight of anyone that could possibly come in the room. Her aches and pains did not like the heat at first, but she knew that once she was submerged, the heat would help to soothe. There was some blood on her breasts, which was to be expected, if what she thought happened did indeed happen... for now though, she banished that thought, and decided to finish bathing. Plenty of time for introspection later.

Sinking down to her chin, Sariah sat in the warm water to think. Sariah heard the sound of wings, and then her crow perched on the edge of the tub. She lifted a finger out of the water to the crow. It nipped at her finger playfully, then rubbed its beak and the side of its face on her finger. "You need a name, little friend. The Crow did not tell me your name, so, I guess we'll have to figure one out for you, hm?" At her question, the crow made her silent caw, and blinked at Sariah. "Your eyes remind me so much of the moon on a winter's night." They were a bright, whitish gray, compared to the shiny black of the average crow. "What about Luna?" She smiled as the crow ruffled its neck feathers, and nuzzled her finger again. "Well, Luna, what kind of mess have we gotten ourselves into?"

"Lady Sariah?" came a voice at her door, followed by a knock. Recognizing the voice of one of the servants assigned to assist the Queen's Ladies, Sariah called out to let the girl know she was welcome. Since Sariah had locked her door, the girl needed to use one of her keys to open it, but that's why the servants had keys to the Ladies' rooms. The girl blinked at the crow, but didn't say anything, and continued into the room towards Sariah's bed. A large four-poster bed, Sariah had it covered in satin and velvet. She loved the feel of lucious fabrics against her skin, and it was one of the few places she could really indulge herself.

"M'Lady, Her Majesty asked me to bring you a fresh gown and stockings. She also wanted me to bring word of your well-being to her. I guess your appearance has created a lot of gossip in the castle." Maddie was the servant girl that helped Sariah most often. She laid the dress on the bed, and stood next to the bed, waiting for Sariah's message back to the Queen. Sariah looked over at Maddie and gave an exasperated sigh.

"Maddie, for heaven's sake, have a seat. You know I don't hold such formalities with you." Sariah was doing her best to break the servants that attended her of all of the little trivialities that other nobles or Ladies might make them observe. She knew that most of the Queen's Ladies had once been servant girls themselves, so they did not observe the formalities of court with the servants. A few of them though thought it was their due to be treated like nobles. She did not begrudge them their feelings. They had all had hard childhoods, and deserved some niceties. They were never rude or cruel to the servants. Neither she nor Queen Elliana would have stood for that.

"Lady Sariah, you know I prefer to stand. Do you need assistance washing your hair?" Sariah shook her head no, and began to think about what she was going to send by way of Maddie to the Queen.

"Maddie, please let Her Majesty know that I am well. I am tired and sore from my journey, but the two men who brought me back were nothing but kind to me. They deserve my thanks, and should be treated as my guests while they are in the Castle." Maddie nodded her head dutifully.

"And what of your assignment, Lady Sariah? Was it successful?" At Maddie's question, Sariah frowned. Her assignment. Her memory loss apparently was impacting more than just what happened to her when her life was taken.

"Maddie, forgive me. I had a fall while I was away, and my thoughts are muddled. What assignment are you speaking of?"

Maddie shook her head and said, "Forgive me, Lady, I do not know the particulars, only that Her Majesty was interested in knowing if the assignment had been completed." Sariah nodded at Maddie, and grabbed a bottle from a table near her tub. She poured some of the liquid into her hands and began to lather her hair.

Sariah thought about what she could remember of the trip. Waking up in the cave... finding Heath and Javier... coming back to the castle. She didn't remember leaving the Castle or going on assignment. She knew that she was repressing the memory of her death, but, did that include everything that happened before her death? No. Not completely. She leaned her head back in the water to rinse the suds out. She remembered life in the castle, Luc and Lara, Luc's wife. Maddie, and her Majesty. She remembered her training and her younger years. She even remembered the cute guard that she brought back to her room the week before she left. She smirked a bit at this one. He had no idea what he was getting himself into.

But the last couple of days? Maybe even weeks? She remembered nothing before she woke up in the cave. "Maddie, please tell her Majesty that I need to speak with her about the assignment. You may explain the fall, and the reason for my lapse in memory." Maddie nodded at Sariah, and asked if there was anything else she needed. Sariah smiled warmly at the girl. "No, thank you Maddie, you may go." Maddie left Sariah's room, and left Sariah to her thoughts.

When Maddie shut the door to Sariah's room and walked away, a man emerged from the shadows, and approached the door. His footsteps were silent. He moved to the door, and paused, making sure no one was coming. The rustle of Maddie's skirts as she hurried down the hallway was the only sign of life he could discern. He heard Sariah murmuring on the other side of the door. He paused to hear if anyone responded, but after a moment, he heard Sariah's voice again. She must be musing aloud.

He took two small metal instruments out of the pouch at his belt. He made quick work of Sariah's lock, and stood there a moment to see if she had noticed the sounds. He didn't hear a stop in her musings, so he shoved open the door. A throwing knife appeared at that moment to the left of his head, half buried in the doorframe. "Was that really necessary?" he admonished, stepping into her room and closing the door behind him.

Sariah was standing in her bath, naked, with a snarl on her lips. "What do you think you're doing here?"

He looked her naked body up and down quickly, before leaning against her door and crossing his arms across his chest. "We need to talk."

Chapter Eight

He yanked the throwing knife out of the door frame and laid it on the table just inside the door. "Nice knife. I didn't know you had those kinds of skills, *M'Lady*." The emphasis on her title made her grind her teeth. Sariah noticed that he kept his eyes firmly on her face. When he pushed open the door, she had stood and grabbed her knife in one motion, letting it lose to hit the frame and give warning.

She still stood in the bath, comfortable in her nakedness. She knew that her young body was pleasing to men. She had used it in the past to her advantage when needed. She raised an eyebrow at him, since he was obviously not going to leave.

"Oh, by all means, please, continue your bath. I do not want to interrupt that." She rolled her eyes and sat back in the water, to continue bathing. If he was going to watch her, she might as well finish what she started. She could tell he was battling with his baser wants since he was being gentlemanly and keeping his eyes on her face. Fine then. If he could ignore it, so could she.

"What do you want, Javier?" He was so silent, she looked up to see if he was still there. He was, and his attention was focused on Luna, who was on one of the posts of Sariah's bed. "She kind of comes and goes on her own it seems. She's good company though." Luna turned her attention to Javier, and gave an annoyed silent caw in his direction. She flew back over to the lip of the tub and perched herself in between Sariah and Javier, ready to do her duty if she were called.

"You are no Queen's Lady. At least not in the traditional sense. No way a gentlewoman could throw a knife with that kind of accuracy." He arched a brow back at her, daring her to try and wiggle her way out of this.

"You don't seem to be a gentleman yourself. Breaking into Ladies' rooms? Especially those who are in the bath?" She was washing her body with soap, lathering up her arms as she spoke to him. The water was deep enough that even if she suffered from modesty, her breasts would be covered. She paused and gave him a pointed look before continuing to bathe.

"Yes, well. I had no idea you were in the bath. I didn't know that the castle had tubs in the rooms." He did look somewhat embarrassed by that. "Are they in all of the rooms? I don't remember seeing one in our room, but to be honest, I wasn't there very long before I came looking for you." He didn't look at all abashed about seeking her out as quickly as he had.

"Queen Elliana had them installed in all of her Ladies' rooms. It gives us more... *privacy* than the average guest or servant. Since we are indeed noble ladies, she thought it was warranted." Having finished lathering, she began rinsing her arms.

He was silent a moment as he watched the water sluice over her arms. She knew he had gotten a good look at her body while she stood before him, as well as a good feel of it as he held her on the ride here. While she had some softness to her as most women do, she was built with a lot of muscle, and muscle that was well used. She wasn't watching him watch her, but she could feel his gaze. Knowing that he was watching her gave a little boost to her pride, and she made more of a show of rinsing herself off than she normally would have.

Having finished her ablutions, Sariah stood up, and reached over to the end of the tub where a white linen dressing robe awaited her. Wrapping herself in it, she took a nearby towel, and started drying her hair with it. "Well, if you're finished ogling me, could you please get to your point? I'm expected in the Queen's quarters in a quarter hour." She really wasn't, but there was no way that he would know that.

"Who are you, Sariah?" He sounded confused, as well as somewhat in awe.

Sariah stopped drying her hair and smiled at him sweetly before resuming her task. "I am Lady Sariah, a member of the Queen's Ladies to Queen Elliana of Blackmore. I have lived here since I was young under the tutelage of a great governess at the request of the royal family. My parents were poor farmers, but I caught the eye of the then Princess early when she attended a festival in our small town. Beyond that, I am no one. I serve my Queen as she wishes, and I happily live here flirting, dancing, and living at her leisure. Just another castle girl." She said this so self-deprecatingly that he laughed when she finished.

"I'm sure that's all true to an extent. And I'm sure if I asked around, your story would be corroborated. But that's not the whole story, and we both know it." He sounded so sure of himself. She looked up at him with fire in her eyes.

"What does it matter to you who I am? You will be leaving in a few days, and will forget all about me. Now please leave my room. I would like to get dressed in peace. She turned away from him and dropped her robe, beginning to get her undergarments and stockings on.

Recognizing a true dismissal when he heard it, he slipped out of her room silently. Sariah knew when he left, even though he did not make a sound. Luna ruffled her feathers once he was really gone, and made her silent caw at Sariah.

"Don't you start with me too. I've never been in a position like this before. I don't know what I'm doing with him." Luna cocked her head at Sariah. "I know. I need to figure it out. Especially since he's seen me in a light that no man other than Luc has. He's seen me with the pretenses dropped, and my guard up. I will have to be careful around him."

Sariah slipped her dress over her shoulders, and worked on lacing up the front of her bodice. The Queen's Ladies were provided with deceptive undergarments that made them look like they were wearing corsets, when the outfits they wore really allowed free and easy movement in case they needed to defend their Queen. Able to get in and out of their garments easily, all of the Ladies usually wore pants and some type of tight-fitting shirt under the gowns, if the cut allowed it. If not, the undergarments they wore were demure enough that no one would bat an eye seeing them sans gown. The gowns were also altered so that the Ladies could conveniently hide weapons in their gowns. Most had hidden pockets that allowed them to carry what they needed at their hip without revealing that they were armed. Plus, pockets were so convenient for carrying general things.

Her gown was a deep blue, and unlike standard ballgowns of the time that ladies wore around the world, Queen Elliana's Ladies wore simple A-Line dresses. They fell simply around the hips, and flared just a bit around the thighs and calves. The dresses were floor-length, allowing the Ladies to wear soft-soled boots which would let them run if they needed to, and the boots also provided convenient places to stash blades.

Smoothing her skirts down, and making sure that none of her blades were visible, Sariah turned towards the door of her room. She realized Luna wasn't with her, and turned to the bedpost where she had seen Luna last. Luna wasn't there. Sariah did a quick perusal of her room, and didn't see Luna anywhere. She looked by her tub, and saw that one of the windows was cracked open. Figuring that Luna went to find some food, and that she'd be back, Sariah left her room to go seek an audience with the Queen.

Chapter Nine

As soon as Sariah had taken three steps from her room, she had to lean against the wall, and she put a hand to her head. She was suddenly very dizzy, and she needed to take a moment. She felt lucky in that the only people that often used this corridor were the Ladies, and their assigned servants. This time of day, it would be almost deserted. Sariah laid her forehead against the cool stone of the hallway, and just stood there for a moment like that. A tiny squeak made her lift her head. All of a sudden, she didn't feel poorly anymore. She felt invigorated. She moved towards the sound she had heard, which was just up around the corner.

Rather than just barging into whatever was coming, she slowly peeked around the corner. She could see that she wasn't the only one who was glad that the corridor was almost empty. One of the castle guards had a kitchen maid up against a wall. His groans of pleasure were easily heard down the hallway. However, the maid was not enjoying herself so much. He had one hand over her mouth, tears were streaming down her face as she tried to plead with him. Sariah could see that thankfully he hadn't gotten too far. He only had his hand up her skirt, which in itself was bad enough of a violation. He must have done something particularly rough, because the maid whimpered and huddled down into herself.

Before Sariah knew what was happening, she was behind the guard with her blade to his throat. "Remove your hands from her. Now." Her voice didn't sound like her own. It sounded like The Crow. And that's when she realized what was going on. The Crow had come into her, and had decided to carry out the justice that she had told Sariah would be coming. Frankly, in this case, Sariah would have been happy to be leading the charge, even though The Crow was the one holding the reins.

The guard growled at Sariah, but lifted his hands from the maid's mouth, and out from under her skirt. "Now back up. Slowly." The Crow did not want him to do anything rash, Sariah knew. If she could avoid taking a life, she would. Sariah wasn't so sure that this life needed to be saved however. This particular guard, once she saw his face, had a reputation of using his position of power to get what he wanted.

As soon as she was freed, the maid ran off towards the kitchens, not looking back. Seeing that he was deprived of his prey, the guard smacked the blade out of her hand, and whirled around, pushing Sariah into the wall behind her. Her back hit the wall hard, and her head followed, bouncing off the stone. Ow. That was going to hurt later. The guard followed her, holding her against the wall none too softly.

She saw stars for a second before leaning forward and cracking her head into the guard's nose. His head flew back, and Sariah pushed herself off of the wall towards him. He had weight and size on his side, but Sariah was fast, and The Crow seemed to be lending her additional speed, and some strength.

"You will never go near the maids again. In fact, you will never touch a woman in anger, nor will you touch one against her will again." All of a sudden, without knowing where it came from, a long-sword with silvery-blue metal appeared in Sariah's hand. The hilt was wrapped in black leather with silver wire wrapped periodically in as well. The blade itself had runes etched into it, and they seemed to glow white as she wielded it. She looked at her hand holding the sword, and swore that she herself were emitting a blueish glow.

"YOU BITCH! I think you broke my nose!" The guard had blood streaming down his face from his nose- it was definitely broken. She'd heard the crunch when her head connected with it. His face took on a new rage, and he charged her. She thrust the sword forward as he ran towards her, wrapping her arm around his back as she pushed her blade as deep into his belly as she could get. The guard turned shocked eyes onto her. His hands clutched his belly as blood, hot and black, spilled from it onto the floor. His eyes turned pleading as he realized he was dying.

Sariah stood over him, looking down on him with merciless eyes. She was concerned that she felt no remorse over what she was doing. Taking a life should have *some* feel to it. She always felt remorse as she had taken lives before. This time though, she just felt... calm. Even. There was no emotion behind it, except maybe a bit of gladness that he would never be able to hurt someone else.

Sariah saw a pale image step out in front of her. It was The Crow. She picked up the dying guard, cradling him like a baby as she took an ethereal blade and used it to end his life. She looked at Sariah and nodded, before turning and walking away, carrying the guard with her. She rounded the corner, and Sariah stood there a moment, her mouth hanging open. Did that really just happen?

Next thing she knew, Luna landed on her shoulder. Realizing that she most likely needed to change again, she looked down at herself and saw... nothing. Her clothes and hands were pristine. She saw no blood on the floor, either. She took a deep breath, and her legs went out from under her. She collapsed against the wall, and sat down on the hard floor. She was breathing heavily and she put her head on her knees for a minute.

What she had just experienced was *intense*. She had no idea what to expect when The Crow said that she would share consciousness with Sariah. She had no idea that she would still be completely in control, but would feel as The Crow did. She still felt no remorse over the guard's death. And where did The Crow take him? What was she going to do with him? Clearly he couldn't just *disappear*, that would be super suspicious, especially after what the maid had seen.

Queen Elliana knew her Ladies were capable of great violence in defense of her person, which meant they'd be capable of great violence elsewhere as well. Sariah knew that the Queen would defend any of her Ladies against anything said against them. Sariah knew that the Queen would support her. However, how was she to explain *any* of this? She couldn't even really comprehend it herself.

Sariah leaned back and tilted her head against the stone wall, looking up, and closed her eyes. She knew she was going to have to get up and get moving soon. While this corridor was empty now, she knew it was almost supper time, and that servants would be coming through here with trays for any Lady or guest that did not wish to eat in the main hall. Sariah contemplated calling for dinner herself, but knew that since she just returned from who knows where in who knew what kind of condition, she would need to show her face in the main hall.

Sariah stayed sitting for a few moments more before taking a deep breath and slowly getting to her feet. She brushed her dress off, looking for any sign of anything that just happened, and, seeing none, she steeled her face, and started walking towards the main hall. She realized a moment later that Luna was no longer with her. She wondered at that a moment before continuing on. Since the bird was a scion of The Crow, she was clearly capable of things not of the norm.

He watched as she walked away. They were going to have to have another talk later. What Javier had just seen was an incredible thing. He rubbed his hand over his mouth, looking at Sariah's retreating form in awe. Luna fluttered her wings before landing on Javier's shoulder. He reached his fingers towards her, and she nuzzled them, giving him a light nip before flying off towards Sariah's room.

Sariah had no idea that Javier had seen her, or had been following her since she left her room. If she had known, she would've considered him a lot more dangerous than she did now. He was the one person who knew her secret. But unbeknownst to her, he had secrets of his own.

Chapter Ten

Sariah had gotten herself mostly composed by the time that she walked into the main hall... only to find it empty. She was a bit early for dinner she knew, and the tables were all laid for it, but usually there were at least a few early comers in there. Sariah debated on what she should do. She had thought to go visit Queen Elliana before dinner, but, since she had been so emotional after her episode with The Crow, she thought it best to put off that visit. However, since no one was yet in the main hall, she thought she might as well go and seek Her Majesty out.

Sariah headed right down the hall to the receiving room. Kind of like a throne room, this is where Queen Elliana received all of her visitors that were not residents of the castle. This is where Sir Javier and Lord Heath would be received when Her Majesty was ready to hear from them. She hoped that the Queen would give her a private audience before their meeting. She had much to explain.

However, as she walked into the receiving room, she saw that wasn't going to be possible. Queen Elliana was sitting atop her "throne," a beautifully carved wooden chair that had been in her family for generations. She was intently listening to what Luc was saying about their arrival and Sariah's appearance. Off to the side she saw Javier and Lord Heath. They were not restrained, thank goodness, but they were flanked by the Queen's own guards. Not a position she herself would fancy. As if he felt her stare, Javier looked up at her just then. She saw hunger in his eyes as he took in her appearance.

Something had changed since she saw him in her room last. She was naked in front of him then, and he only showed a mild interest. Now he looked like he'd take her where she stood if they were alone.

And she was dressed from head to toe. The scary thing for her is that she didn't know if she'd try and stop him. The thought of his arms around her as they rode brought color to her cheeks. Seeing that, Javier gave her a wicked smile.

If she were going to explore these feelings at all, she needed to stop the proceedings. Before she stepped further into the room, Luna landed on her shoulder. Luna had been timing her entrance into Sariah's doings quite interestingly. Sariah ran her fingers down the back of Luna's neck, took a deep breath, and walked into the room.

Since the Queen and most of those in the room holding court with her were so focused on what Luc was saying, they didn't notice Sariah as she approached. She came up behind Luc and let him finish speaking before she herself spoke up. "Your Majesty. I beg pardon for being late." Sariah went down into a deep curtsey and held it, not sure what to expect from the Queen.

"Lady Sariah. Sir Luc has been explaining your appearance with Lord Sandram and Sir Javier. I see he was not exaggerating on some of the changes he beheld in you, such as your voice. Pray tell, what happened to you these last few days that you've been missing?" There was an odd tone to her voice, and Sariah cast her eyes up to the Queen while staying in her curtsey. What she saw in Elliana's face was rage. Pure, unadulterated rage. This was not good. It would not be easy to explain, especially in front of the whole court. But she had to do something, or the Queen was likely to take that rage out on Lord Heath and Javier.

"Your Highness, I have had a few difficult days, and I suffered a fall. I don't remember most of my trip away, but I'll relate what I do. I woke up in a cave about- well, I'm actually not sure how far away. It was close to where Lord Sandram and Sir Javier were camped down for the night. I couldn't remember how I'd gotten to the cave or what I was even doing in that part of the country. I assume I was thrown from my horse, and whatever escort I had moved me to the cave for safety before going after it."

Elliana was listening intently to Sariah, and she relaxed a fraction in her chair as Sariah continued her tale. "I climbed down from the cave, realizing as I went that there was a good amount of blood on my clothes. I must have hit my head in the fall. You know how head wounds are wont to bleed." At this, Sariah touched her hair near her temple. She was glad that she had just pulled her hair back in a simple braid- it would explain away not seeing any cuts at the back of her head.

"I came across Lord Sandram's camp, as I mentioned, and while we were discussing the best way to get me home, I must have fainted from blood loss, shock, or maybe even hunger. When I awoke next, I was on a horse in front of Sir Javier. He was keeping me steady as we went. My hands were bound to the saddle horn, but that was only to steady me. The bindings were very loose and I could have pulled out of them at any time, but worried that I might fall asleep or faint again, I left them as they were." Sariah risked a glance at Javier, who was looking at her appraisingly.

"Your Majesty, I owe these two men a debt of gratitude for saving me from the forest, and for returning me safely to your court." Sariah bowed her head at this, waiting to hear what the Queen would say to this. Sariah knew that the two men would not be let off free and clear until she had spoken with the Queen privately, but with this story, Elliana would be able to give the men a bit more reign of the castle. Behind her, the room was silent. All that Sariah could hear was the rustling of Luna's wings as the little bird looked around. Sariah was breathing slowly and calmly, but she was very much on edge.

"Lady Sariah, I agree that these men are owed a debt. I will allow them to remain here as your guests as long as they wish, and as long as they abide by the rules of the house. I trust yourself or Sir Luc to explain those rules to them, and see that they are followed. If they break the guesting rules, they will be punished based on the severity of the crime, followed by swift expulsion from Blackmore. Now, please, all of you, head to the main hall for dinner. Sariah, I request you stay for a private audience." Queen Elliana had spoken, so the crowd followed. Sariah stayed in her deep curtsey, listening to the courtiers file out of the receiving room and head into the main hall.

When the door was shut behind the last one, Sariah stood up, and looked around the room. Finding only herself and the Queen left in the room, Sariah approached Her Majesty's throne, and knelt to kiss her hand. "Your Majesty. I apologize for not sending word before my arrival." Sariah was pulled up into a tight hug. Luna was dislodged, and flew over to a decorative table where she perched, glaring at the Queen.

"Sariah! Where have you been?! After sending you on your mission to handle Lord Darian, we heard nothing of you for weeks! Finally, we receive a missive from you that you're coming home, but you didn't. And then you turn up, covered in blood, with a scar across your throat, and your voice sounding damaged..." Pulling back, She looked Sariah over, and gently touched the mark on Sariah's throat. "Who did this to you? What happened? Sir Luc was fit to be tied when he came storming in here to tell me of your arrival. He and Lady Lara will have much to discuss tonight, I have a feeling, including her talking him out of killing your escort. He still believes that it was they who harmed you."

At this, Sariah shook her head. "I do not know who harmed me. All I know is that I woke up in a cave. Someone was there with me, but my weapons were gone. The next thing I knew, I was waking up in a pool of sticky liquid, which I have since realized was blood. I found Lord Heath and Sir Javier, and they were kind enough to escort me back. I remember nothing of leaving here for Lord Darian, or spending weeks in his company. I do not even remember why I was sent to him."

Queen Elliana pursed her lips, as if deciding what to say. Finally, she began, "I don't know how much you remember from your time before you were gone, but I had sent you to Lord Darian to try and gain information from him in any way you could. If he took you to bed, and later proposed a marriage alliance, it would have given me an out. He is a dangerous man, a known womanizer, and not one that I would prefer to be wed. Do you remember anything of your time there?" The Queen looked hopeful, but her tone sounded dejected.

"Unfortunately, Majesty, I do not. I can't pinpoint my last *known* knowledge before I left, but as I said, I do remember my life here. I know who I am, I know what I am for you. I remember all of my training, my family, everything. Recent memory is just a fog, until I woke up in that cave and tried to find my way home." Sariah frowned. This lapse in memory was really getting to her. Luna flew over to Sariah and landed on her shoulder. Sariah stroked her neck feathers absently while she contemplated what the Queen had said.

"This is a charming bird." Queen Elliana reached a finger out to Luna, and stroked her as Sariah was doing. Luna rubbed her beak on Elliana's fingers before giving her a gentle nip and leaning back against Sariah.

"I'm not sure how she found me, but she's become sort of a pet. Her name is Luna. She has not truly left me since I woke up. She comes and goes as she wishes, but she always seems to be there when I need her." Sariah reached back up to Luna, and looked over at her. Luna ruffled her feathers in pleasure, and flew back over to the table she had previously vacated. Sariah continued to look at her, thinking about everything she had just relayed. She turned back to the Queen when Elliana began to speak again.

"Do not fret over the lost memory of the mission. I was hoping for intel and an in with Lord Darian, but I need to treatise with him no matter what happens, so, I guess I will just invite him to court, and see what we can manage." Queen Elliana put her hand on Sariah's cheek affectionately. "I am so glad you are returned to us safe, if not whole." She leaned down and kissed Sariah's cheek as a sister would. "Come now, let's go to dinner before they've eaten the whole feast without us." Queen Elliana stood up, and took a step towards the door. Sariah followed suit, staying three steps behind her Queen, as was custom in public for one of the Queen's Ladies.

Chapter Eleven

Dinner went on without incident. Since Sariah sat with the other Queen's Ladies at a table near Her Majesty's, it was not hard for her to see that Javier often turned his gaze to her. After dessert was served, Sariah gave her excuses to the Queen, and instead of moving to the theater with the rest of the courtiers for the evening's entertainment, she headed towards her room. She had not seen Luna since she and Elliana had left the receiving room, but she had a feeling that she'd show up as soon as she felt needed. Luna was becoming dependable in Sariah's mind, and she was glad to have her.

When she got into the passage just outside of the main hall, she felt like she was being followed. She turned around to find Javier following at a discrete distance. "Can I help you, Sir Javier?" Sariah gave a small curtsey in deference to his rank.

Bowing back to her, Javier replied, "I was hoping to escort you back to your room, M'lady." He held out his arm, and she took it, knowing that to argue would look strange if anyone were watching. Lowering his voice, he said, "Thank you, Sariah, for what you said in the receiving room, and for the graciousness that you've shown since we've returned to your home. I know that you did not have to do that, and Lord Heath wanted to pass along his gratitude." His head was leaning close to hers, since he was considerably taller than herself. She was average height for a woman, around five and a half feet tall, and Javier had a good eight inches on her.

Sariah wasn't sure when he'd had time to bathe today, but he obviously had. And he was either wearing some kind of cologne, or his personal scent was just that good. He smelled musky, and somewhat spicy. Similar to how he smelled on the journey here, but enhanced. It was intoxicating. She knew she herself smelled of lavender. A girl in the village made special soaps and lotions for the Queen's Ladies, and Sariah loved the smell of fresh lavender, so she had the girl make all of her scents with it. She began to walk again, not wanting to start gossip if they were found standing in the hall so close together, apparently speaking of intimate things.

Sariah continued the conversation that he had started. "You may pass along my gratitude to him as well. Without the two of you, it would have taken me a lot longer to return to Blackmore. And since I was unarmed, and apparently injured, who knows what kind of shape I would have been in when I got here." Sariah was keeping her pace deliberately slower than normal, since she was enjoying being close to Javier.

"You seem more than capable of holding your own, M'lady." Javier stopped walking, and turned to face Sariah. "In fact, I don't know why you didn't fight me on the journey here, or even that night in the forest." His eyes were boring into hers. He was all she could see. She stepped closer to him. His smell surrounded her, and she acted almost without thinking.

Sariah stood on her toes and leaned in close, as if she were going to kiss him. Just before her lips touched his, she murmured, "I could have, yes, but I didn't want to hurt you." She smirked at him as she turned down the hallway and continued towards her room. Javier's grin was pure evil as he followed her. Sariah knew she was playing with fire where it came to Javier. But in all honesty, she wasn't sure she'd mind being burned.

Javier quickened his pace to come even with her again. "I have no doubt of your ability to wound me, Sariah. There are many other ways I would like to spend time with you, however." His invitation was blatant. This flirtation would lead to bed, Sariah was sure. But she wasn't sure she wanted the chase to end. She was enjoying herself immensely playing with him.

"Mmm, well, I do tend to spend many *pleasurable* hours alone. I'm sure you could come up with some things for us to do together." He was watching her, so she quickly darted her tongue out to moisten her lips. She saw his lips purse, and his fists clench. Oh yes, she was going to enjoy this flirtation immensely. She began thinking of her wardrobe, and what she could wear to drive them both crazy while he remained at Blackmore. Then her thoughts paused. He would be leaving soon. She mentally shook herself. It didn't matter. She would enjoy him while she could.

As they reached the door of her room, she turned to him to wish him goodnight. He stepped into her, and very gently pushed her against the wall. He waited as if for permission before pressing his body fully against hers. She arched her body a bit, pushing her breasts into his chest, and leaned her head back some, exposing her neck. He lowered his mouth to her neck, and kissed it. Then he gave a gentle lick, and nipped her neck. Sariah gasped, and then gave a little moan. She felt wet. It had been a while since she'd had boundless pleasure, both given and taken. Most of the other lovers she'd had were merely scratching an itch. That wasn't to say they were bad, but they didn't affect her the way that Javier did.

She tilted her head back more, giving him better access. He kissed his way up her neck, nipped at her jaw, before taking her lips. His lips were fire, and she opened her mouth in pleasure and invitation, wanting him to deepen the kiss. He had one hand on the wall near her head, and the other was kneading the small of her back. If he took her right here where anyone could come across them, she wasn't sure that she'd care. Her reputation would be ruined, but she was sure that having him would be worth the price.

After what felt like an eternity later, he pulled back from the kiss. Her lips were parted, her cheeks flushed with pleasure. He gently opened the door behind her. He was holding her, thankfully, otherwise she would have fallen on the floor. She felt utterly boneless, and wanted nothing more than to take him into her room and into her bed. With his body still pressed against her, she could tell that he also wanted her. He leaned down and took her lips again, this time gently, rather than the burning kiss they shared before. Slowly, so that she could gain her balance, he released her, and stepped back. She made a sound of desperation, then realized what she was doing, and brought herself back from the brink. Javier was giving her a very courtly bow, which she returned with a curtsey. Then he closed the door. Her mouth opened in surprise, and she yanked the door back open, but he had already turned the corner, and she was left standing in the hallway alone.

"You have got to be fucking kidding me!" she exclaimed heatedly. He left her here, all worked up, and nearly panting for him. And he just *walked away*?! She huffed at the empty hallway before whirling around and going back in her room. She slammed her door shut, and stalked over to her wardrobe. She saw Luna perched on the top of the wardrobe, cocking her head at Sariah as if trying to figure out what was wrong.

"He just *walked away*! And left me feeling like *this*!" Sariah's blood was up, and she knew she needed to get out some frustration. She changed into her black leather breeches and a loose cream linen shirt. She pulled her soft black leather boots on, and grabbed several of her throwing knives, and fighting blades. She strapped the throwing knives in her boots, her short sword she put in its scabbard and then tied that around her waist, and she stuck the sheath of her dagger in the other side of the scabbard tie. Glaring at Luna who she imagined was giving her an amused look, Sariah turned around, and stormed out of the room.

Chapter Twelve

Sariah moved quickly through the castle until she reached the kitchens. She grabbed a water skein, and headed out one of the doors that led to the back of the castle. The guards had training grounds to the back, but since the Ladies were supposed to be demure and elegant, she wasn't able to practice on the main training grounds. Luckily, the Ladies were permitted to wear pants and shirts when they went out riding, otherwise there would have been a lot of questions as to why they were frequently seen out of dresses.

The Ladies' practice grounds were a ways from the castle in the woods. Sariah usually took a horse to them, but with as worked up as she was tonight, she knew she'd need the exertion. She made her way across the small field of sweet grass, and into the woods at a fast walking pace. As soon as she wasn't able to be seen from the castle, she took off at a run.

Sariah loved to run. The wind in her face, her muscles loosening up as she put everything behind her, it was so freeing compared to the structure of castle life. She jumped over tree roots and fallen branches as she made her way back to the old barn that the Queen had refitted for the Ladies' use. Sariah had a feeling she'd be alone there tonight. There were only six Ladies currently, and of the Ladies, Sariah was the only one unmarried. Several of the other Ladies' husbands were guards or soldiers, so they usually helped to keep their wives in shape.

If Sariah had asked one of the other Ladies to come, they would, but she was fairly self-sufficient. She had developed a practice routine she could do solo for working out, and if she needed a sparring partner, could usually count on Luc. He never pulled punches with Sariah, and she often had the bruises to prove it. But a good thing about sparring with Luc was that she learned how to become faster, and good ways to get out of the hold of someone who outweighed her by about seventy pounds. Sariah was no waif- she had thick thighs, large breasts, and a fairly large yet shapely ass, but Luc was built. When he wasn't on duty, he was with his wife or working out with the other guards. Being in shape was part of his job, and he took it seriously.

By the time Sariah got to the clearing where the barn was, she was fully loosened up from her run, and had a light sheen of sweat all over her body. Night was just starting to fall, so she went inside and began lighting candles in the hanging lanterns and on the chandeliers so that she'd have plenty of light to work with. Once she had lit both chandeliers, she raised them up using the pulley system so that she'd have ample light. Once she was finished with that, she untied her scabbard and tossed it and her dagger off to one side. She took a healthy drink from the water skein before setting that aside as well. She rolled her head on her neck and jumped in place a few times to make sure she was still ready to go before breaking out into a hand-to-hand combat routine with an invisible partner.

She threw punches and delivered kicks that would have been devastating to anyone who faced her. The barn was laid out with the center of the floor completely clear. This is where Sariah was currently practicing. Along the sides of the open area, there were support beams holding up a second level that ran around the edge of the building, but left the center open to the roof so that the chandeliers could be raised or lowered depending on which floor was being used. In the wings of the lower level, there were hay-filled dummies that were good for practicing blade work, while upstairs there were various objects to help keep their muscles strong, such as various weights. Sariah's personal favorites were the old cannon balls. She had wrapped rope around them and created handles. She was able to lift them straight that way, or to swing them around. There were also ropes that dangled from the roof, to allow the Ladies the ability to practice their climbing skills.

As Sariah finished up the first part of her workout, she was lamenting not having a partner. She felt that having someone there to take her rage out on would be key to getting her calm. She walked over to her water skein to take a drink, wiping the sweat from her brow. She had gotten a good start on her workout, that was for sure. She was glad that her injuries hadn't hindered her too much. She did a couple of arm stretches before she took a nice big gulp from the water skein. She heard a slow clap behind her. Whipping around, she saw Javier leaning against the side of the barn. She grabbed her short sword from her feet, growled at him and charged.

She had to give it to him, he was quick. He had his sword out and ready to block by the time she reached him. Rather than looking surprised or taken aback, he had a smile on his face. She wanted to smack it off. She backed off, giving him a bit of room before thrusting again. He parried her blow, and got in one of his own. He moved to the side, and, catching her off balance, she stumbled a bit as she went by him. He took the moment to smack her ass with the flat of his blade. The world came to a screeching halt. She very slowly turned around to face him. She was seeing red. The look on his face was one of amusement, but no apology.

She came at him charging again, yelling this time. He was ready to block her, but at the last possible second, she whirled away from him in a dazzling move that allowed her to get back over to where the water skein was, and to get her dagger. She now held two blades to his one. She was hot, and sweaty, and worked up in more ways than one. From the look of him, Javier was feeling the same way. She awaited his next move, and the look that she gave him made it very obvious that she knew what effect she had on him. Her confidence was glorious. It was like seeing a warrior goddess.

Sariah couldn't help the smirk she gave him. Even though that smack on the ass made her see red, she knew that Javier was the perfect sparring partner for her. He had the same intensity of strength that Luc carried, but he also moved like a dancer- light on his feet. Javier did not practice fighting to stay fit, this was a man who was used to fighting for his life. As much as she could tell he was aroused by their fighting, so was she. She launched into a fast attack of swinging blades. He fended her off, and then grabbed her by the waist and kissed her. It was a very quick, yet passionate stolen kiss. But Sariah wasn't going to give in that easily. Biting his bottom lip quickly but gently, she dashed away from him. He put his hand to his lips as if to see if she had drawn blood. He gave her the evil smile she was coming to love before launching into his own attack.

They were fairly evenly matched, skill-wise, and while he had a physical advantage on her, she was just the tiniest bit faster. If this were a real fight, she wasn't sure who would win. She didn't know if he knew, either. After a while, they were both breathing heavily, and were slicked with sweat. Neither one had given an inch. Sariah couldn't take much more of this. Something had to give. She threw down her blades and charged him unarmed. He dropped his blade when he saw her coming. She jumped on him, wrapping her legs around his waist, and securing her mouth to his. He put his hands on her ass, holding her weight easily.

His kiss was salty with sweat, and yet he tasted amazing. She let go of him quickly, and pulled her shirt off over her head. She had her breasts bound with linen strips to allow her easier movement while fighting. He lowered his head, licking, biting, and sucking his way from her neck down. She gave her hips a little twist, grinding herself against him. He moaned in pleasure, or maybe it was pain. She knew if he didn't get inside of her soon, she would go mad. He lowered her to the floor, and pulled her breeches off. Her skin had a lovely flush to it from their fight, and her passion.

He undid the ties to his own trousers, and got down on the floor with her. Seeing her there, open for him, glistening, he couldn't help himself. He had to taste her. He leaned down and licked her slit, his cock twitching at the sound of pleasure she made. Even here she smelled like lavender, but she tasted sweet, like fresh honey. That one taste drove him wild, and he got up on his knees, shifted her hips, and thrust into her. She was so wet, and the feeling of his fullness inside of her was intense. Seeing her pause, he took a moment to let her get used to his size, slipping his hand under her bindings to find her nipple. He rolled it around in his fingers, loving the way it made her arch into him.

He was driving her crazy with his little touches. She tightened around him, and then lifted her hips to take him deeper. As soon as he was as deep as he could be, they started to move together, their passion building. She felt him rise up with her to the peak, before they both shouted in pleasure, and tumbled over together. He quickly rolled over, putting her on top of him while he was still inside of her so they could catch their breath. She leaned down and kissed him, before collapsing against him.

As they laid together on the floor, Sariah was thinking about the best way to sneak Javier into her room. Javier suddenly stilled beneath her. "What is-" he put his hand over her mouth, and half carried, half dragged her into the wings of the barn. Sariah heard what had startled him- footsteps, loud and fast, were headed towards the barn.

Thankfully, Javier had the presence of mind to grab her clothes when he got them over to the side. Sariah slipped her breeches on quickly, super thankful that they never tore her breast bindings off. She pulled her shirt over her head, quickly kissed him on the mouth, and then shoved him towards the back of the barn. "Sariah!" Sariah's head whipped towards the door. That was Luc coming, and he sounded very angry. Sariah moved back into the center of the barn, and grabbed her blades. She stepped back over to her water skein and took a deep drink.

"Sariah!" Luc yelled again as he pushed open the barn doors. She was right- Luc was *PISSED*. "Sariah. Where the *hell* have you been?! I went by your room to check on you when you left dinner early, and you weren't there. Lara went to find you within the castle, and sent me here." He was breathing heavily and was slicked with sweat. It looked like he ran the whole way to the barn from the castle.

"Luc, calm down. I got back to my room and was too anxious to stay there. I decided to come train for a while." Sariah put her hands out to encompass the barn. "And here I still am." While she loved Luc and Lara like a brother and sister, she wasn't about to let Luc get away with acting like her father or guardian. "I'm a big girl. And a trained killer. I can handle myself." Being almost interrupted apparently returned her frustration- there was bite to her voice.

Luc stalked forward and put his hands on Sariah's upper arms. He was holding her firmly, but not so tight that he was causing her pain. His voice cracked when he said, "You were gone. No one knew where you were. Lara couldn't find out any answers and neither could I. We figured you were on a mission, but none of your missions have ever lasted that long." He looked at her with pain in his eyes. "We thought you were dead. And then you turned up, looking like *that*, tied to that man's horse like a prize of war?" Luc paused and took a breath. "I almost killed him. Did you know that? I followed him to his room after you left the courtyard. I didn't believe that he didn't harm you. I had my sword in my hand and I was going to run him through for what he did to you..." Luc suddenly released her arms, and pulled Sariah into a tight embrace. "I can't lose you, Sariah. You and Lara are all I have in this world."

There were tears in his voice, and it affected Sariah deeply. She returned his embrace. "Luc, I'm so truly sorry that you were hurting. I promise you, that while I don't remember what happened while I was gone, you know me. You know that I'd never intentionally hurt you or Lara." Her heart ached for this man. He had been through hell while she was gone. And tonight, after everything, she had disappeared on him again. She completely understood where his feelings were coming from, and she didn't blame him at all.

"If you need to finish up here, I'll wait for you and walk you back." Luc started over towards a bench against the wall of the barn. He was gaining his composure again.

"No, it's alright. I was just finishing up, actually. And I think a walk with you would be perfect. She strapped her blades back on. He grabbed her water skein. She put out the chandeliers and lanterns on the walls with his help. They shut the barn and began the trek back to the castle.

In the dark of the barn, Javier stood up from where he hid near the back doors. "She is extraordinary. You will never find another woman like her." Javier didn't jump. The Crow had been coming to him for a while now, long before he had met the beautiful Sariah.

"Does she know that you come to me as well as her?" Javier looked over at the beautiful goddess standing next to him. She was partially transparent, as if she were not fully part of their world. It was how she looked when she had stepped out of Sariah and carried the guard away.

"She doesn't need to know. Sariah is mine now. She's given herself over to my cause." The Morrigan said it with such a finality as to brook no argument. "She will remain in my service as long as she stays pure of heart, and as long as she wishes." She paused, and turned a sly look his way. "I could always use a second. While no man can be considered mine, I could take you under my wing as a guardian of the protector."

Javier still looked at where Sariah had closed the door. He looked back to the goddess, but she was gone. He sighed, and started to walk towards the front of the barn. He would be missed in the castle if he stayed any longer.

Chapter Thirteen

Sariah woke alone in her own bed the next morning. Luna hopped across the pillow next to her so that she could nuzzle Sariah's outstretched hand before flying up to one of the posts of the bed. Sariah stretched her body, reveling in the delicious soreness from the night before.

When she finally climbed in bed last night after visiting with Luc and Lara, she almost wondered if she had imagined her interlude with Javier. She put her hand to her lips, and smiled. Her body this morning told the story of their lovemaking on the floor of the barn the night before. And oh, how pleasurable it was.

She had a feeling that Javier's experience with women was great for him to be so skilled in those arts, but she in no way held that against him. As long as she was on the receiving end of the fruits of his labor, she didn't care how many women he had slept with. If they were married, or in a committed relationship, he'd have to be only hers, but since he would leave soon, she wasn't going to exact any promises from him.

Sitting up, she saw she wasn't alone in her room. The Crow was in her room, in her human form. She was standing at the foot of Sariah's bed, just watching her. "Good morning, My Lady." Sariah wasn't overly surprised to see her, especially since she had been The Crow's arm of justice the night before.

The Crow tilted her head this way and that. Sariah was starting to get used to the birdlike movements on a human woman. "Sariah. You conquered the evil in one man last night, but now it's time to take it further. Starting in Blackmore is fine, but there are many in the world who should be excised." Sariah flinched at that last word.

She wasn't overly happy with The Crow sharing her body at times, but she knew what she was getting herself into when she agreed.

After a moment, she nodded to The Crow. "Yes, my lady, I understand." Sariah knew that her ability to travel as a Queen's Lady would help her carry out the mission that The Crow had bestowed upon her. While she was not scheduled out again for some time, she might be able to help out those in need locally. The human Crow nodded, and transformed into the corvid version of herself. Her transformation was interesting. It was like a fog came around her body, and then quickly cleared, leaving whichever form she chose to be in. Sariah hadn't even seen that much before. She had been transfixed by the place and time she had been in.

Sariah stood up, walked over to her windows, and opened one so that The Crow could fly out. The Crow hopped over to the window, and then made a small flight up to the sill. She eyed Sariah with one of her onyx black eyes before leaning towards her, and nuzzling Sariah's hand with her beak. The Crow definitely showed some affinity for Sariah, and Sariah had a feeling that it would grow the longer she was in the Crow's service.

The Crow began to spread her large black wings and pushed her feathered body off of the window sill. Sariah watched as she flew away. Last night, The Crow was almost ethereal. She was transparent and hazy, and Sariah would have said she'd seen a ghost if she had not recognized The Crow's face. Today however, she seemed almost completely human. And the bird version of The Crow was as solid as she was. She wondered a bit at that, and how it all worked. But she had a feeling that the workings of a goddess were not meant to be understood by humans.

Sighing and turning away from the window, Sariah knew she needed to get mentally prepared for the day. Since she was back in the castle, she would need to get back into her daily routine. Her Majesty held daily office with all of her Ladies privately before moving to the receiving room for business. After that, unless she needed one of her Ladies for a private project, or was looking for companionship for the day, the Ladies were free to do as they wished. It would be then that Sariah would be able to head out into the village proper, and see if she could not find any justice that needed serving up.

Sariah washed her face and switched out of her nightdress and into a dress suitable for court. She wore soft-soled slippers for the morning, since she would be coming back and changing into her riding clothes before heading out into the village. The sleeves on this gown were specially made with small slots on the inside so that she could equip herself with some throwing daggers as she moved about the castle. She blew a kiss to Luna, who was dozing on her bed post, and then Sariah slipped out of her room, and headed for the Queen's personal chambers.

Walking the halls of the castle felt a bit strange after her absence. Nothing had overtly changed with the castle that she could tell. She, on the other hand, had changed completely. She looked down at the stones beneath her feet, and then to the walls that made up the hall she was walking down. She had seen very few people on her walk towards the Queen's rooms, other than those that graced the paintings on the walls. It was fairly early in the day still, but most of the castle's inhabitants were already up, about, and working on their day. She mounted the stairs that would take her to the Queen's hallway and chambers.

Outside of Elliana's chambers, Sariah saw the other five Ladies. They were waiting in a group and chatting about the most innocuous things. When Sariah walked up, they all fawned over her, and wanted to make sure that she was alright, and that she hadn't suffered too horribly during her ordeal. Lara was looking her over, as this was the first chance that any of the ladies could really get a good look at Sariah since she had returned. Having spoken to Luc, Sariah guessed,

Lara's gaze lingered on Sariah's throat, raising her color. However, seeing that Sariah was mostly unharmed, she just placed a hand on Sariah's arm before continuing to chat with the other ladies, as Sariah was now.

Lara, much like her husband, was quick to anger, and she could be twice as lethal. Where Sariah worked primarily with blades, Lara's specialty was needles. Deadly ones that were coated in different kinds of poison. Her targets never saw her coming. She would hold a needle in the palm of her hand until she was ready to strike. She'd reach out, prick her target with a needle, or, alternatively, if she were in a fight shove the needle into her target as far as she could. With the coating of poison, even if the target were able to get the needle out, they were doomed. Since Luc was such an up front fighter, it had always amused Sariah that Lara's specialty was subterfuge and quiet assassination.

Each of the Queen's Ladies specialized in different tactics for protection and information. They were spies as much as they were bodyguards and loyal friends. The hard part was not doing the missions they were sent to do. The hard part was making themselves seem like they were not dangerous at all, and instead just flighty women with nothing more in their heads than the latest hair or dress styles at court. As Javier had proved, not everyone accepted their guise, even when they were playing it off flawlessly.

Sariah frowned when she thought of Javier, and tuned out the chatter around her. She wondered just how he was able to see through her guise. She had done nothing until yesterday when he entered her chamber that would suggest she was anything but the lady she pretended to be. Sure, she had managed to sneak up on their camp, but as ladies tended to walk softly, and she had the excuse of a head injury, he should have fallen for it. Sariah smiled. Javier was more than just good looking and talented. The man was sharp. She had a feeling that he knew so much more than he was letting on. She looked up from her thoughts to see Lara watching her, a small smile on her own face.

The Queen's chamber doors opened just then, and Sariah and the other Ladies entered the Queen's room for the morning meeting. The Queen's chambers were about as sparse as the rest of the castle. Settling down on a few couches that the Queen had in her chambers, the Ladies awaited the words of their leader. Sariah looked around to see if any changes had been made since she was in the room last. The carpets on the stone floor were still the same. There was a writing desk in the one corner of the room near a window that the Queen often used when writing her letters and missives, but also just to sit and think. The couches in the room were plush, and had a lot of pillows piled up on them. When Sariah had attended the Queen in the past, she could often be found relaxing on one of her couches with a book. Queen Elliana walked out from her dressing room fully dressed for her day, fixing her circlet over her intricately braided mahogany hair, interrupting Sariah's perusal of the room.

No one could accuse Her Majesty of being homely. She was quite beautiful. Emerald Green eyes, milky white skin, and lips the color of a summer rose blossom. She seldom wore makeup, as the warmer weather in Blackmore caused it to run. She requested her Ladies follow suit, but would not argue if they chose to touch up their appearance with some cosmetics. She was young, in her early twenties, the same age as Sariah.

She looked around at her Ladies and clasped her hands together in front of her. "Good morning my Ladies, my friends. Sariah, we have missed you these past weeks, and are so very grateful to have you back with us. We have some guests staying in the castle currently as you all know. Lord Heath and Sir Javier are owed a debt from us for returning Sariah to us. Ladies, please make them feel as comfortable as you can."

Sariah bristled a bit at that statement, but she wasn't sure why. She had no ties to Javier other than some shared kisses, and some extremely satisfying sex. They weren't in love, and he wasn't hers. She had just thought to herself earlier that she was going to require no oaths from him, so why should she care if any of the Ladies entertained him? Sariah frowned, and she knew she'd revisit this later when she didn't have to pay attention to her Queen.

"I've sent word to Lord Darian Thomas of Langton, asking him to join us for a time. As you Ladies know, Sariah was to be on business in Lord Darian's land, but due to extenuating circumstances, her mission was unable to be completed. I expect to hear back from him in a few days, and I invited him for next month. I expect he'll bring a large party of his men as well as his mercenaries, so we'll have our hands full keeping him happy and his men content." Queen Elliana paused here, as there was a knock on her chamber doors. She frowned at the doors, not used to being interrupted except in the most dire of circumstances. "What is it?" Elliana, usually very friendly, had a bit of fire in her voice.

"Your Majesty! We are cancelling today's court session! Sir Robert Lightly was just found at his home. He is dead!" One of the guards was outside Elliana's room for good reason then. While Sir Robert had carried a reputation about him, Elliana had never been able to get anyone to speak out against him so that she could banish him.

"Please, come in and explain yourself." Elliana's voice was much gentler this time, and the guard who walked into her room was very young, and looked very intimidated. "What happened to Sir Robert?"

"Your Majesty, he was found face down at his table. He had left a letter detailing atrocities towards several maids at the castle as well as young ladies in town. I will not risk your Ladies' constitutions by detailing. It seems like he committed suicide. Poison is thought to be the culprit. Several of the guards are protesting this, insisting that a man as strongly willed as Robert could never have done such a thing. They say the note looks like his handwriting, but they've called in his sister to identify it."

During the young guard's speech, Sariah felt the blood drain from her face. She knew she needed to keep it together until she was alone, but, how did The Crow manage to pull this off? She had stabbed Sir Robert in the belly last night, and held him until he left this world. He was a miserable son of a bitch that the Ladies knew to steer clear of. What if this somehow came back to her, or worse yet, what if someone tried to frame Javier for it?

It wouldn't be out of the realm of possibilities for sure. A stranger shows up out of nowhere with Sariah appearing as a hostage to everyone who looked at them, and then the next day, a guard is found dead? Props to The Crow with the way that she set things up, but, Sariah had a bad feeling about the whole thing.

"Thank you, so much, Sir...?" The young guard was not one that Sariah remembered encountering before, and the Queen always preferred to call her guards by name if she could.

He blushed profusely before replying, "Sir Lane, Your Majesty... I've only just lately joined your forces." He bowed regally to the Queen.

She gave him a gentle smile. "Yes, thank you Sir Lane. Please have Sir Luc put together a plan for Sir Robert, and to make sure that there will be no gaps in our defenses. Also have him pay my respects to Sir Robert's family." Sir Lane bowed again, stepped out of the room, and closed the door.

Queen Elliana waited a few moments to make sure the guard was out of hearing distance before she continued. "Well, this is an interesting turn of events. Ladies, I don't have much else for this morning. Please, go about your business. If any of you hear anything about Sir Robert's incident, please do not hesitate to bring it to myself or to Sir Luc. For the moment, you are excused." Queen Elliana motioned to the door with her hand, and watched as her Ladies shuffled out of the chamber.

Chapter Fourteen

Sariah walked back to her room in a daze, and sat down heavily on her bed. There was nothing she could do now about what she had done. It was done. She remembered her promise to The Crow, and decided that the best thing she could do was to stay busy. She pulled her dress over her head, and got out a clean set of riding clothes.

Similar to her workout clothes in style, her riding clothes were dove grey leather, and also had a morning coat that went with the breeches. She pulled on a pair of soft black boots with a nice hard sole, and discreetly armed herself. Since she was only going into town, and not out on an actual ride about the country, she needed to stay as demure-looking as possible for her reputation.

She quickly braided her long black hair, and then pulled the tail of the braid up into a twist at the back of her neck. Glancing at herself in her looking glass, she saw that she was still pale but she felt about as ready as she could be to go out. She grabbed a small leather pouch and affixed it to her belt for her money, and turned to head to the door. She paused, her hand on the door.

She didn't know why she was stressing over the death of Sir Robert so much. She knew she had been justified in her self-defense. She also knew that stepping in and stopping him from further abusing that young girl was the right thing to do. Queen Elliana would not censure her at all, nor stand for her to be punished. And yet... something still wasn't right. She felt very uneasy.

She knew that stalling wouldn't help the situation any, though, so she took a breath and pulled open her door. Javier was leaning on the stone wall across from her door, one foot on the ground, the other on the wall behind him, with his knee bent in front of him.

His arms were across his chest, and he was looking down. Hearing no movement after the door opened, he looked up. Her breath caught in her throat again at his beauty.

"We need to talk. Do you want to do so here, or somewhere else?" He looked grave, and there was something behind his eyes. Something had happened. Sariah hoped it was nothing more than him wanting to talk about the death of Sir Robert, but if he wanted her alone, she didn't think that was all he had to say.

Quickly shifting her plans a bit in her head, she responded, "I was just heading down to the stables. I was going to ride into the village proper to do some shopping. Maybe we could ride by the lake first, if you cared to join me?" The lake was often deserted this time of day, with the exception of some kids who were brave enough to play near its edges or to fish its waters for food. They would be alone there, or at least alone as they could be. Sariah also thought that maybe some fresh air would do them both good. This time of year there was usually a nice crisp breeze that came across the lake.

Javier pushed himself forward off the wall, and held his arm out for Sariah. Sariah stepped out of her room, locked the door behind her, and took his arm. As they began to walk, she turned them towards the back of the castle. "Are your rooms comfortable, and to your and Lord Heath's liking?" Thank goodness for small talk. Hopefully Javier would take the hint.

"Thank you, m' lady. Yes, they are very well-appointed and comfortable rooms. Everyone has been particularly hospitable." Javier had put on quite the unaffected air. He was smiling, and walking with her as if they were out for just any old daily stroll. They nodded to several servants they encountered as they made their way through the castle.

"Have you been to Blackmore before? Forgive me, I do not know where Lord Sandram calls home." Sariah was wondering if she could glean information about her intriguing companion as they walked.

Neither Javier nor Heath spoke with accents, and looks-wise, Heath could be from anywhere. Javier had warm-toned skin, most likely from the deserts of the western world or the jungles of the southern world. However, he honestly could just be someone who spends a lot of time outdoors. Sariah didn't think so, though. There was something exotic, something *other* about Javier.

"As you know, Lord Heath has been to Blackmore many times, when he was betrothed to the Queen's sister. This is my first visit, however. But it will not, I think, be my last." Javier looked over at her with a smirk. "Lord Heath is from Belrick, not too far from here. His family has owned land there as long as anyone can remember. He is the steward of the land, as their country has no traditional King. Since he travels a lot on business, his sister has the keeping of the country most times. She is quite the capable ruler. Truth be told, it suits them both well. He doesn't like this to be common knowledge, but he never wanted to rule. He loves having the ability to travel, and make alliances with new lands. He's a businessman at heart. Lady Margaret makes a fantastic regent. She's extremely honest and fair. She is also quite beautiful. It is a surprise that neither she nor her brother have made a marriage alliance for her yet."

Sariah smiled at his obvious admiration of the siblings. "Lord Heath is no slouch in the looks department himself. His long dark hair, and striking green eyes give him a roguish look that I have a feeling has quite a few women chasing after him."

Sir Javier chuckled. "Indeed. However, his Lordship prefers the company of gentlemen to that of women." He had a twinkle in his eye as he looked over at her.

"Well, good that his marriage to Princess Ariana never went through then, hm?" Sariah smiled at the thought, and then was saddened by it too. If his parents had been trying to force him into a traditional marriage, they most likely were not thrilled by his inclinations. "Did his parents know he was gay?"

"His father did not, hence the creation of the engagement. However, after his death, if you recall, his mother broke the engagement. She knew her son well, and loved him until her death. His sister knows as well, and loves him all the more for it." He had a genuine smile on his face. Sariah could tell that he looked at the family he worked with as more than just a client. He had said he was a friend as well as a guard for Lord Heath.

"I can tell you love the family very much. Have you been with them long?" Sariah wanted to learn as much as she could of Javier before they turned to speaking of graver things.

"Most of my life." Javier gave such a short answer compared to what he gave about the Sandrams.

Sariah tried again, "Are you from Belrick?" They were moving at a fair pace, and would be out of the castle soon.

"Not originally, but I call it home now." Again Javier gave such short answers. Sariah had a feeling that he was not one to talk about himself. As one who kept her cards close to her vest, she understood the feeling. "Are you from Blackmore?" He was apparently going to try to turn the tables on her.

"I am." She decided to play along with his game. Maybe she could get a quid pro quo bargain with him.

He shot her one of his grins, realizing what she was doing. "I guess I deserved that. I'm just not one to talk about myself. I don't feel like my life is very interesting."

Sariah pursed her lips, deciding what to say. She was still trying to figure it out when they walked outside. She steered Javier towards the large stable behind the castle, where her mount was housed. Sariah wasn't sure if his and Lord Heath's mounts had been moved to this stable as of yet, but she figured the stable boys could find a spare horse for Javier to ride.

As they walked across the field she had all but run through the night before, he asked, "Did I make you angry?" He ducked his head to see her expression. The earnest look on his face reminded her of a little boy who had been naughty. He was trying to figure out how bad his punishment would be.

She threw her head back with an honest laugh. "I'm sorry to laugh at you, but you just looked so innocent then. Like a child caught stealing cookies. It was very cute." She smiled at him, laughter in her eyes.

He took her chin in his hand, turned towards her, and kissed her. This was not the fiery, passionate kisses of the barn, nor was it the quick kiss she gave him as she shoved him out the door. This kiss was sweet. And as it continued, it started a slow burn in both of them.

Sariah wrapped her arms around Javier's neck, and stood on her tiptoes to get better access. Javier's hands landed on her waist, and with that, she deepened the kiss a bit. After a few moments, she ended the kiss by nibbling on his bottom lip. They both were feeling the effects of it, but they were unable to act on it, being in the middle of a field, and in view of anyone who cared to look.

Sariah felt that if she really were a Queen's Lady in the traditional sense, she'd be embarrassed by what they'd just done in such a public place. Being who she was though, she just felt achy, and wet. She wanted him again. And she had a feeling that he wanted her just as much. Sariah wondered when she'd be able to get him alone again. She also wondered if her feelings for him were remaining purely physical. He was indeed a fine specimen of a man, but he was also sweet, and kind. His danger made him all the more intriguing. Was she starting to fall in love with him? She'd have to think on it. For now though, he held his arm out to Sariah, and they continued on to the stables.

Chapter Fifteen

The stable boys had two horses saddled in no time at all. Sariah set them off towards the lake at a canter, wondering what Javier needed to talk to her about. It could be any number of things, really, but she had a feeling it was about who she really was, and her role as a Queen's Lady. Sariah wasn't forbidden from telling someone who she really was, and what she did for the Queen, but she needed to be selective about who knew. A spouse or partner for example, would need to know, for their own safety. Queen's Ladies sometimes made very powerful enemies, and living with one or loving one could be very dangerous.

Sariah was not worried about Javier's safety if he knew her secret. Her concern was that he'd be leaving. And then he'd know. She'd really need to trust him if she were going to tell him what she was. She'd been given no reason *not* to trust him, but at the same time, she'd been given no reason *to* trust him, either. She knew this was going to come down to a gut decision.

As they came up to the lake, they slowed their horses. Cantering made talking prohibitive, so, Sariah had had time to think on their journey over. By the solemn look on Javier's face, he'd had time to think, too.

As they slowed the horses further, down to a walk, and started a path around the lake, Sariah waited for Javier to begin. She turned her face to the breeze, enjoying the fresh and crisp air. Some strands of her hair came loose from her braid, and swirled around her face.

Javier looked at her for a long time. Sariah was wondering what he was thinking. "I heard about Sir Robert. I wanted to ask you how you were." Sariah was taken a bit aback by this comment.

Her face very carefully and quickly shut down. "It was a shock to hear this morning, to be sure, but I'm doing fine. I didn't know the man really well, so his death, while sad, has no real impact on me."

Javier looked at her for a long time before speaking again. "Of course. Lord Heath and I believe that they might try to pin his death on us. What do you think? Is this a possibility?"

Sariah thought about his question for a moment, even though it was a question she had asked herself that morning. "I had heard his death was a suicide. If it is truly deemed such, there would be no way to place the blame on the two of you. If that is untrue, and they determine he was murdered, it *is* possible."

Javier was again silent for a long time. Sariah watched Javier as he ran things through his head. She got the feeling he was disappointed about something. Maybe he was expecting a different answer from her. But, she wanted him to be prepared. If the Queen or her guards moved against him, it could be a while before she heard about it and would be able to step in. And she would step in. There is absolutely no way that she'd let him or Lord Heath take the fall for what she did.

"I wouldn't let anything happen to you. I know you did not kill him, nor did Lord Heath. My opinion holds a lot of sway with Her Majesty. I'd never let you take the fall for this." She was seeking to reassure him, and apparently what she said did somewhat. He turned to her with less grave of a look.

"Thank you, m'lady, for once again offering to stand up for complete strangers. Not many would bother." They were riding close enough that Javier reached over, grabbed her hand, and kissed it.

When she took her hand back, she placed it near her leg on the horse. She didn't want him to see the reaction he had on her. But she stretched her fingers out, before putting them into a tight fist. How a simple thing like that could have such an affect on her was beyond her. But it did.

They had come to a part of the lake that was particularly deserted. While the day had started out clear and sunny, clouds had rolled in as they were riding, and rain threatened. The wind had picked up more, and the temperature was dropping. Sariah was about to mention heading back before the weather as they came around a bend of trees and they saw a young woman carrying her infant. Sariah thought this was an odd place to take a walk with such a young child.

As they got closer Sariah saw that the infant was dressed in the lightest of clothing, and that the young woman was headed with the infant towards the water. Without knowing what she was doing, Sarah kicked her mount's flanks, and took off quickly towards the woman and child.

Her head was spinning, and the blood was pounding in her ears. She knew she was not alone, and in that moment, she knew what she had suspected was right. The young woman was going to rid herself of her child. Sariah called out to the woman, who started, and pulled the child closely to her.

The woman turned away from the water, and looked like she was going to run, but Sariah was determined not to let this woman get away. As soon as she was close enough, she dismounted without even slowing. "You have come here to rid yourself of a burden." She spoke to the woman, but the voice was not hers.

"Your husband is away, and has been for some time. The child is not his. You didn't want him to learn of your infidelity, so you chose to take an innocent life rather than to face what you've done." Sariah reached out, and took the child from the young woman. The woman was too shocked to object. It was a little girl, she saw, with bright blue eyes, and strawberry blonde hair. The infant smiled up at Sariah before yawning, and slipping into a deep sleep. Sariah had no doubt in her mind that The Crow helped the child into slumber.

Javier was behind Sariah, having caught up to her while she had been speaking to the young woman. Sariah backed up to him, and handed the child over to him. He reached down and took the infant into his arms without complaint, and continued to watch the proceedings. He knew what was going on.

"You have made your choice. You will deal with the consequences of it." The ethereal sword appeared again in Sariah's hand. The woman dropped to her knees on the ground, fervently praying for forgiveness. "I will make sure your child is taken care of." The woman looked up at Sariah in surprise, her mouth open some, when Sariah swung the blade.

The woman fell to the ground seconds later. She had been cleanly beheaded in one stroke. She had felt no pain as she died. Once again, Sariah saw The Crow step out of her body, and gather up the woman's remains. Sariah had so many questions for The Crow. However, The Crow just put her finger to her lips, her face solemn, and, carrying the woman's body, started off towards the village.

Sariah dropped to her knees once The Crow was out of sight. She had started this event. She knew what would have happened to the child if she hadn't stepped in. She thought of the feel of her blade as it went through the woman's neck. Sariah leaned over to the side, and vomited.

Chapter Sixteen

Luna landed on Sariah's shoulder. She nuzzled the side of her face with her beak. Sariah took comfort in the fact that the little crow was trying to ease her pain. Where Sariah felt no guilt about Sir Robert, she was sick over this death. Even knowing that she saved the life of that innocent little girl, she did so at the cost of the girl's mother.

She slowly stood up, and turned to look at Javier. "Are you alright?" His concern was evident in his eyes, although his voice was steady and held no emotion. He looked down at the child for a moment before looking back at Sariah.

Sariah nodded her head and felt more bile rise in her throat. She held up one finger, asking him to wait a moment, and bent over holding completely still. Finally, the nausea passed, and she stood up slowly. "I'm fine." She did not truly believe what she was saying, and this knowledge came out in the way she spoke.

Javier looked her over, from her overly pale visage to the slight trembling in her hands. "You said you'd see the child taken care of. Do you have a place to take her?" He apparently wasn't going to comment on what had just happened, so, Sariah would do her best to ignore it for now as well.

Sariah nodded, "I do. I know a family who would love a child, but have not been successful in having one. They are in the village. We can take the little one to them on our way back. Please, let me do the talking." Sariah sounded exhausted, and sad. She looked it, too. She was moving slowly and unsteadily.

Javier nodded his head once, and looked down at the sleeping infant in his arms. They made quite a picture. He had pulled a shawl from a pouch at his belt, and wrapped the tiny baby in it. Due to

Sariah's intervention, she would hopefully get to live to be an old maid. Javier looked over at Sariah. Luna left Sariah's shoulder and landed on Javier's. He held his fingers up to Luna for her to rub or nip them as she would. She did both, making him smile.

Sariah climbed up onto her mount, and turned it towards town. She was clearly in shock, and she felt that she needed to be alone for a while. Since Her Majesty had called a halt to all things court related until Sir Robert's death was worked out, after getting this girl to her new home, she'd be able to shut herself in her rooms and just be alone as long as she needed.

As they made their way into the village, Sariah straightened her posture, and plastered a smile on her face. As a Queen's Lady, she would need to be happy and cheerful. What did a Queen's Lady need to worry about? Sariah felt sick inside. But she could not show any hint of it outwardly.

Several people in the village tipped their hats to her, or curtseyed as she passed. She was well-known in the village. It spoke well of her, that she didn't shun the people around her due to her status. As they reached the edge of the village, she slowed her horse outside of a larger house. There were farmlands just beyond its fence.

Sariah dismounted and headed back to where Javier had stopped his horse. She reached up to him for the baby without saying anything, and he handed her over. The look on Sariah's face was unfathomable. She was in so much internal pain. Without looking him in the eye, Sariah turned towards the house with her bundle.

She knocked on the door and waited. Soon, a plump young woman answered the knock. She was plainly dressed, but quite beautiful. She had blonde hair and bright blue eyes. She saw Sariah and smiled. "Lady Sariah, what a pleasant surprise! I just laid tea. Would you care to come in?" The young lady had a beautiful smile.

"My thanks, Eleanor, I cannot stay. But I have brought you a gift. My companion and I were out riding today, and discovered this abandoned among the grass near the lake." With that, she pulled the covering down so that Eleanor could see what she carried. Eleanor gasped. "I know how long you and Charles have wanted a child. I know that you haven't been blessed with one yet. Since this little girl seems to be unwanted by her birth parents, I thought maybe you and Charles would be able to give her the home that she deserves."

Eleanor held her hands out for the infant, longing in her eyes, but still speechless. Sariah carefully handed over the little girl, who opened her eyes, and looked at her new mother. She smiled and yawned, and snuggled into Eleanor's arms. "Oh. Oh my. Lady Sariah. She's so beautiful. She's truly a gift. And you're sure she was abandoned? No one will be looking for her?"

Sariah's smile faltered but for a second. "No, Eleanor. No one will be looking for her. She is truly alone in this world. Please, love her as your own, and give her a good home." Sariah needed to finish this business and get back to her room. She was barely holding it together.

Eleanor nodded profusely. "We will. I promise we will."

Sariah pulled a small bag of coins from her pouch. "For her keeping." She curtsied and turned away from the house. When she reached her mount and Javier, she put her foot in the stirrup and mounted without looking at him or speaking.

"Lady Sariah?" Javier sounded very concerned for his companion. She merely nodded, and turned her horse towards the castle. Javier followed suit, but Sariah could still feel his eyes on her. She worried that he would try to stay with her.

When they reached the castle stables, Sariah dismounted quickly, and handed her mount over to the stable boys. She felt like she was in a fog as she walked back towards the castle. She had one goal at this point: to get back to her room where she could fall apart in peace. She was thankful that Javier had been there with her that day, but she needed away from him.

THE QUEEN'S LADY

Regardless of how rude it was, she left him at the stables and took off across the field they had kissed in earlier. She knew she was faster than him, and once she was in the castle, she could lose him with shortcuts.

Sariah made it through the castle without meeting anyone, thank goodness. She locked her door, walked over to her wash basin, and ran some cool water into it. She splashed some of the cool water on her face and ran it over her wrists. She felt too hot, and yet she was freezing all at once.

She pulled the cord over her bathing tub for hot water, threw in some of her chamomile as well as her lavender bubbles, and immediately stripped out of her clothes. She climbed in the tub without checking the temperature first, and pulled her knees to her chest. She put her hands around her knees, and just sat there in the water, trying not to think.

Chapter Seventeen

Javier headed to Sariah's room. When he reached her door, he paused outside of it, to see if he could hear anything. He thought he heard running water, but couldn't be sure. He pulled out his picks and made quick work of the lock. He gently opened the door.

She didn't even register that the door had opened. She was still in the bath with her knees to her chest. She was looking straight ahead and her mind was somewhere else. He walked into the room and shut the door behind him, locking it. Sariah heard him, but did not acknowledge that he was there. He walked over to the tub and pulled the cord to turn off the water. The tub was almost full. She looked up at him with unseeing eyes. "Oh, baby." He said, compassion in his voice. She wanted nothing more than for him to pick her up in his arms and hold her. Let her know that it was going to be alright.

Since she was in the bath, he looked over the lotions and creams on the side of the tub, picking out a lavender shampoo and soap, and he took her hair down out of her twist and braid. Since she didn't stop him, he got her hair thoroughly wet, and washed it, just like one would a child. Then he used the soap on her shoulders and arms, sliding his hands under the water to rub it across her belly and down her legs. He was completely innocent in his quest to get her clean. She let him clean her. She just sat there and let him take care of her. It was nothing like she, as strong as she was, ever thought that she would need. He grabbed her robe from the chair near the tub, picked her up out of the bath, carried her over to the bed partially wrapped in it, and laid down, pulling her into his arms. At this point, he was completely soaked, but he didn't seem to mind. Sariah laid in his arms with her eyes open.

Luna fluttered her wings a bit, making enough noise to let them know she was there. Dusk was falling, and her room was getting quite dark. As he laid there with her in his arms, the candles around the room flickered into life. The room took on an ethereal glow in the growing darkness. Sariah's mind did not register this bit of magic, as shocked as she was. She just focused on staying present in the moment.

After a little while, Sariah started shaking. It wasn't a shaking like she was cold, but a rhythmic shaking, like she was quietly sobbing. He just pushed her hair back away from her face, and continued to hold her. Eventually the quiet sobbing turned to actual crying. When this started, she grabbed him tightly, and buried her face into his chest.

At one point he looked up towards the foot of the bed, and saw The Crow standing there, looking at them pensively. She just watched them, saying nothing and not moving. Sariah did not register that The Crow was there, nor that Javier was looking at the goddess. He just nodded at the goddess who looked at him speculatively before disappearing from sight. Once she was gone, he tightened his arms around Sariah and let her cry.

After their unexpected visitor, Sariah eventually cried herself out and laid still in his arms. Her room was temperate, and neither of them was too warm or too cold. He scooted down a bit on the bed carefully, so as not to jostle her too much. Once he was in a fully supine position, he saw that she had fallen asleep. Not wanting to leave the candles lit, he waved his free hand, and all the candles in the room went out at once.

The next morning, Sariah woke up to a knock on the door. Figuring it was Maddie coming in for the day to launder her clothes and maybe give her some news about the day, she called out consent for the girl to enter. She snuggled down deeper into her bed. She'd never slept more comfortably than the night before.

The second that the spicy musk registered, she sat straight up in bed. Javier was in bed with her, and she was wearing only her robe. He was fully dressed, but the fact remained that she had a man in her bed. As a Queen's Lady, her romantic partners were not looked at overly closely, but she was expected to be discreet. Since she was unmarried, if Maddie saw Javier in her bed, she worried what the consequences would be. Unfortunately, she was out of time and options as Maddie came bustling into her room.

"Good morning, M'Lady. The skies are clear, the sun is out, and the day promises to be warm." Maddie went straight to the bath, and hadn't looked at the bed yet. Sariah looked over at Javier, who was still asleep. "Did you forget to drain your bath last night? In all your excitement, I'm sure you were tired. Mistress Eleanor Baker was in this morning already, asking to thank you again for bringing that baby to her. What a joy!"

Maddie added some new washcloths, checked the levels of Sariah's soaps and lotions, and cracked the window by the bath before turning towards Sariah. "Oh goodness my lady!" Maddie put her hands to her mouth. Sariah closed her eyes in fear of what was coming next. "Your hair is quite a mess! It looks like a bird's nest. Would you like me to stay and help you arrange it?"

Sariah opened her eyes with a start. Maddie had a huge grin on her face, though she was doing her best to cover it with one hand, and was looking directly at Sariah. There's *no way* she could not see Javier. Why wasn't she mentioning him? Well, if Maddie wasn't going to mention it, Sariah most assuredly was not going to. "No thank you, Maddie. I must have been tossing and turning last night. It shouldn't take me too long to fix it." Sariah smiled with what she hoped was warmth and thanks at the girl. Maddie nodded and went over to the laundry basket that Sariah kept by her wardrobe.

Sariah stole a glance behind her, and saw Javier awake, propped on one arm, but still spread across her bed. He held one finger up to his lips. She nodded mutely. Maddie turned back to Sariah. "I've brought some of your gowns back, M'lady, but you're down to one set of riding clothes. Were you planning on going anywhere in the next few days?"

Sariah started to answer in the negative, but the gentle nudge behind her changed her answer. "I've been riding out with Sir Javier, showing him the country. If you could have the laundry maids focus on my riding clothes first, please, I would appreciate it." Maddie nodded at this, grabbed the basket and set it out in the hall. She came back in with an empty basket, set it where the previous one had been, curtseyed, and made her way out of the room. As soon as the door closed, Sariah bolted off her bed and across the room to lock it.

"What did you do, bribe Maddie to stay quiet?" Sariah asked as she turned to face Javier. Her tone was incredulous.

He pursed his lips and shook his head. "I'm not without talents, you know. I have my ways." With this cryptic little speech, Javier stood up, walked over to Sariah, and put his hands on her shoulders. "Are you okay?" His question was an honest one.

Sariah looked at him blankly for a moment, and then she remembered the night before. She blushed down to her roots, and tried to squeeze out of his grasp, but he tightened his hands. She realized that he was not going to let go until she answered. "Yes. I'm fine. Thank you." She cleared her throat and he let her pull away this time.

"Sariah, you have nothing to be embarrassed about. What you did yesterday- it was a hard thing. I know it's not your first time, not with the way that you wield your blades, but taking a life should never be easy." Sariah looked at him for a moment before frowning and turning away.

"I don't know how to do this, Javier. I don't know what I'm doing with my life. It was set up so neatly before. Yes, it was mundane, and yes, I'm sure I could have been doing more to help make the world a better place, but it was *my* life. Now I feel like I'm living someone else's life." While she had started out quiet, by the end of her speech, she was almost yelling.

Javier came up behind her and put his arms around her. This time she didn't pull away. She let herself relax back into his chest for a moment, soaking in his warmth, and letting him comfort her. She twisted around in his arms, took his face in her hands, and kissed him. It was a short, soft kiss, but that kiss said so much about how she felt for him- thankful, sweet, and honestly? Loving. She realized she was starting to fall in love with him.

Chapter Eighteen

The thought that she was falling in love with Javier was like a splash of ice water to her system. So as not to concern him, she gently pulled out of his embrace, when what she really wanted to do was run in the other direction, and never look back. How was she going to be able to make this work? She was a Queen's Lady, and required here, in Queen Elliana's Court.

He was not only a bodyguard for Lord Heath, but from what he had told her of Heath's family, they were like his family as well. And now, with her bond to The Crow, she didn't know how to balance it. She had a feeling that she could go anywhere and carry out The Crow's mission, but, how did she tell Javier about it?

She played the scenario between the two of them out in her head, and it didn't come out in her favor. She was still in Javier's arms for the moment, and didn't want to leave them. She let out a big sigh, and pulled back a little and turned to look at him. "That was quite the sigh." Javier brushed some stray hair from her brow and kissed her forehead.

Sariah decided to put off making any decisions for now. "What would you like to see today? Since you gave me a story so that I could spend more time with you, I might as well make the best of it." He chuckled at her, seeming amused by her discomfort.

"Am I really that unpleasant to be around?" He asked teasingly.

Sariah quickly backpedaled. "Oh, goodness no! I'm so sorry if I made you feel that way. I'm just not used to taking orders from anyone but Queen Elliana. I've been my own person for so long now that leaning on someone else just feels funny."

Javier seemed to take pity on her since she was sincerely worried that she might have offended him. "I was only teasing you. I know that you're not upset by spending time with me." He tilted her chin up with his finger. "Besides, if you were really sick of me, I know you could just figure out a way to get rid of me. You're very resourceful." He smiled at her, but she started a bit at what he said. Realizing how he had sounded, it was his turn to backpedal.

Sariah stopped him before he could get too far into his apology. "Javier, let's agree to stop apologizing, or we'll never get anything done." She smiled at him to show him he was forgiven.

He smiled back at her. "Deal."

Sariah realized that she was still only wearing a robe, and so she turned away from him to get some clothes on. She still didn't know how on earth he was able to either evade Maddie's notice or have her ignore him, but she was going to find out. She dressed quickly, and when she turned back around to see Javier still sitting on her bed.

He wasn't looking at her, but instead was looking down at Luna, who had made herself comfortable in his lap. He was gently stroking her, and she was making almost a purring noise from his attention. Sariah made a small noise of pleasure, and he looked up at her and smiled. This man kept surprising her. She had chosen a forest green dress today, knowing that jewel tones suited her. He hadn't seen her in color yet, outside of a navy blue so dark that it was almost black. His gaze roved over her, and he clearly approved of the change of color.

"Since I'm apparently almost out of riding clothes, I'll need to stay close to the castle today. We could walk into the immediate village outside the gates, but that would be about as far as I could really go." Sariah was twisting her hands a bit, and looking down. She was nervous, though she wasn't sure why.

"Staying close to the castle is fine by me. I'd actually love for you to get to spend some time with Lord Heath. I really think you two would get along." Sariah smiled at the suggestion. She had only spoken to Lord Heath briefly, and she would love to get to know him more. Maybe he could provide some insight into the mystery that was Javier.

"I would be honored to spend more time with you both, Sir Javier." Sariah wasn't sure why she made the response so formal, but she was happy she did so. Lara chose that moment to come into the room.

Outside of Maddie, Lara was the only other person to have a key to Sariah's room. Lara was astounded to find a man in Sariah's room, and sitting on her bed. She looked from Sariah to Javier, then took in the state of the room. Seeing that the bed was made, and Maddie had obviously been there recently, she was able to relax a bit. She walked over and hugged Sariah, ignoring Javier for the moment. "I came to see how you were doing. A lot has happened in the last few days." Lara pulled back, but kept her hands on Sariah's arms, seeming to want to get a good look at her.

Sariah, who was always pale, seemed a bit more so today, and the dark circles under her eyes, which were still puffy, made Lara frown. Sariah knew that her friend was prone to mothering, especially when she thought Sariah was not taking care of herself. Sariah worked up a genuine smile for her friend to help ease her mind before turning her attention back to Javier. "Lady Lara, I'd like to present you to Sir Javier. Sir Javier, Lady Lara is one of my best and oldest friends."

Javier stood up with a flourish, Luna having vacated his lap when Lara walked in. He stepped over to the ladies, and bowing deeply over Lara's hand, he laid a kiss on it. "M'lady, it is my pleasure to make your acquaintance."

Lara looked him over skeptically until she saw that Sariah was giving her a dirty look. She plastered a smile on her face and responded cordially to the introduction. She turned to Sariah and arched a brow in question.

"Sir Javier has invited me to spend the day with himself and Lord Heath. I was deciding whether to entertain them here, or if I should take them into town. I believe there's a market today." Sariah wanted to gauge Lara's reaction, to see if she would be able to be alone with the gentlemen if she stayed, or if Lara would hover the whole time.

Lara took the bait that her friend was laying for her. "Yes, there's a market in town today. Quite a large one, with vendors from around the country. I might go with you if you decide to go today."

Sariah hadn't been expecting that. While she figured that Lara would hover if she stayed here, she didn't count on Lara going to the market with them. She wasn't opposed to this, since she hadn't gotten to spend much time with Lara, and it would be interesting to see her take on her feelings for Sir Javier. "As long as Sir Javier and Lord Heath do not object, I think that would be wonderful."

Sariah and Lara both turned to Javier, awaiting his response. "I have no objections, and I doubt his Lordship will, either. We'll get to escort the two most beautiful ladies there!" He smiled at them both.

Sariah was pleased with how quickly he responded to her inquiry, and Lara seemed pleased by it as well. "Lara, will you need to let Luc know where we've gone, or is he already out and about for the day?" Luc did not keep a super close eye on his wife. He trusted her implicitly, and he knew she could defend herself if anything were to happen, but he did still like to know if she'd be going out. Lara expected the same courtesy from him.

"He's out on patrol today. Won't be home until after dinner, most likely. But I'll pop into our room and leave him a note before we leave. Sir Javier, if you'd excuse us, I had some things I'd like to discuss with Sariah." Lara nodded at him in dismissal. He smiled at Sariah when Lara was turned away from him. He was amused by Sariah's friend.

"Indeed. I'll just head back to Lord Heath and my room to make him aware of our plans. Should we just meet you ladies at the gate, or would you like us to come back here and escort you?" Again he flashed a grin at Sariah.

Before Lara could say something to embarrass herself, Sariah interjected. "We'll meet you gentlemen at the gate. Thank you, Sir Javier." Sariah dropped into a curtsey, knowing that Lara would feel compelled to do so as well. When she did, Sariah gave Javier a smile in return, and he bowed to both ladies before leaving the room.

Chapter Nineteen

Once Sir Javier left the room, Lara surveyed it more critically. Sariah rolled her eyes at her friend, and said with exasperation, "Well...?" Lara looked at her with an amused grin.

"Well what? What am I supposed to think when I walk into your room first thing in the morning and find him here?" She put her hands on her hips and looked at Sariah disapprovingly.

"He was not here first thing. Ask Maddie. She was here just before you. And unless you think he was hiding under the bed, she can vouch that I was alone except for Luna." Sariah motioned to the small crow.

Lara looked at Luna before narrowing her gaze and turning back to her friend. "What happened, Sariah? You were gone. And now you're back, and you've changed." She stepped forward, and touched the scar on Sariah's neck with her fingertips. "Your voice has changed, you brought back a strange pet, and you arrived tied to a strange man's horse! A man who now looks at you like my husband looks at me! I think he's in love with you." At this last part, Lara's mouth quirked up into a knowing grin.

Sariah shook her head, looking serious. "I don't know, Lara. I can't remember anything before waking up in a cave, apparently laying in a pool of blood. Well, nothing distinct anyways. I *know* things about my life before, but I can't pinpoint *when* the memory loss begins. I won't deny things have changed, because I know they have. I know *I* have." Sariah wrapped her arms around herself and started pacing.

"Javier is- I don't know what he is to me yet. I'm still figuring it out. But there's heat and passion there. I can tell you that. Love? I'm not so sure. I think I might be falling in love with him, but I've only known him for a few days. It makes no sense." Sariah stopped next to her friend.

Lara laid a hand on her shoulder, and smiled at her. "Sometimes you just know. It was that way for Luc and I. While we knew right away, we had a long courtship before we married though. Do you think a marriage could potentially work between you two?"

Sariah moved her arms down to her stomach and fisted there. She didn't like the pain she felt in the pit of her stomach when she thought about not being able to be with Javier. "Honestly? I don't know. I feel needed here, with Queen Elliana. And he's been with Lord Heath's family most of his life, he said. They're like family to him." Sariah looked at her friend with pleading eyes. "I'm not sure what I can do."

Lara put her arms around Sariah and pulled her into a hug. "If it comes to it, my dear, Elliana will find another Queen's Lady. She would want you to be happy. You know she would."

Sariah wasn't so sure she could just leave the place she'd known as home for her whole life to head off with a man she barely knew. She decided it was something that she would need to think on. "Well, we need to head towards the gates, or the gentlemen will be waiting on us." Sariah needed to change the subject. She could not ruminate on this anymore right now.

"It's okay for them to wait on us. Gives them character." Lara winked at Sariah and put her arm around her as they headed out. Sariah laughed, and locked her room behind them.

When they got to the gate, the men were indeed waiting for them, but it didn't look like they'd been waiting long. Sir Javier made introductions of Lord Heath and Lady Lara, and then the foursome headed out the gate towards the village. Markets usually took place on the outskirts of the village, not far from the castle gates. They had originally taken place on the other side of the village, but when vendors realized that a lot of the castle inhabitants couldn't get the time off to make it out there, they relocated.

Consisting of mostly local farmers, but also a few traveling artisans, the market always had a bit of a festive air to it. There were often performers there as well- local villagers who dusted off their instruments, or dancing shoes, and felt the need to show off. They performed for free, but always had a container out for tips. Sariah's money pouch was full today, and she intended on spreading it around the market as much as possible. While she didn't really need the items that she bought, she loved to be able to support those who lived in the village. The Queen often gave her Ladies extra money when she heard they were going to the market so that she too could support those in the village, but anonymously.

Since their village was a fairly productive farming village, and Blackmore did a good amount of trade with surrounding lands, their village was fairly well off. They had families who struggled, for sure, but the majority of the families could not only feed themselves with the monies they made from their farming or production, but they were able to enjoy some finer items than would normally be found in a village. Interestingly, Queen Elliana kept very few luxuries in the castle, beyond the ability to have hot running water, and some items with nicer fabrics. For the most part, she put the country's wealth back into its economy, and its people. She was a beloved monarch.

As the foursome walked, Sariah and Lara told the men about various interesting aspects of the country in which they lived. The gentlemen were attentive listeners, and asked questions about different facts that they found particularly interesting. As they walked up to the market, the men looked around with interest. While some of the traveling vendors had tents they pitched to display their wares, most of the local vendors had created makeshift wooden tables that they left up between markets.

There were a lot of vendors this morning, since the weather was nice. People selling honey and jams, butter and dried meat, milk, leather goods, wool items as well as raw wool, all the way to intricate glass beads and forged weapons. Since the traveling vendors changed regularly, you never knew what you'd find at the market. One of the first stalls they came to was a flower vendor, and Lord Heath bought each of the ladies a small wildflower bouquet.

The group wandered around, and while Sariah would have loved to have visited the blade vendor, she knew that in such an open atmosphere, she could not. However, since the men wanted to go look at the blades, the ladies just *had* to follow their escorts. They made a decent show of objecting to wanting to go check out the weapons, but in reality, both of the Ladies were completely happy to go along and peruse the wares.

Sariah, having lost a full set of her blades, was particularly intrigued. Sir Javier held his arm out for her as they walked into the vendor's open-sided tent, and she obliged him. The lust in her eyes as they walked by well-forged steel, and decorative blades was hard for her to hide, especially from Javier, who was walking so close to her. Some women loved flowers and chocolate, but this woman? Give her a sharp blade, and she'd be thrilled- that is until you made her angry... then she might use it on you. He smiled at Sariah as they walked through, and he saw her eyes stop on a particular item.

A simple short sword with a polished, double-sided blade, there was nothing overly decorative or beautiful about it, except for the fact that it was well-crafted. Her fingers ached to touch the blade. This one reminded her so much of the one that she had lost that she knew she had to have it. She would have no real way of being able to purchase it though, not with her image. Javier led her over to the blade though, and started looking it over. He picked the blade up, and looked down its length, making sure it was quite straight. He tested the edge of the blade on each side, as it was a double-edged sword. Holding his hand flat, he tested the weight of the blade as well as the balance.

Sariah watched Javier as he looked over the blade, wondering at his motives. Could he tell how much she wanted it? The blade was not a blade she'd have picked for him, after seeing him wield a long-sword in practice with her. The hilt of the sword was very simple, wrapped in black leather, and not so bulky as to cause discomfort in the grip, even for hands as small as hers. Javier motioned the vendor over, who was the blacksmith who made the blades, and began to ask about pricing. While he was doing that, Sariah saw that Lara had a small dagger that had caught her eye. Lord Heath was looking over the dagger with her, and they seemed content for the moment. Luckily for Lara, daggers were very acceptable for women to purchase, even if they were shopping on their own. Daggers were used for more than defense, although, as a Queen's Lady, defense and offense were mostly how they were employed.

Sariah turned her attention back to Javier as he finished the purchase of the blade. He took the blade and scabbard from the merchant, and handed over a small pouch of money. The vendor's eyes got wide, but he just nodded his thanks. Sariah realized that Javier must have overpaid for the sword. Javier continued down the tables of blades to see if anything else caught his or Sariah's eye, but nothing seemed to. Looking back at Lord Heath and Lady Lara, Sariah saw that they too were finishing up a purchase. Javier leaned down close to Sariah's ear and whispered, "Seeing how you looked at that blade reminded me of how you were looking at me the other night. I knew I couldn't leave without getting it for you." Sariah quickly turned to him, a shocked look on her face. "Hopefully I get to see that look turned towards me again." He glanced around, but since no one was looking, he stole a quick kiss before walking out of the tent.

Sariah flushed as much at his words as the stolen kiss. He was keeping her off balance alright. And she knew she wanted to turn that look on him again. In fact, as soon as she could get him alone, she'd love to get her hands on him again. For more than just a quickie. She'd love to be able to take her time with him. And she had a feeling that he would love taking his time with her. She cleared her throat, and fanned herself a bit. "It's warm today."

Javier chuckled, and she realized she was not fooling him at all. "Indeed. Quite warm." She was grateful that he was playing along with her. With his little smirks and grins as they exchanged banter, she had a feeling that he enjoyed the chase as much as the reward.

When Lara and Heath joined them again, Sariah had herself under control. Apparently there was something in her face though, because she saw Lara arch a knowing brow in her direction. Sariah stole a glance at Javier, but all seemed in order with him. It must be her face that was giving something away, since they were just standing outside of the tent with her arm in his. Completely innocent.

The group moved through the rest of the market, Sariah and Lara spending coins liberally. The men noticed what they were doing, and found occasion to spend as well. It spoke well of Blackmore to Lord Heath that the Queen and her Ladies sought to promote its citizens through commerce as well as general support. It was something that his sister strove to bring to Belrick as well. Finding nothing much more of interest, however, they agreed to head back to the castle so they could break for lunch.

Chapter Twenty

Javier had been taking Sariah's purchases as she made them, so that when they were back at the castle, he had a very easy excuse to head back to her room with her. Both Lara and Heath gave the couple knowing looks, but said nothing. The foursome were getting ready to split and head their separate ways.

Lara said goodbye to Sir Javier, Sariah, and Lord Heath, and headed back to her room with her small amount of purchases. Where Sariah preferred to buy small gifts here and there while giving the vendors a little extra money, Lara usually would only buy a few items and vastly overpay for them. Sariah didn't keep most of what she bought. She gave gifts to the various maids and guards that she'd come across. She also tended to buy handicrafts, or homemade goods, knowing that this would give the vendor the highest possible profit. She was constantly leaving small jars of jam or honey out for the guards on their watches, or giving the maids small bits of carmel or other sweets. In the cooler months, she tended towards buying gloves and scarves, knowing that the maids needed them on their daily outdoor chores. She favored bright colors and beautiful patterns, knowing that the girls often wore drab or undyed items.

Javier's arms were laden with small packages that she had purchased. He didn't seem to mind. He followed Sariah to her room, letting Lord Heath know that he would be back to their room later. Sariah felt bad with Javier carrying all of her packages, but he had reassured her several times that he didn't mind. She didn't press the issue after he gave her a stern look when reassuring her the last time she had apologized. As they made their way through the castle, the few people they came across smiled after they had passed. Sariah was one of the few Queen's Ladies who didn't have a steady relationship.

Sariah was well-loved among the castle staff, so seeing her happy would make all of them happy as well.

When they reached Sariah's room, she unlocked the door and walked in, holding the door open for Javier. Once he was in her room, she laughed a little. "Oh, dear. I bought too much again. It's a habit. I apol-" at the look on his face, she swallowed her apology and laughed again. "I give the staff and guards a lot of small gifts." She motioned to a cleared floorspace by her wardrobe where he could set the packages.

He walked over to the spot she had indicated, and gently set down all of the items but one. When he stood up and faced her, he had the sword in his hands. "Your sword, m'lady." He bowed a bit when he presented it to her.

She swallowed deeply, a wave of emotion coming over her. She gently took the sword out of his hands. He stood up so he could watch her with the blade. The fire was back in her eyes. She unsheathed the sword, loving the almost hiss it made as it slid out. This blade was so beautiful. The weight was perfect for her. She tested the balance with a few small swings, seeing how the weight felt as she moved around with it. She couldn't wait to train with it. She knew immediately that this was going to become her favorite and primary blade. And the fact that he had purchased it for her... that he saw how much she wanted it... She looked up at him.

His eyes showed raw need for her. She sheathed the sword and set it next to her bed. She put her back to her bed, plastering a pleasant smile on her face. She motioned to the door, like she was going to show him out.

He swallowed his disappointment. She could tell that he wanted her, and yet there was no way that he would push the issue. He smiled back at her, and moved towards the door. When he reached the handle, and started to open the door, her hand was suddenly there, shutting it. She turned the lock, and he turned to face her.

She moved forward towards him. He leaned back until his back was pressed against the wood of the door. She looked up at him with half-lidded eyes. She walked forward and pressed herself against him, going up on her toes so that she could put her arms around his neck and kiss him. And oh what a kiss... It was a slow burn, building the flames inside of each of them. She licked and nibbled at his mouth in addition to just kissing, and she felt as his desire rose in addition to seeing it. He was holding his hands at his side, flat against the door. She grabbed hold of his black shirt with one hand, and started backing up towards her bed.

She stopped before she reached it, and turned them around, so that his back was to the bed. She kissed him again before giving him a gentle push. He fell backwards onto the bed, offering no resistance to her wants. She climbed up on top of him, straddling his hips. She leaned down and kissed him, reaching down for his hands. She took his hands in hers, and raised them up above his head, and used her weight to hold him there. She pulled back and looked at him.

This man, this very dangerous man, who outweighed her significantly, and who could easily make her do whatever he wanted, was giving all of that up, and submitting to her. He was giving her all of the power, and it was an intoxicating feeling. She released his hands, and reached down to the hem of her dress, which had ridden up on her thighs. She lifted it over her head, revealing nothing but pale creamy skin beneath. She threw her dress off the bed, and before she could lean down again, Javier had sat up, and taken one of her rosy pink nipples in his mouth.

He gently licked and sucked, driving her pleasure even higher. Gently, so that she could object at any time, he sat up more, and rolled her over, pressing her into the bed with his weight. He mirrored the gesture she had made with him earlier, putting her hands above her head, and holding them there, but he was able to hold her in place with one hand. He leaned down and kissed her deeply, then trailed kisses across her jaw, down her neck, and back to her nipples. He was rock hard by this point, but he wanted to focus all of his attention on her. A mere thought, and all of the candles in the room were lit.

After spending ample time on her nipples, he moved lower, licking and kissing his way down her belly, across her hip, before dipping his head to the vee of her legs. Using his tongue and fingers, he drove her higher and higher, until she climaxed, then he licked up every drop of the honey she had spilled. As he moved up her body, she realized that he too was naked, and had no idea when he had taken the time to strip. The moment he entered her though, she didn't care when he had taken the time.

They fit so well together. She twisted her hips a bit, smiling wickedly at the tensing of his jaw. He saw the smile and returned it with one of his own. Then they began to move. It was a give and take, gasps and deep breaths, kisses and touches. They drove each other harder and higher until they came together, and collapsed in ecstasy on her bed. Sariah let out a contented sigh before rolling to the side, and dropping her head onto his chest. Javier kissed her head, moving her hair out of her face, and then they both drifted off into sleep.

Chapter Twenty-One

Sariah dreamed of The Crow. She was back in that meadow of heather where she had met her the first time. "He loves you, you know." The Crow looked at Sariah and smiled kindly.

Sariah shook her head. "He can't possibly love me after such a short time." Her voice carried a bit of an echo in this place, and unlike in her waking world, here it sounded like her voice had before the scar appeared.

"Some people just know." Sariah started at The Crow's words, since they were the same as what Lara had said earlier that day to her.

"Can it ever work though? How will I be able to be with him? I belong here. He belongs there." Sariah was wringing her hands a bit. As soon as she noticed it, she made a point to stop.

The Crow smiled and cocked her head, much like her bird form would have. "Do you? Are you really sure you're meant to be apart?"

Sariah thought about that. She and Javier got along so well, it was like they'd known each other forever. They moved well together, and they fought well together. She would love to see them battle together against a real opponent. She would not envy them. She smiled at the thought.

The Crow saw the smile and nodded. "You see it too. You know he is yours. All you need to do is take what's in front of you."

Sariah thought wryly, Isn't that what I just did?

The Crow's mouth quirked into a smile. "Not quite what I meant, but it is a good start. You two are so good together. Celebrate love in my name, always."

Sariah woke with a start. She looked around her room and saw that all the candles were lit. She did not light them, and she knew that Maddie hadn't been in. It was full-dark out, though she had no idea of the time. She looked over to the other side of her bed where Javier slept. He was so beautiful. He had just a smattering of chest hair over his broad tanned chest, which turned into a small line of hair just below his belly button. That hair trailed down to his manhood, which was quite a sight to behold. Even asleep, he was quite large. She smiled at the thought that she had just enjoyed him completely as he had her. She looked at his muscular arms, letting her gaze travel down his biceps and his forearms to his very skilled fingers. His legs also were extremely muscular. Since he was on his back, she could not see his ass, but she'd felt it, and it was an amazing ass.

Taking her eyes off her lover, she thought back to the Crow's dream. It was a confusing one, in that The Crow seemed to suggest that Sariah maybe didn't belong in Queen Elliana's court. Where did she belong then? This place had been her home as long as she could remember. She was offered a position as a companion to the Princess at a very young age, and once Elliana became Queen, Sariah was offered the training to become a Queen's Lady.

She laid back against the pillows again, enjoying being completely at ease in her room. Javier definitely was showing signs of courting her, so maybe he *did* have feelings for her as The Crow suggested. But he had not said anything outright, and he would need to ask her to come with him if that's really what he wanted. Based on what The Crow was hinting at, that is indeed what she thought should happen.

Sariah looked over at Javier again, only to see his dark eyes looking back at her. She smiled at him, and he rolled on his side, putting a hand on her thigh. "What were you thinking just now? You had this look of longing and sadness on your face." Sariah wished Javier wasn't so insightful or attentive to her. If he weren't, she'd be able to hide some things from him.

She turned to face him. "I had a strange dream, and was thinking about it, that's all." While not completely a lie, she did not like the way it left a bad taste in her mouth. She didn't want to lie to him. She hadn't exactly lied to him, but she hadn't told the truth, either.

Javier looked down at his hand on her thigh for a moment. "Lord Heath and I are going to head back to Belrick in a few days." Sariah suddenly found herself swallowing back tears. She knew this was coming, but she didn't expect it to hurt as much as it did. She did her best to hide her disappointment. "I would like you to come with us."

Sariah's whole body froze. She swore that her heart didn't beat for a moment. "I'm sorry?" She was hoping she had heard him correctly, but at the same time, she was also afraid that she had heard him correctly.

He smiled at her shocked voice, and sat up, taking her hand in his and looking her in the eyes. "I would love for you to come to Belrick with us. I want to show you where I live, and I think getting away from everything here could do you some good." The hand on her thigh was massaging a bit as he talked with her. It was distracting.

"Umm, I'd have to get permission from her Majesty to leave." His hand was moving up her thigh, ever so slowly.

"Lord Heath offered to help with that. He was going to request your presence at his court for a time." Javier leaned down, and started laying kisses where his hand had been.

All thoughts flew out of Sariah's head. She had an amazing, sexy, god-like man in her bed, naked, with his hands on her naked body. No one would blame her for not being able to think. As his hand kept moving up, she lifted his head with one of her hands, and took his lips for her own. They spent the rest of the night giving and taking pleasure, finally stopping only because the sun was coming up over the horizon, and Javier could not be found in her room by anyone.

He quickly dressed, and she put her robe on, and she kissed him passionately as he left her room. Sariah turned around and pressed her back against the door of her room. She felt blissfully used, and she knew that he must feel similarly, as she gave as good as she got.

She took a deep breath, hoping her legs would hold her, and she stumbled back over to her bed, where she collapsed into blissful sleep. She didn't notice that as soon as Javier left, all the candles in her room went out simultaneously.

Chapter Twenty-Two

When Sariah woke up, she could see through her windows that the sun was high in the sky. She rolled over onto her back from her belly, placing her clasped hands on her midsection. She stared at the ceiling, thinking over the night and day before. Had he really asked her to go back to Belrick with him? Considering they were in bed, naked, and about ready to have some really steamy sex, she wasn't sure if he did. Maybe after her dream, she imagined it. If he did ask her, would she go? Would Elliana give her the permission to go?

"Well, good morning!" At the voice, Sariah sat up so fast the room spun. She looked over at the chair by her wardrobe and gave Lara a dirty look. Then she let herself fall back onto the bed again.

Lara chuckled, and came over and sat on the edge of the bed. "Well, it's a good thing you finally caught up on your sleep. Her Majesty thinks so too, which is why you're not in trouble for missing her morning meeting and court this morning." Lara stopped here and looked over at her friend. Sariah was still laying on her back looking at the ceiling, so Lara continued.

"A very interesting thing happened in court this morning, in fact. Lord Heath and Sir Javier said their goodbyes to Her Majesty-" Sariah cut Lara off mid sentence.

"They did what?! When did they leave? I have to go." Sariah jumped up out of bed, throwing off her robe and digging through her undergarments in her wardrobe.

"Calm down please. What you didn't let me say is that they said they would be leaving in a couple of days. And Lord Heath has petitioned you to visit his court for a while." Lara looked like a cat with cream, her smile was so smug.

Sariah dropped the items she had in her hands, and turned to face her friend. The blood had drained out of her face, and Lara's smile faltered. "Sariah? I thought you'd think this was good news. I can only assume he asked on behalf of Sir Javier. It's obvious that the two of you have become close. Aren't you happy?"

Sariah walked back over to her bed slowly, and sat next to her friend. "He asked me. Last night he asked me to go back to Belrick with them. I thought I was dreaming. That's what I was thinking about this morning. Whether or not he had really asked me, and what I was going to say if he indeed had." Sariah's hands were limp in her lap.

Lara grabbed one of her friend's hands, and held it between her two. "Pack."

Sariah looked at her in confusion. "What?"

Lara smiled brightly at Sariah. "Pack. Pack your things right now, and don't look back. Sariah," Lara put one of her hands on Sariah's cheek, "you've been miserable. Anyone can see it. Whatever happened to you while you were gone has caused you undue pain. You need happiness too."

Sariah felt a glimmer of hope. "What did Queen Elliana say?" She knew that without the Queen's approval, if she left, she'd never be able to return. She'd be expelled from Blackmore, and never be allowed to return.

Lara smiled again. "She said she'd need to speak with you, but as long as you didn't object, she saw no reason to say no. I told you she wanted to see you happy!" Lara wrapped Sariah in a hug before releasing her to dig Sariah's travel trunk out from under her bed. "Get dressed. Go seek an audience with Her Majesty. Don't worry about packing, I'll get started for you!"

Sariah wondered if she should be offended with how quickly Lara wanted to get rid of her, or if she should kiss Lara for helping her secure her hopeful happiness. Sariah picked up the undergarments that she had dropped, and began to dress. She pulled on a simple black dress and boots over her undergarments, and armed herself lightly.

Sariah kissed Lara on the cheek and thanked her for being such a good friend. She walked to her door, put her hand on the handle, and froze. Or rather, the world around her seemed to freeze. Sariah looked around to see what had happened. Lara was at the end of her bed, the trunk half open, and frozen in place. Luna was on the bedpost, wings spread a bit as if she were disturbed.

Sariah expected to see The Crow in her room, but no one else was with her. She reached out and tried the door handle. It opened easily enough under her hand. She opened the door a crack and then paused. Something was definitely wrong here. Maybe she was dreaming?

Slipping one of her throwing daggers out of her sleeve, Sariah used the point to prick the pad of her first finger. "Ouch!" It had definitely hurt. She rubbed the small spot of blood between her thumb and forefinger before sticking the finger in her mouth to stop the bleeding.

Sariah heard a shuffling in the hallway and froze. She was not the only one unaffected by whatever was going on. Maybe it was just her room. Sariah carefully opened the door and saw Javier propped up on the wall across from it. He looked up when the door opened, and smiled at her. "Was that you that said ouch a moment ago?" His tone was amused, but the question was genuine. At Sariah's nod he continued, "What happened?" He did not sound worried for her at all.

Sariah held up her finger, the small cut visible on it. "I wanted to make sure I wasn't dreaming. Something strange is going on in my room. Everything seems frozen." Sariah motioned to her door which was still partially open.

Javier suddenly looked a bit nervous. "Yes, well, about that. I need to speak with you. Without anyone listening." He was looking at the floor at this point, avoiding Sariah's gaze.

Sariah caught on, but at first didn't believe it. Then she remembered that she was the scion of a battle goddess. Who was she to say something was impossible? "Magick? You have magick?" As much as she didn't want to, she sounded a bit shocked.

"I do." Javier cleared his throat. He sounded so nervous and wary. "I've had magick since I was a very young boy." He stopped there, risking a glance up at Sariah. While she looked confused, she wasn't running away. "It's how I was able to see you take care of Sir Robert. And how Maddie wasn't able to see me-"

Sariah held up a finger, cutting him off. "The candles. And your clothes the other night?" At his nod, she continued, "You said you saw me with Sir Robert. And I know you saw me with the girl by the lake. Can you see her when she comes to me?" Sariah was almost trembling by the time she got the question out.

Javier nodded. "I can't see her when she first comes to you, but when she leaves, I can. The Crow has been coming to me for many years, ever since my mother died. Her people were magickal. It's where my magick comes from."

Sariah's legs gave out on her, forcing Javier to catch her. He sat down on the floor, and pulled her into his lap. "I thought I was going crazy... and you could see her. You saw what I did. You saw how I was suffering. And you said *nothing*?" Sariah turned to look at him, her eyes like silver fire.

Javier winced at the look. "I did. That's why I stayed with you that night. I was worried about you, and what you were going through. I've been there. I've taken young lives before. I know how it can cut. Sariah, I'm sorry I didn't tell you. I see now that it would have given you someone to talk to. It would have helped to alleviate your burden." Sariah turned her face away from him. "But at the time, I thought it would drive you away from me. I didn't want that, and at the time, I didn't think you wanted that either." he took her hand in his, and she couldn't bring herself to pull it away. She was hurt by his actions, but she wasn't cruel.

"So this is what you needed to talk to me about?" Sariah was a bit disappointed. She thought maybe he'd come to renew the sentiments he shared the night before, and to ask her again to go with him to Belrick.

"Some of it, yes. If you're thinking of traveling with us, and if you're developing similar feelings to the ones I am, I thought you deserved to know the truth about me." He paused for a moment to let that sink in. "I also came because a body was found in the lake early this morning."

Sariah had been looking at her hands until now, but at this statement, she quickly looked up at him. She didn't say anything though, so he continued. "From the sound of it, it's the young woman from the other day. I don't know much more than this, since I heard the guards talking about it. This death though doesn't seem suspicious at all though, since they found a couple of rocks in the pockets of her apron. They think she weighed herself down, and walked into the water. After she died, they think some of the rocks fell out, allowing her to float to the surface."

Sariah felt sick. She had a slew of questions that only The Crow could answer. She felt like she was running at full speed in a forest, and was about to hit a tree. She needed some direction. With that thought, she remembered what The Crow had said in her dream the night before. "Are you really sure you're meant to be apart?"

The Crow had given her a direction. And in her first conversation, she had told Sariah that there was always choice. So, what was she going to choose? She looked down at their entwined hands, before looking back up at him. "Do you really want me to go with you to Belrick?"

Without pausing to think, Javier responded, "I absolutely do."

Sariah nodded and was silent for a moment before saying, "Then I will go with you. Let me know when you're ready, and I'll be there." Javier leaned forward and kissed her, before helping her to stand. A moment later, Lara poked her head out of Sariah's room.

"Oh! Sir Javier, Sariah. I heard someone out here, and thought that it might be Maddie. I was going to get her assistance in packing Sariah's trunk for your journey." Looking at the pair, she saw their joined hands and smiled. "Sariah, I believe you were going to speak with Her Majesty about the trip. I'll go find Maddie to assist with the packing, shall I?" With that, Lara closed Sariah's door and headed down the hall to the right of Sariah's room towards the servant's hall.

Sariah looked at Javier and smiled. "Thank you for releasing them."

Javier smiled back at her. "I never intended on keeping them that way for long. I just needed you to tell me what I hoped to hear."

Sariah gave him a quick kiss and headed down the hallway opposite the way Lara had gone. She needed to speak with Queen Elliana.

Chapter Twenty-Three

Not knowing exactly what the Queen was going to ask her or say, Sariah really had no way to plan as she walked towards the receiving room. This time of day the Queen could be in one of several places, so it might take Sariah a while to track her down.

Sariah entered the receiving room and found she was in luck. The Queen was just finishing with petitions of villagers. Sariah stood in the back as a man told the Queen his grievance. Apparently his neighbor's pig broke down his fence, and ate many of the vegetables in his garden, trampling anything it did not ingest. The man's neighbor stood a little ways away from him in front of the Queen, waiting for his chance to tell his side of the story.

Sariah had a feeling that she knew how this would end, but she waited patiently to hear both sides. Sure enough, the neighbor came up and claimed that the man's garden fence had been left open, and the pig had not broken it down. He did agree that the pig made a mess of the garden, and offered to pay for those damages, but refused to pay for the fence.

Her Majesty let the man with the original grievance rebut his neighbor before making her decision. She stated that the neighbor was to pay damages on the vegetables from the garden, but both men were to fix the fence, that way maybe they could build a better fence so that the pig would find it harder to escape in the first place.

Sariah nodded her head, as she agreed the ruling was fair. The neighbors shook hands, and walked off semi-cordially. Business being completed, Elliana called the session closed, and thanked all for coming.

Sariah moved off to the side, letting people shuffle out of the room. After a moment, the Queen saw her there and motioned that she should approach when she was able. As the room started to clear, Sariah began to move towards the Queen.

Out of the corner of her eye, she saw a dark spot against the wall to her left. She turned her head and saw Javier leaning against the wall, his legs crossed at the ankles and slightly out in front of him, his arms crossed over his chest. He was watching her approach Elliana. When he realized she saw him, he put his finger up to his lips. Sariah looked forward again, and kept going towards Elliana.

She had no idea what Javier was doing there. But if he wanted her to keep quiet, it meant that she was the only one who could see him. Sariah had to stop and wait as a few people finished up speaking to Elliana. As she was standing a ways away from the Queen, Luna landed on her shoulder. Luna pushed her beak into Sariah's hair and nibbled at it a moment before just sitting on her shoulder like a statue.

Having both Luna and Javier there made her more nervous than she had been before. Why would they both be there if this was going to go well? Suddenly, Sariah both wanted this conversation to be over already, and at the same time to never happen. The moment that the final petitioner turned from the Queen and bowed to Sariah as he walked out, Sariah felt herself break out in a cold sweat. Why was she so nervous about this? Elliana smiled at her, and Sariah smiled back, trying to regain her resolve as she walked forward toward her Queen.

"Lady Sariah." Elliana stuck out her hand smiling warmly, and Sariah curtseyed and kissed it. Since the Queen was still using formalities, Sariah figured that someone was there who could possibly see.

"Your Majesty," Sariah said as she came up from her curtsey, "I would like to request an audience, if you have a moment to spare." Sariah stood completely still, her hands clasped in front of her, her gaze cast slightly down. Luna wasn't moving at all either. It was like the little bird knew just how much was riding on this meeting.

"Of course, Sariah. Please, come with me to my private receiving room." Elliana motioned to a small entryway just behind her. It was off to the left of the platform where the throne sat, and still in the room. Sariah knew that it led to a very small sitting room, with only two chairs and a small writing table. The Queen did not often use this room, but when she needed to speak to someone privately, and would not be able to make it back to her chambers, she could take them here.

Sariah gave a small curtsey again, and waited for Elliana to turn from her and head to the room. Sariah once again waited the requisite three steps before following. She did not look behind her to see what Javier did. With the possibility of someone watching them, she did not want to alert them to his presence. She knew that he could handle himself, even among the Queen's guards, so she had to leave him to his own devices while she faced the Queen.

Sariah followed Elliana into the small room, and shut the door behind her. Luna ruffled her feathers. She did not like small, closed spaces, but she was there now, so she would have to deal until Sariah was ready to leave, or figure out a way out on her own. With the way Luna seemed to pop in and out of existence, Sariah wouldn't be surprised if Luna did just up and disappear while they were in the room.

Elliana and Sariah each took one of the chairs, and faced each other. The silence was so heavy in the room that it started to feel almost physical. Sariah broke it first, since that's what Elliana seemed to want. "Your Majesty, I hear that Lord Heath has approached you about me coming to stay at his court. Lady Lara said that you wanted to speak with me before you officially gave your answer. I was wondering if you had questions or anything in particular you wanted to speak about?" Sariah had to force herself not to wring her hands.

She was not normally a nervous person, but with someone that she felt safe with, she had a habit of letting some of her nervous ticks show.

Queen Elliana smiled warmly at Sariah. "I did indeed want to speak with you about this. It took me a bit by surprise, to be honest with you, but at the same point in time, I have been hearing reports of you spending quite a bit of time with Sir Javier. Some of the reports have made comments that the two of you have become particularly *close*. Lady Lara believes that you might be in love with him." Elliana raised an eyebrow and gave Sariah a knowing look. "You know, Lady Sariah, that I would like nothing more than to see you happy, but I wanted to make sure that you knew what you were getting yourself into, and that you were not being coerced." Queen Elliana looked a bit concerned. "You have not been the same, my friend, since you came home."

Sariah sat for a moment, really thinking through what she wanted to say. Elliana was waiting patiently, which Sariah greatly appreciated. "Yes, Majesty. I am much changed." The words came out slowly, as if Sariah had to force each one out of her throat. She wasn't sure where this reticence was coming from. It was so opposite of her normal personality that it just seemed wrong.

Sariah thought of seeing Javier out in the hall, and potentially being in earshot of this conversation before she decided that it couldn't be helped. If he heard this, so be it. Her words started tumbling out of her mouth very quickly. "I cannot say that I'm in love- yet. I definitely have feelings that are there for him, and that seem to be growing, but, I'm not sure that it's love." Sariah paused to take a breath, and leaned back in her chair, her eyes becoming unfocused.

"I have to be with him though. There is something that is drawing us together…" Sariah trailed off, realizing what she was saying. She sat back up, and looked at Queen Elliana expectantly.

Elliana wasn't smiling anymore, but she wasn't angry. She looked sad. "Sariah, I have never seen you like this before. It is indeed an interesting sight to behold. But I can hear the sincerity in your voice. And I can see the look in your eyes. You had decided to go whether I gave permission or not, hadn't you?" Elliana arched a brow at Sariah.

Sariah looked down at her hands before replying. "I have, and I will. Regardless of what you say here. As much as I don't wish to lose you as a friend, or my connection to Blackmore, I have to go." Sariah did not look up from her hands. She was fighting back tears, and did not want to show such emotion if Elliana decided to banish her.

"So be it." Elliana had decided.

Chapter Twenty-Four

Sariah walked out of the small room looking a bit dazed. Javier saw her, and followed her out of the receiving room. Sariah knew he was behind her, and wondered how much he had heard. She needed to go back to her room to pack, since she knew they were leaving soon.

She said nothing all the way back to her room, avoiding anyone in the hall she might come across. Surprisingly, Luna had never left her, even though the bird was extremely uncomfortable in that room. She reached up and touched one of Luna's feet, needing some type of connection.

Her conversation with Elliana had brought some of her strength back. She'd been feeling it leave her a little bit at a time since she had to take the life of the girl at the lake. But making her mind up about going with Javier and sticking to that no matter what helped to remind her of who she was.

As she reached her room, she paused at the door, taking a deep breath. She stood up straight and pushed her shoulders back before opening the door. Lara and Maddie were both in the room, and Sariah's travel trunk was almost full. Both women looked up at her entrance. Maddie took one look at Sariah's face, curtseyed and excused herself from the room.

Lara had stopped what she was doing, and was still holding a piece of clothing in her hands. "How did it go?" Lara didn't move from her spot.

Sariah swallowed once. "Lara, you need to go. Please. I'll finish that." She said this with kindness and sadness both.

Lara's face fell. "Sariah, no. What happened?" Lara dropped the item of clothing into the trunk and walked over to Sariah. Sariah stepped away from Lara. The hurt on Lara's face at this was like a knife to Sariah.

Sariah's voice broke as she said, "Lara, please. I- I can't." Her eyes filled with tears as she did the only thing she could- send her friend away. "I need you to leave. Please. Just go." Sariah looked down at the floor. She would not be able to look Lara in the face. She heard Lara's footsteps as she walked to the door. They paused at the door, as if Lara had turned to say something, but then the door opened, and the footsteps retreated down the hall.

A moment later, Sariah heard her door close and lock and looked up. Javier had come in, and he looked distressed. "Are you packed? We need to leave. Heath has our horses ready."

Sariah looked at her trunk. All of her worldly possessions were in that trunk, with the exception of her blades. Without speaking, she walked over to her wardrobe and pulled out the last clean set of riding clothes she had. Maddie had not had a chance to restock her outfits.

Sariah turned her back on Javier and pulled her gown over her head. She quickly dressed in the riding clothes, and then opened a compartment in the side of the wardrobe. Sariah looked over what was left of her blades. She grabbed several throwing knives and daggers, and slipped them into her bracers and into the loops in her boots. She picked up the sword that Javier had purchased her and tied the scabbard and its belt to her waist. Finally, she affixed the sheaths of a couple additional daggers to this belt.

Next, she pulled a small pouch out, and closed the compartment. Closing the wardrobe door, she walked over to one of the posts on her bed. Using her nails, she pried open a hidden cache, and removed gold coins, which she put in her pouch. Having completed that task, she turned to Javier.

He had been watching her silently this whole time. "Now I'm ready." Luna flew to Sarah's shoulder and made a silent caw in Javier's direction.

Javier nodded at Sariah, and moved towards the bed to grab her trunk. "Leave it. There's nothing in there that's truly mine." The sadness in her voice caused Luna to nuzzle Sariah's cheek with her beak. Sariah stroked her neck in a gesture of thanks.

"Alright then. We'll leave immediately, and ride through the night. We have provisions enough to get us to Belrick." Javier took Sariah's hand and kissed it. "Are you ready?"

Sariah took one last look around the room that had been hers for over a decade. She nodded at Javier, set the key to her room on the bed, and shut the door behind her as they left.

Javier and Sariah moved through the castle quickly, thankfully not running into anyone. With it being dinner time, most of the castle was in the main hall. Heading out the front of the castle instead of the back, they came into an empty courtyard, except for Heath and the two horses that the threesome had ridden in on.

Lord Heath took in Sariah's appearance before handing Javier the reins of his horse. Sariah was thankful that neither of the men seemed particularly chatty. She wasn't sure what she could say to them at this point. Her world had irrevocably changed, and she honestly wasn't sure exactly how she felt about it.

Lord Heath mounted his horse, and waited for Javier and Sariah. Javier put a foot in the stirrup of his saddle and swung his leg over the horse. Sariah watched this exhibition of grace and male beauty, and realized what she was giving up for him. Javier held his hand out to Sariah, and she knew that this was truly the point of no return.

She didn't hesitate, and put her hand in his. He pulled her up onto the horse in front of him. Lord Heath set out through the gate. Javier cleared a small lock of hair off of Sariah's neck just below her ear and laid a kiss there. She shivered a bit at his touch, which made him chuckle.

The sound of male pleasure made her smile, and knowing what she was doing was right, she did not look back as they rode under the gate and onto the road that would take them to Belrick.

Queen Elliana watched the threesome's progress from the window in her chamber. She was seated at her writing desk with only a candle lit in front of her. Her eyes were dry, and she smiled a bit as she saw the trio round the bend of the road. "Godspeed." She blew out the candle, and walked into the dark of her room.

Chapter Twenty-Five

Sariah was very quiet on the road as they left Blackmore. Javier had come even with Heath so that they could talk or plan as they rode. They talked of what had happened while they were at Blackmore, and what the plan was now that Sariah was returning with them to Belrick. They would not have time to send word ahead, so her arrival would be as much a surprise as their return.

Sariah just listened as the two men chatted about other matters as well. She tuned them out as they turned to talk of business and trade, and watched the countryside as they went. She didn't know when or if she'd be able to come back to Blackmore. She wanted to commit everything to memory that she could.

She hadn't been to Belrick, and had heard little of the country before meeting Javier and Heath. As they rode, she let her mind wander, trying to imagine life in a kingdom where the ruler didn't really rule and the regent didn't really have full power.

Javier kissed her just below her ear again, and she realized both men were focused on her. They must have been talking to her while she was daydreaming. "I'm so sorry. I was far away. What did you ask me?"

Lord Heath smiled at her preoccupation while Javier ran a hand down her arm. She knew she'd have to start paying attention to the men, especially Javier, or he might start wondering if she were regretting her decision to leave. Sariah leaned back into Javier a bit, enjoying the feeling of his muscular arms around her, and the play of his stomach muscles on her back.

Once full dark hit, the group got especially quiet, not wanting to draw extra attention to themselves. Heath pulled a couple of mincemeat pies out of his saddle bag and handed them over to Javier and herself. He dug another out for himself, and they ate in silence as they continued on their journey.

Sariah found herself dozing as the moon rose high in the sky. Javier kissed the top of her head and said, "Sleep. I won't let you fall." The words that were so similar to those he said to her on their first journey made her smile. She closed her eyes and did as he bid.

When Sariah next opened her eyes, she found herself in the meadow of heather, The Crow at her side. "Are these really dreams, or are you and I actually in a field of heather conversing?" Sariah had a feeling The Crow wouldn't answer her, but she figured she might as well try.

"You've made a decision that will change your life. You've forsaken your home and family to be with him. Do you love him?" The question from The Crow threw Sariah for a moment. Did she love Javier? She frowned.

"I don't know. I don't know if I even know what love really is. How is one to know if they love someone?" Sariah looked at The Crow with confused and pleading eyes.

The Crow gave her a gentle smile. "Love cannot be defined by the words of men. It is a matter of the heart, not the brain. While the path you've chosen is a difficult one, it is the one you needed to take."

Sariah nodded slowly, digesting what The Crow had told her. She had felt that this was right for her, that it was what she needed to do. But will it be worth the cost? She thought of Javier. His smile, his touch, his lips on hers. She knew so little about him. What if this was just physical attraction?

"You know that it's more than that. Come, now. You cannot lie to yourself, or to me." The Crow cocked her head to the side, and gave Sariah a knowing look.

"Yes, there are feelings there. You're not wrong. But as I said, I don't know what they are." Sariah sighed. The Crow nodded sagely.

"It's something that you'll come to, I'm sure." The Crow leaned over and kissed Sariah on the forehead.

Sariah's eyes fluttered open. The sun was coming up over the horizon, and she was laying on the ground in the forest. Javier's arms were around her, and was laying at her back. He was gently kissing up and down the side of her neck. She hmmm'ed in pleasure, and rolled over to face him. "Where are we?"

He kissed her gently on the mouth before responding, "somewhere between Blackmore and Belrick. We've been riding all night, and stopped to grab a quick nap before continuing. Are you okay?" He brushed some hair away from her face before continuing, "You were very deeply asleep."

"Mhm. I had a visit from our lovely feathered friend. I believe she keeps those she pulls to her in a type of deep sleep so she can speak to them as she needs." She kissed Javier back with interest. "Where is Lord Heath?" Javier had been kissing her neck while she was speaking. Sariah tilted her head back to give him better access. When he didn't respond right away to her inquiry, she nudged him with a laugh.

"He's over there, sleeping." Javier motioned off in a direction away from them while getting back to his kisses.

"As *you* should be." When he hit a particularly sensitive spot, Sariah gasped. "Then again, I can always direct the horse and follow Heath..." Javier made a low noise in his throat. Sariah closed her eyes and made a similar sound.

All of a sudden, Javier stilled. Sariah went to ask him what was wrong, and he clamped his hand over her mouth. The look of seriousness on his face made her realize something was wrong. Putting his other hand to his lips, telling her to be quiet, she nodded and he pulled his hand away. He motioned for her to stay where she was, and he very slowly and quietly got up, and headed into the direction he motioned where Heath was resting.

Sariah fingered her bracers and ran a hand over her boots, making sure that her weapons were easily at hand. Soon, she heard it. A clatter of hooves on the road just out of sight. Lots of armored men as well, marching along. Just like Javier had, Sariah got up very slowly and quietly, and made her way towards the road. She was very careful not to step on any sticks or rustle any leaves, although she doubted that would be heard over the procession.

She crouched down in the brush just before the road, and peeked through a small opening in the leaves. What she saw made her mouth drop. An army of men was marching past. Mounted soldiers, walking soldiers, big wagons of items, and men that were not soldiers at all. They were separated a bit from the discipline of the army, but still with the group. Mercenaries, Sariah realized.

The thought of mercenaries made her think of Lord Darian Thomas. The army wore no crests, and carried no flags, but she had zero doubts that was who they were with. Remembering that Queen Elliana had sent a missive asking him to visit had her wondering. The Queen had said she had invited Lord Darian for the following month, but the timing would be right for him to have received the missive and headed out for a visit.

Sariah watched in awe at the amount of men that walked past her. They just seemed to keep coming. All of a sudden, a hand clamped over her mouth, and she was pulled back against a hard body. "Well, well, well. What have we here?" The voice sounded excited, and the grip on her tightened almost painfully. Sariah went limp.

Chapter Twenty-Six

Thinking that she had fainted, the man loosened his grip on Sariah to turn her around and see what he had found. Using the moment as a feint, Sariah slid a throwing knife out of her bracer and into her palm. Even though she hadn't recognized the voice, Sariah wanted a visual of her captor before she committed any violence.

Once she was facing him, she saw that he was a stranger to her and clamped her hand over his mouth before hitting him hard in the head with the hilt of her throwing knife. Not expecting it, the man took the blow squarely on the temple, and went down like a rock. Sariah didn't stick around to see if he was okay. She as quickly and quietly as possible got deeper into the trees.

In case the man wasn't alone, Sariah deliberately moved away from the spot where her trio had bedded down. She didn't want to end up leading someone to Heath and Javier. Sariah frowned at that thought. She hadn't heard anything from either of the men since Javier had left her.

Sariah replaced the throwing knife in her bracer, and took the dagger off of her belt instead. A much wider and heavier blade than the small and slim throwing knives, her dagger was about the length of her forearm. Crouching down in the underbrush, she paused to see if she could hear anyone moving around. When all she heard was the group of men moving past still, she started heading deeper into the trees, hoping to circle back to her camp without alerting anyone.

Periodically Sariah would stop and hold her breath, trying to see if she could hear anyone sneaking up on her. Holding the hilt of her dagger in her hand so that the blade pressed against her forearm, she shielded the fact that she was armed to anyone who might come across her.

As she came up to the campsite, Sariah felt a blade pressed against her throat. Hoping that Javier was continuing their foreplay, but not willing to risk her life on it, she froze. The person holding the blade put a hand under her elbow and slowly started lifting her up. Sariah moved with the hand, not wanting to get cut, and looked into a face that was vaguely familiar.

She couldn't place where she'd seen this man before, and she didn't linger. Not seeing any sign of Javier or Heath made her panic, and she executed a quick back handspring, bending backwards so that her assailant wouldn't be able to cut her neck, and then pushing off with her arms, enabling her to kick the blade out of his hand and disarming him.

She came up out of the back handspring and flicked her wrist forward, allowing her to quickly arm herself with her dagger. She planted her feet firmly apart, one slightly in front of the other so that she could launch herself at the man if needed. She was in a partial crouch, and when she looked up to locate her attacker, there was no one there.

She turned about quickly, making sure he wasn't able to sneak up on her, and, seeing movement out of the corner of her eye, whipped around, throwing one of her knives with her left hand.

Thankfully Javier was quick. He plucked the knife out of the air by the flat of the blade, and arched an eyebrow at her. She stood up, panting, and put a hand over her heart. "You scared me!" She whispered just loud enough that he'd be able to hear her.

She quickly moved back to where the man had been standing with the blade to her throat. She was looking at the ground, and moved a bit away, figuring that the blade she kicked out from the man's hand would have landed a little ways away from where he had been standing.

She searched around, gently pushing the leaf debris with the toe of her boot. Javier came up behind her and handed her throwing knife back to her. She tucked it into her bracer, and kept looking at the forest floor. Moving forward a bit more, she saw a glint in the leaves. Bending down to pick up the blade, she brushed the leaves aside, and froze.

Javier saw her freeze, and leaned down to pick up the blade she had uncovered. It was a very simple blade, well forged, with a simple gold-colored guard, and a black-wrapped hilt. There was nothing special about it, but the elongated dagger had caused Sariah undue stress.

"Sariah, what is it?" Sariah didn't look at Javier, but she could hear the concern in his voice. "What's wrong?"

Sariah swallowed down the bile she felt rising in her throat. "The man. He was holding that blade to my throat." she swallowed again.

Javier didn't even try to mask the venom in his tone. "Did he now?" He cast his eyes about the forest, but seeing no one, he turned his attention back to Sariah. She was still visibly shaken. "You weren't this upset when I held a blade to your throat." His voice turned teasing, and she realized he was trying to get her to smile, "Should I be worried?"

Sariah tried, but she couldn't manage a smile for him. "That's my dagger. It was taken from me. On the day that I died." She turned her face up to Javier, but she felt lightheaded. All of the blood had drained from her face. She collapsed into Javier's arms, but didn't lose consciousness. She was just in complete shock. Javier held her to his chest.

Sariah now knew where the vaguely familiar man was from. He is a high ranking official of Lord Darian's guards. Sariah now knew that her death had something to do with Lord Darian or his court. While she had an inkling before, the confirmation was indeed startling. The fact that this man, who's name she couldn't remember, had her dagger. Her personal dagger, that she never would have loaned out or given to anyone, concerned her deeply.

Javier looked down at Sariah. "Sariah, what do you mean by 'the day that you died?'" He looked at Sariah with almost a little bit of horror on his face.

It hurt Sariah's heart to see that. She closed her eyes for a moment, trying to figure out what to say. "Javier, I don't remember everything. Let's get back on the road, and I'll tell you what I can, honestly."

Javier nodded slowly at her. "The procession has passed. A few guys stumbled out of the woods at the end, but they are all gone now. I'm not sure what it was for, but I have a guess."

Sariah nodded back to him, pushing off his chest so that she could stand on her own two feet. "It was Lord Darian's men. Queen Elliana sent him a missive asking him to stay with her next month. Apparently, he didn't want to wait. I hope she's ready for him."

Javier frowned at this. "Lord Darian and Queen Elliana? Is she seeking an alliance with him?"

Sariah responded in the affirmative. "She's afraid he's going to insist on a marriage alliance between the two of them, which Elliana does *not* want. She knows he's a womanizer. She also knows he's dangerous."

Javier was looking very seriously at Sariah. "He is extremely dangerous. He's known for violence against women. Not sexual violence. He is not one to commit rape from what is said of him. But he has been known to be cruel. If someone crosses him, they had better hope he doesn't find out, or he'll take the price out of their hide." Javier's face got darker. "You said you know that these are his men. And you found this dagger. Was there a man here that was carrying it?"

Sariah looked down at her hands and took a deep breath. She vowed to herself to be honest with him. "Yes, there was a man here that I recognized from his court. One of his personal guards. I never would have given him this blade. I don't know how he got it, unless he was the one who took my blades from me and murdered me." She looked up at him before continuing. "We need to get on the road. If you don't mind, I'd like to put some distance between us and those men."

Javier nodded at Sariah. "I would like to put as much space between you and them as I possibly can. Come along. Heath was gathering up our stuff when I left him to come find you." Javier kissed Sariah's forehead and pulled her into a bone crushing hug. "I'm so very glad you're alright." He pulled apart from her, leaned down, and kissed her very tenderly. "Come along, trouble." He gave her a smirk, and started off in the direction of their camp.

Sariah took one last look around, looking at the spot on the forest floor where she found her dagger before turning and following Javier towards their horses and goods.

Chapter Twenty-Seven

As they got back on the road, Heath stayed close to them. She didn't know how much she'd be able to say about herself with him so close, until Javier seemed to realize what was causing her reticence. "I have no secrets from Heath, and he has none from me. He knows all about my magick. You can trust him. He will not betray it."

Sariah nodded, and began the tale as she could remember it. She left nothing out except for the last couple of conversations with The Crow where she discussed her feelings about Javier. By the time she was done, Javier's hands were clenched so tightly on the reins that they were shaking. "When you find out *who*, you *will* tell me." Javier gave her no option in that statement. His voice and body were both wound tightly with rage. Sariah was surprised that he did not self-destruct from the rage he contained.

Looking over at Lord Heath, she saw that he was not much better. Lord Heath was a very sweet man who had taken to Sariah quite nicely. She couldn't call them exactly friends yet, but she had a feeling that his connection to Javier had something to do with his feelings towards her. And much like one man would protect the wife of his brother, Heath seemed to want to protect and defend Sariah. She loved the look of pride on both of the men's faces when she told them about disarming Lord Darian's guard.

Try as she might, she could not remember the man's name. She knew that she should know it, as she had spent time in Lord Darian's court, or, at least she should have, if she was able to carry out the mission that Queen Elliana had sent her on. And yet, anytime she tried to think of him, or even focus on the idea of him, all she could see was the glimpse she had gotten of him that morning.

Javier and Heath looked at each other before turning their attention back to the road. She had given them much to think about, and she was slightly concerned still that Javier or Heath would think she was crazy and lock her up somewhere. Although Javier had told Sariah about his magick and the fact that he had also been seeing The Crow, everything still seemed so surreal to Sariah. Thinking of The Crow made her pause. She did not see or feel The Crow this morning when she was facing the mercenary and Lord Darian's guard. She knew these were not good men. Why did The Crow not come to her to exact justice?

It was at this moment that Sariah also realized that she had not seen Luna since she had set off with Javier and Heath either. Had The Crow decided to forsake her? The idea made Sariah's heart skip a beat. While she had questioned her choices since she decided to be The Crow's scion, the idea of being abandoned by her was almost unfathomable. She knew that she would try to call The Crow when she laid down to sleep that evening. She hoped that she would not be shut out.

Javier tightened his arms around Sariah as they rode. Sariah started asking questions about Belrick to pass the time, but neither Javier nor Heath were feeling particularly chatty, so she soon grew quiet herself. Ahead of the group, the road forked, with a signpost at the center. One direction pointed towards Belrick, and the other pointed towards Langton. Sariah knew they were going to turn towards Belrick, but she also knew that if she went towards Langton, she could possibly complete the mission that Elliana had sent her upon. She remembered the last words that Elliana said to her, and a wave of sadness came across her.

In a dark mood, Sariah leaned back into Javier, enjoying the feel of his arms around her and his hard body behind her. "How long until we reach Belrick?" She wondered if they would be sleeping outdoors again.

Javier looked at the sign post and then over at Heath. "If we ride through, we should reach the castle a couple hours after dark." Heath nodded at Javier. "We will have beds to sleep in tonight." Javier kissed the top of Sariah's head.

Sariah didn't mind sleeping on the ground, but after the day she had, it would feel good to have solid walls around her, and know that she was safe in a castle with a man who would give his life for her. Sariah lowered her voice, hoping that Lord Heath would only hear murmurings from the couple. "What will my sleeping arrangement be?" Sariah wanted to know before they reached the castle so that she knew what to expect.

Javier stiffened behind her. "I had hoped that you would stay with me in my rooms." He sounded very tense and unsure.

Oh, stupid stupid man. "Of course I will stay with you if that is what you wish. I wanted to ask to make sure that there would be no awkwardness once we reached the castle. I would hate to plan on sleeping with you and then be escorted to a guest chamber down a women's only corridor, for example."

Javier chuckled in her ear. "I dare any man to try and take you from me." His words sent shivers down Sariah's spine. "But you need not worry. I am well-respected and feared in Lord Heath's court. No one will speak against either you or I."

Sariah frowned at the thought that anyone would speak ill against her. Then again, she could see why he thought she was questioning that. She was an unmarried woman now traveling with two men, and she would be sleeping in the rooms... well, in the bed... of one of the men. If things were similar to what they were at Blackmore this would cause quite the gossip, and the young lady's reputation would be quite ruined.

"It needn't concern you though. Lady Margaret will love you as well. You will be the talk of the castle, but in a very good light. A new face, a beautiful and dangerous one at that, who is as sweet and kind as she is deadly? I will be the envy of every man there, and every woman will be tripping all over themselves to become your friend." His words sounded calm and even, not as if he were speaking about things out of the ordinary, but instead things that he knew would happen.

It sounded completely foreign to Sariah. But, then again, she was going to a new country and a new way of living. As they came up to the fork in the road, Javier slowed their horse down a bit. He looked at the road sign intently. Sariah was doing the same, until a wave of exhaustion hit her. She would find out the truth another day. "Javier?"

Absent-mindedly, he responded, "Hm?"

"Take me home, please." It was not just the words although she was sure they had an impact on him, but the way she delivered them. She added a little more tiredness to her voice than she probably needed to, but she also really did not want Javier to go off on a vengeance quest. The Crow had said that Sariah would need to decide what to do about the man that murdered her. She had implied that Sariah would need to be the one to face him, and either deliver justice or vengeance.

Javier took one last look at the road sign before turning his horse to follow Heath down the road to Belrick.

Chapter Twenty-Eight

The rest of the journey was spent in quiet companionship. All in the party were tired, but occasionally Sariah would have a question about something that they rode past, or a question about how the court at Belrick worked. Having no memory of her time spent in Sir Darian's court, all that Sariah knew of courtly life came from her time spent at Blackmore.

From what the men said, life in Belrick was similar to that of Blackmore, but women had more freedom here. Where Queen Elliana relied on social courtesies carried through generations, Heath and Margaret smashed the old ways to bits, and brought about a social revolution. Much to their surprise, things went over fairly well, and while some of the older members of the court still used the old ways and verbally pined for them, most had easily adapted.

Just as the moon was creeping up over the trees, the men turned the horses off of the main road, and onto a smaller lane. Looking around, Sariah saw discrete iron fencing lining the lane, and the vegetation quickly became less wild and more cultivated. Soon the trees opened up to a grassy expanse, and Sariah's breath caught in her throat. "What do you think?" Javier was clearly excited to show his home off to Sariah, and what a home it was.

Built less like a forbidding fortress and more like a comfortable manor home, the castle ahead of them was made of light stone, and it gleamed in the moonlight. The lane curved around a lake to the front door of the building, which was a large decorative wooden door. Sariah had a feeling that door could withstand a battering ram. "It's amazing." Sariah's response came out as a whisper, and Javier kissed her neck before he and Heath pushed the horses towards the castle.

As the group approached it, the door opened, and a man dressed in a smart uniform stepped out. He bowed to the gentleman. "Sir, Lord Heath. So wonderful to have you back. Please, leave your things, and I'll see to it that they and the horses are taken care of." Heath smiled and dismounted, looking more than happy to be rid of his horse for a while.

Javier swung his leg over the back of his horse and reached up to swing Sariah down. As they approached, the servant bowed to Sariah with a, "m'lady," before motioning to another servant just inside the door to take care of the horses.

Sariah followed Javier through the door into a grand entryway. The floors were polished wood and the walls were the same light stone as the outside of the manor. Sariah looked around and saw many tapestries hanging up on the walls with some paintings interspersed. Seeing her look of wonder, Javier took her hand with a smile to lead her deeper into the manor.

The entryway culminated in a large staircase and two hallways, leading to either side of the steps. A young woman walked out of one of these hallways. She curtseyed to Javier. "Evening, sir. Your room is ready for you whenever you like. Would you like your dinner in the dining room, or would you prefer it be delivered to your room?"

Javier looked at Sariah and raised a brow in question. She shrugged her shoulders at him. "Thank you, Mairi. We will have dinner in my room. If you could let the cook know to plan on another place setting for the foreseeable future, I would appreciate it." He smiled warmly at the girl. She smiled back, nodded, curtseyed, and moved off quickly to carry out his orders.

Javier led Sariah up the stone steps towards the upper levels of the manor. When they reached the first landing, Sariah froze in place, staring at a very large painting of a woman. She was young in the painting, with glossy dark curls, dusky skin, and the most amazing chocolate brown eyes. Javier was the spitting image of her.

"*You* live here. This is *your* home. Not Heath's." She turned to face Javier with a look of incredulity on her face.

Javier had the grace to look sheepish. "My mother descended from royalty where she is from. The magick her family carried was only carried *by* the royal line. They did quite well for themselves. When she came here to marry my father, she brought much of her fortune with her. They built this house." He paused for a moment, looking up at the picture.

"When my mother died, I had already been boyhood friends with Heath. His family took me under their wing, and between him and myself, we've done quite well for ourselves in business. Money is not something I ever have or will ever have to worry about." He gently squeezed Sariah's hand.

Sariah looked from the portrait to him and back. She had no idea that this man was the son of royalty. Nor did she have any inkling that he was wealthy. And yet his home rivaled the size and splendor of Blackmore castle. "Do Heath and Lady Margaret live here as well?" Sariah could not imagine that a country could hold more than one manor such as this.

"No. Lady Margaret lives in Sandram Castle, which is up the road a ways. Heath comes and goes as he pleases. I keep rooms for him here, and he's welcome anytime he desires." Javier started back up the stairs.

Sariah didn't know what to think. No wonder he said no one would judge her. She was basically sleeping with a prince in his own right, and a noble as well. She looked at the man leading her in a whole new light. She wondered just how much power he actually held in Belrick, and if he was expecting her to just bend to his whims as those around him seemed to.

At the top of the stairs, Javier led Sariah to an ornately carved door. It pictured lush jungle plants, and a large cat with spots. A snake hung from one of the trees near the top of the door, while exotic flowers spread across the bottom. The wood was polished to a shine, and was a very dark red wood. Sariah felt that she could stand there running her fingers over the carvings for days, and she'd still never discover all of its secrets.

Javier pushed the door open and led Sariah into his suite of rooms. His bedroom was large enough that it had its own sitting area with a few bookshelves. There were some very comfortable looking leather chairs in the sitting area that sat upon a gorgeously woven ornate rug. A small fireplace made the area seem cozy, and she itched to get her fingers on those books.

His bed was raised on a stone platform. It was the centerpiece of the room. Sariah took the step up the platform to get a closer look. It was a very large bed with a wooden headboard. Sariah walked around it and ran a finger over the covers. Chills ran down her spine at the luxurious satin feel of his bedclothes.

She turned towards the door to find him still standing just inside the room, watching her. His eyes were hungry for her. She toed off her boots next to his bed. She took the bindings out of her hair and let it fall to her waist. When she went to lift the hem of her shirt, his hands were there with her, branding her like fire. The next thing she knew, she was naked and so was he. He was very obviously aroused.

Sariah put one finger on his chest, a silent request for him to stay there. She climbed up on his bed and propped herself up on his pillows, splaying herself out to be at the best advantage for him to see. She licked her lips and the fireplace and all the candles in the room lit. She crooked her finger at him, and he stalked her around the bed, climbing lithely onto it, reminding her a lot of the jungle cat that was carved into his door.

He climbed up her body, leaving trails of kisses in his wake, and then he lost himself in her for what seemed like forever.

Chapter Twenty-Nine

When a knock on the door came, Javier wrapped his hips in a sheet and walked over to the door. Sariah watched him, but in the blink of an eye, he was no longer wrapped in a sheet, but was fully dressed. Looking down at herself, she saw that she was dressed again as well. At her small sound of surprise, Javier shot her a wicked grin over his shoulder.

Sariah sat up in his bed as he opened the door. She couldn't see who was at the door, but when Javier turned around, he was holding a tray of food. Sariah's stomach rumbled at the sight and smell of the freshly baked bread, roasted vegetables and meat. There were two mugs of some type of liquid on the tray as well.

Javier walked over to the sitting area and set the tray down on the small table. He moved the table between the two chairs, and sat in one of them. Sariah slid off the side of the bed and headed over to the sitting area. "Mmmm, smells delicious." She sat down in the other chair, and took a deep breath.

Javier handed her one of the mugs, and she took a testing sip. Fresh, cold cider filled her mouth. The taste of crisp apples made her smile. "Delicious, thank you." She set the mug down and reached for one of the plates.

"The apples are grown locally. In fact, all of the items on your plate are also locally sourced." The pride in Javier's voice was obvious. Sariah smiled at him and took her plate.

Roasted chicken, potatoes, root vegetables, fresh bread with butter, and some greens. Sariah began to eat, noticing that Javier only started eating after he was sure she was going to eat, and that she enjoyed what she was eating. "After dinner, if you want to clean up, I have a tub in the bathroom. It's through that entryway." Javier motioned to an entryway to the left side of the bed.

Sariah nodded. "Thank you. Cleaning up would be nice." Sariah felt awkward. This was his home. She was staying here with him. They'd made no promises to each other, and even though there was fire there physically, Sariah wasn't really sure exactly how he felt about her. The Crow said that he loved her. But he'd not said anything to that effect.

She looked up and realized Javier was watching her. "I know this situation may seem awkward. But I want this to be your home too. I want you to be happy here. Anything you need, just ask, and if we don't have it, we'll get it." He smiled warmly before resuming his dinner.

Sariah smiled back and resumed her own dinner, although it didn't taste quite as good now. He said he wanted this to be her home, and wanted her to be happy. He said nothing about love though. Sariah sighed mentally. At least he said he wants her happy and comfortable. That showed caring if not love.

While Sariah knew she was probably asking for too much at this point, she felt lost and adrift. She was without a home, at least a permanent home. Sure, right now Javier wanted to take care of her, but what if that changed? They'd known each other for such a short time.

As Javier finished his dinner, he brushed his hands together and stood up. "I need to go over some things with my staff. Please take your time finishing your dinner, and then go relax with a bath. I'll be back as soon as I can." He stepped over to her, leaned down, putting his hand on the back of her chair, tipped her chin up, and laid a gentle kiss on her lips.

Sariah watched him walk out of his room and shut the door behind him. While she was still hungry, her curiosity was getting the best of her. She set her food aside and made her way towards the bathroom. Stepping through the arched doorway, Sariah was thrilled by what she saw.

Javier had gone all out in here as well. She saw a closed doorway, which she stepped over to and opened. It was a private water closet. She shut the door to it and looked around the main bath area. The floor was stone tile, in a gray so dark that it was almost black. The walls were a lighter gray, and there were several stained glass windows in different shades of blue.

There was no rhyme or reason to the design of the stained glass, but the effect of the light coming through it made her feel as though she were under water. She walked over to the very large tub that was near the windows and across the room from the door.

The tub was the largest one she'd ever seen. It could easily hold two people. It was copper colored, and there was a spout like the tub she had at Blackmore. Sariah hadn't counted on warm running water when she came here, but it seemed like she was going to be pleasantly surprised.

Sariah pulled the cord near the bath and sure enough, hot water came out of the spout. She let the tub start filling and stripped out of her clothes. Climbing into the tub, she leaned back and groaned in pleasure. The hot water was easing the aches and pains of being on the road, and loosening her stiff muscles.

She saw a few bottles nearby and opened them one by one. They all smelled like Javier- that spicy, musky scent she'd come to love. She'd have to see if she could get some lavender soap at some point, but right now she hoped that Javier didn't mind her smelling like him.

Sariah poured a little of each bottle in her hand to see if she could figure out the difference between them. She was pretty sure she figured out what was shampoo and what was soap by the consistency and viscosity. She lathered her hair, taking time to wash every inch of it very well. Traveling on horseback and in the woods is not conducive to having pretty hair. Once she was satisfied, she dipped her head back into the water, rinsing out all of the shampoo. When she sat up again, she found herself staring into the eyes of The Crow.

A slight flutter of wings and she saw that Luna landed on the side of the tub next to her. She was genuinely happy to see her little feathered friend. She was also happy to see The Crow, even though lately The Crow did not always help her. "My lady." She acknowledged The Crow while she petted Luna, sending the little bird into ecstasy.

"Sariah, I'm glad that you've found your way here to Javier's home. You look good in his home, and he enjoys having you here. I know that you are concerned about your place here, and in his life, but you need to be patient. You are still learning each other and figuring out the scope of your relationship. You have nothing to fear though. He would never abandon you." The Crow was silent for a moment, letting what she said sink in. "Also, you always have a home. I am your home." The Crow reached out and placed her hand on Sariah's cheek, smiling at her like a mother would a child.

Sariah smiled back at The Crow. She heard the bedroom door open and turned her head to look that way. When she turned back, realizing she couldn't see who it was, she saw that she was alone with Luna.

Chapter Thirty

"Sariah?" Javier walked into his suite of rooms and didn't see her in them, although he saw the dinner trays left in the sitting area. He cleared the trays and set them outside his door.

"Did you get everything finished?" Sariah called out from the bathroom. She had heard him clearing their dinner mess, and was curious how long she had been with The Crow. The water was still plenty warm, so she didn't think it had been too long.

Javier walked into the bathroom and smiled at seeing Sariah and Luna together again. "I did. I just needed to inform my staff that I would be home for a while, and to prepare things for the three of us until Lord Heath decides to depart. My maids are awaiting your orders on any clothing you may need, or luxuries you may want." He walked over to the tub and knelt by the side of it. "Mmmm. You smell like me." He gave her a heart-stopping smile.

"That doesn't bother you?" She wanted to make sure that he was okay with it. She'd have the ladies make or get her some lavender soap, but, this was really all she had right now.

"Quite the contrary. You smelling like me is very alluring. It shows me that you consider yourself *mine*." The possessive look he gave her sent shivers down her spine. He leaned over the tub and gave her a quick and gentle kiss. "I'll let you finish your bath." Javier got a towel from a closet that Sariah hadn't noticed, and sat it within her reach. He walked out of the bathroom, looking back once to smile at her.

Sariah sighed after he was gone. The Crow was right. She had feelings for Javier. And they were not simple feelings that she'd be able to sort out in a day or two. Javier was also right, Sariah did in some way consider herself his. At the same point in time, she considered him *hers*, which was something that they would have to work on getting straightened out in the near future. Sariah picked up the bottle of soap and a cloth laying near the tub and scrubbed herself clean. It felt so good to get the dirt of the last few days off of her.

Once she was finished, she drained the tub, and stepping out, grabbed the towel he left her. She looked at her small pile of clothes on the floor and bundled them up. She wasn't sure what she was going to do now. This was the only set of clothes that she had with her, and they definitely would not work to put back on. She walked out into the bedroom with the towel wrapped around her and the bundle of clothes in her arms.

Once she walked through the door, she stopped in awe. The room was lit with what seemed like hundreds of candles. She had never seen so many candles in one place in her life. The fireplace in the sitting area was lit, as was a bigger fireplace that she hadn't noticed earlier near the bed.

Turning her attention to the bed, She saw Javier splayed out, nude, across his bed. His body really was a thing of beauty. All strength and grace, Sariah had a feeling that it could exact great violence, or, alternatively, as she knew, it could bring great pleasure. Sariah's brain stayed on the idea of pleasure as she stepped further into the room, and dropped her clothes next to the bathroom door. She'd worry about them later.

She took a few steps toward the bed and dropped her towel. She had his full attention. She knew that he loved her seduction. He set the scene for seduction this evening, but she would be the one taking charge. Or so she thought. She climbed up on the bed on her hands and knees, and he sat up to meet her. She began to straddle his hips when he flipped her over on her stomach. Before she could even comprehend what had happened, he had his hands on her neck and shoulders.

He was working on knots she didn't know she had. She moaned in both pleasure and pain as he got a particularly tender spot. "While we were riding, I noticed how tense you were. You just got out of a nice warm bath, so your muscles are particularly pliable. Tonight? You just need to relax."

She tried to sit up to look at him, but he firmly and yet gently pushed her back down. She didn't fight him. Javier began moving down her spine, going towards her lower back. She arched her upper body into the bed a bit, wordlessly asking him to go deeper.

She had never had anyone show such care towards her before. If she came back from a particularly rough mission or training session, she would usually hole up in her room alone. Maddie would bring her whatever herbs or poultices she asked for to help soothe her aches, but she'd never had someone just take charge and say, "I'm taking care of you now."

As he massaged, he'd occasionally drop a kiss, but other than that, he was all business. Once he'd finished on her neck and back, he moved to her arms, then her legs, then her feet. She felt utterly boneless by the time he was done.

She felt herself starting to doze when the light from the candles dimmed then went out. The fires too. She heard the creak of a window being cracked open, and then the bed dipped a little. Strong arms came around her and pulled her back into a chest that was just as strong. Sariah fell asleep with his spicy musky scent surrounding her.

Something woke Sariah, but she wasn't sure what. She was laying on a stone floor. But this wasn't the stone tile of the bathroom, this was a smooth stone. Her hair was loose around her head, and she was dressed. She moved a bit to try and look around, but it was like she was paralyzed. She heard a voice that she recognized, but she couldn't place it, and she couldn't tell what it was saying. All of a sudden, she was pulled up by her hair.

She woke up with a start, sitting straight up in bed. Her hand was on her throat, and she was breathing heavily. Javier was sitting up with her, rubbing her back, murmuring calming words. Sariah put her head in her hands. She could never remember a moment in her life having such a vivid nightmare.

She felt eyes on her and looked up. The Crow was standing at the foot of the bed. Sariah froze. Javier looked up at this and sighed. "That wasn't a nightmare... was it?" Sariah had a sick feeling in the pit of her stomach.

The Crow shook her head sadly. Looking at Javier, she said, "She will need you now more than ever. Help her stay strong in mind and body. The time is coming where she will need all her strengths to face death and choose."

Javier nodded to The Crow and then turned his attention to Sariah. "What do you need from me?"

Sariah shivered. "Just hold me. Please?" Javier wrapped his arms around her and pulled her tight to him, just as he had when they fell asleep before. Sariah looked out the window and saw it was still dark. She lay there for a while, wide awake, thinking about what The Crow had said. Her time was coming. And soon. She'd need to be ready.

Chapter Thirty-One

When Sariah awoke the next morning, she was in bed alone. She looked around the room from her spot in bed, but didn't see him. "Javier?" When she received no answer, she decided to get up and see what her new home looked like.

When she went to the water closet, she saw a pile of clothes laying near the tub. She poked her head back out of the bathroom and saw that her traveling clothes she had piled there were gone. The clothes near the tub were neatly folded, and there was a note on top.

Sariah picked up the note. Scrawled hastily across the front was her name. She opened it and read. "One of the things I took care of last night was to send someone to the castle. You and Lady Margaret appear to be of a size. She has sent some of her clothes for you to wear until we can get some made for you. Wear these today as I'd like to spar with you this afternoon. I had to head out and check on a few things this morning. Have some breakfast and explore the Manor. I'll be back by late morning. Yours, Javier."

Sariah smiled at the note and set it aside. When she picked up the clothes, she could tell that Javier was right, she and Lady Margaret were very similar sizes. It appeared that Lady Margaret was a bit taller and thinner than Sariah, but Sariah felt she could make the breeches and linen tunic work.

She was very excited by the idea of getting to spar with him again. She was hoping for some hand-to-hand combat, as well as the chance to use her new sword. She had a feeling that Javier would take what The Crow said quite seriously, and that they would train physically until they dropped. She wasn't sure yet what she could do for mental training. She'd figure something out though.

Once she was dressed she headed out of the suite of rooms. Outside of the foyer and the Grand staircase, Sariah had no idea where anything in the Manor was located. She remembered the maid from the night before, Mairi, and which hallway she had headed down to speak to the cook. If she could find someone, they could direct her to where she needed to be.

Sariah took the stairs quickly, and turned down the hallway to the left, which was the one Mairi had disappeared down the night before. Several feet down the hall, and she knew she was headed in the right direction. She scented bacon frying, and pastries with fresh fruit straight from the oven. She poked her head into the first door she came across to find a small office.

The office was well, if sparsely furnished with a large desk, a chair opposite it, and several bookshelves holding what could have been household or financial ledgers. Sariah wondered if Javier kept his own books or if he had an estate manager.

She moved on down the hallway, poking her head in doorways as she went. She found a sitting room and a library before discovering the dining room. Finding no one there, she made her way towards the end of the hall where a plain wooden door stood.

Opening that she found herself in a bustling kitchen. A cook was working some type of dough while some kitchen maids were prepping fish and vegetables for what appeared to Sariah to be a soup or stew based on the large pot on the stove.

Not wanting to interrupt their process, Sariah spotted a larder or storeroom near the entrance of the kitchen. Using all of her stealth abilities, she snuck in to grab some food so she could head out. The conversation she overheard made her pause.

"It's about time the Master brought home a lady. Maybe it will keep him home more often, instead of galavanting off with Lord Heath." The voice was a deep male voice, with a touch of an accent.

One of the young girls came back, "She's quite beautiful. And they're obviously together. They're not married though. Oooh! Maybe we'll get to have a wedding!" The young maids started talking rapidly, but the cook interjected quickly.

"Bite your tongue! The type of work that a wedding would cause! Bah. Hopefully he'll just keep her here, and come home regularly to her bed." Sariah was surprised that none of this was said with malice towards her. While she had believed that no one would talk badly about her at the castle due to fear, these servants obviously adored Javier, and seemed to want nothing more than to see him happy.

Not wanting to get caught eavesdropping, Sariah quickly found some hard cheese, a hunk of bread, and a couple of apples. Not having grabbed a bag or anything to carry her contraband in, she used the bottom of her shirt to carry her goods. She peeked out of the storeroom only to see the three kitchen workers facing the opposite direction. Sariah slipped out quietly, and decided to eat as she explored.

Heading back towards the foyer, Sariah decided that she wanted to check out the land that the manor sat on. As long as weather permitted, she preferred being out of doors anyway, and while cloudy, the day looked quite pleasant.

Opening the front door, Sariah found herself on the same lane they had come in on the night before. Rather than see where it led, she decided to follow the wall of the manor to see if she could manage to find Javier's training grounds.

As Sariah walked around the manor, she noticed that the grounds were well maintained. There were lush beds of herbs out behind the kitchen, and there was a small orchard of fruit trees as well.

Around the front and down the sides of the manor were flowering bushes that were left to grow mostly wild, appearing to only be cut back when it became a nuisance. Walking to the back of the manor again, Sariah saw lush tree growth just beyond the cultivated orchard. She smiled and headed for the tree line.

Sariah loved being in the woods. And being in Javier's woods, she had no concerns about safety. She walked for a ways before finding a semi-clear shaded spot where she sat down to eat her food. She wondered what Javier was doing, but, as a man with a manor of this size, and as a protector of the ruling family, she had a feeling he did a lot.

Luna fluttered down and sat on Sariah's knee. Sariah rubbed the little crow's head and offered her a small piece of the bread she was eating. Luna gently took the piece of offered bread in her beak, hopped off of Sariah's knee, and a little bit away from her where Luna could put the bread on the ground to eat it.

Sariah leaned her head back against the tree as she ate. She felt so peaceful where she was. The peace allowed her to think. The Crow said the time was coming where she would need to face death and choose. Did that mean she was going to die? Or that she could choose to end someone's life or save it?

Sariah sat forward, and leaned into a stretch. She put her legs out in front of her, and bent over, leaning as far forward as she could. And what of that dream last night? It had to have come because of the man she saw, and her reclaiming her dagger.

Sariah sat back, and pulled the dagger off her belt. She held it in her hand by the hilt, turning it this way and that. It was definitely her dagger. But there was nothing special about it. It was a simple, utilitarian long dagger. Sariah looked at Luna. "I need The Crow." Luna took flight instantly, and disappeared into the trees.

Sariah didn't know how long it would take for Luna to find The Crow, or how long it would take The Crow to come to Sariah. She knew that The Crow would be able to find her anywhere though, so she stood up, having finished her lunch, and brushed the crumbs from her pants.

She turned back the way she came and headed for the manor. As she got to the cleared space behind the manor, she realized that she had been in the forest longer than she thought. Based on where the sun was in the sky, it was close to midday. Hoping that Javier hadn't been waiting too long for her, she ran into the manor and hurried to the grand staircase, taking the stairs two at a time.

By the time she got to Javier's suite of rooms she had a nice sheen of sweat on her brow, and her breathing was just starting to get labored. Bursting through the door she slid to a stop upon seeing Javier.

He was sitting semi-reclined in one of the chairs in the sitting area, his feet propped up on the other. He had a book in his lap, and seemed perfectly calm. Except for his outfit (he was in the black leather attire she'd come to know him in), he appeared to be the wealthy country gentleman, spending an afternoon of leisure in his study.

"So sorry to have kept you waiting. I lost track of the time." Javier put down his book and smiled at Sariah.

"You didn't. If I'd needed you, I'd have found you." Javier gave her a slow head to toe look over. "I see I was about right on your sizes. You're a bit more shapely than Margaret, but I can't say that I mind that..." the suggestive look that he gave Sariah told her exactly how much he didn't mind her curves.

"Mmhm. We're going to get me some properly fitting clothes soon so that I can avoid showing my ass off to everyone? Hm?" she walked over to Javier, and bent over to give him a kiss. Standing back up, all of a sudden, she felt a hand on her ass. Raising an eyebrow at him she stepped away, and knocked his feet off of the other chair so she could take a seat.

"Your note said something about sparring? And unless it was verbal sparring you meant, I don't think we're going to get much done in here."

He gave her a wicked grin. "Yes, you're right. We wouldn't be able to get the type of sparring done I had in mind when I wrote that note..." he leaned forward and ran a hand up her leg. She just laughed at him. "Well, my lady, since you're so business minded, your sword is over on that side of the bed. Grab it and follow me, and we'll head towards the training grounds."

Chapter Thirty-Two

Javier had two sets of training grounds. One was an outdoor obstacle course with training dummies set up periodically. The second, which is the one he led Sariah to, was an indoor room in the lower part of the manor. There were thick lush rugs on the floor as well as pillows. Since the floors here were stone, sparring by hand would be quite painful if you took a hard enough fall. There was also an area with no padding for swordplay.

Sariah was impressed. With his training area being indoors, he didn't have to go out in bad weather to train. He could train day or night without disturbing anyone. "Who do you usually spar with?" Sariah doubted that any of the servants in the house could take Javier on.

"Heath spars with me sometimes. I can usually pull some of the royal guards over as well with promises of a good meal." He walked over to the center of the padded part of the room. He motioned her over. "I want to start with some hand-to-hand combat to gauge your training. I know you're well trained with a blade." He smirked at her. "I need to see how you do without one."

He jumped in place a few times and rolled his head on his neck. Sariah laid down her blades, took off her boots, and started stretching. She started with her arms, and then did some bends and lunges to get her legs loosened up. She bounced on the balls of her feet a bit, then went up as high as she could on her toes. She looked over and saw Javier watching her appreciatively. Not as a man watches a woman, but as one athlete watches another.

Deciding she was about as ready as she could get, Sariah took a warrior stance across from Javier. She was in a partial lunge with one hand stretched out in front of her, and the other behind. This pose allowed her to shift her limbs any way that she needed to to defend herself.

While a heavily offensive fighter with weapons, Sariah was a primarily defensive fighter hand-to-hand. Luc had called her a patient hunter. She'd wait until the moment was exactly to her liking before she struck with an offensive move.

Javier walked around her, his arms across his chest. Sariah realized he was looking at her form, so she held it. She had a feeling that he would correct anything amiss before he started fighting.

Sure enough, once he was back in front of her, he nodded once, got into his own fighting stance, and prepared to fight. His stance was very different from hers. He was balancing on the ball of one foot with the other flat. His hands were up in front of him, partially open fists so that they looked like hooked claws.

He struck very quickly, kicking out with his legs and trying to throw her off balance. But the beauty of her warrior pose was that she was able to jump up and back, avoiding his kick. He came forward with a closed fist. She kicked it away. Ow. She knew he was made of muscle, but she didn't realize how much those muscles would hurt to fight. It was like kicking a brick wall.

Javier smiled at the grimace on her face and chuckled. "Your last partner a bit softer than myself?" He asked, running a hand down his bicep to demonstrate that his muscles were not just for show.

Sariah knew how strong he was, but seeing that he used his muscles as a weapon made her rethink her strategy a bit. She didn't know if she'd be able to tire him out before she would, and if hitting him hurt just as much as if he'd hit her, she really needed to figure out a way to use his strength and size to her advantage.

She was thinking all of this while dodging blows he was aiming at her. Just like when he was using a blade, his footwork was fantastic. Agile and quick, like a dancer. But once again, she found that she had speed on her side. And while she was starting to peg his fighting style, to him, she was still an unknown. "Never let them figure you out." Luc's voice rang in her head.

Deciding to try and throw Javier off balance, Sariah suddenly dropped into a crouch and swung her leg out in a sweeping motion, hoping to take Javier's legs out from under him. He hadn't been expecting the drop, but once she was down, he was quick enough to jump. He hadn't, however, expected her to quickly shift and shoot her other leg out in the same sweeping motion.

Using her momentum, Sariah rolled forward and jumped up to her feet, kicking out, and stopping just shy of Javier's throat with her foot. He looked up at her from the ground in astonishment. "You fight dirty." He sounded proud. "Good. I'm glad you were taught something."

Sariah laughed. "If we were in real hand-to-hand combat, I'd be kicking the shit out of you right now. Luc taught me to focus on avoidance, but to strike if I saw an opening. In most cases I was going to be smaller and not as strong as my opponent. Speed and surprise need to be on my side." Leaning down, she held out a hand to help him up. "He also taught me to never pull my punches, and to fight each battle as if I'm fighting for my life."

Javier gave Sariah a surprised but pleased smile. "If we'd have met under different circumstances, I think I'd really have liked him." He took Sariah's hand, and let her help pull him up. "Good. Now let's see some of those punches." He stood in front of her with his hands up, palms out, and arms bent at the elbows. He cupped his hands slightly, giving Sariah a target for her punches.

Sariah put her hands up in fists, and started throwing punches at his hands. He made sure that he didn't hurt her hands with his, but he made sure she knew she wasn't going to hurt him. A couple of times he held on to her fist. "I thought you didn't pull punches." Or, "come on, the cook punches biscuit dough harder than that." Sure enough, his words did the trick, and she was punching full force.

He got her angry enough that she landed some kicks to his hands too. She stopped, realizing what she had done, but he made a bring it on gesture, so she let loose. She set off on a flurry of blows, mixing up her punches and kicks. Once they both had a good sweat worked up, she slowed down and stopped. Javier walked away from her and opened a small door she hadn't noticed before.

When he came back, he was holding a pitcher and two mugs. Handing a mug to Sariah, he poured some water into it and then his own. She took a sip and let out a delighted gasp. The water was icy cold. "There's a natural underground spring that runs near the manor. We've tapped into it. The water is always fresh, pure, and very very cold." He smiled at her as he took a long drink of his own water.

Sariah was too wound up to hold still, so she wandered around the training area while she drank her water. As she walked over to the weapons area, she saw that he had all kinds of weapons up on the wall. You couldn't see them from the entry, but now that she could see them, she was fascinated.

He had swords of different lengths and sizes, maces, flails, whips, floggers, morning stars, axes of varying sizes and styles, daggers, throwing knives, and some weapons she didn't even recognize. His collection was quite extensive, and she wondered if he trained with all of those weapons. "I have to keep a variety or the guards and I get bored."

Sariah jumped a bit. He had come up behind her, and she hadn't noticed. She realized it was because without boots on, he moved extremely silently. He would have made an excellent thief or assassin. "It's about dinner time, or a little after. Let's call it for now, clean up, and grab something to eat. We can come back later tonight or first thing tomorrow if you'd like."

Sariah nodded. She hadn't realized how late it had gotten. She grabbed her boots and then held her hand out for his. He put his hand in hers, flipped it so that her hand was on top, and then kissed it. Her heart skipped a beat. Sariah was finding it hard to *not* fall in love with this man.

Chapter Thirty-Three

That night, as they lay in bed together, Sariah woke up, and found that the room she was in had frozen, much like her room at Castle Blackmore had when Javier wanted to speak with her. She slid out from under Javier's arm, hoping that she would be able to return soon.

She quietly walked to the door and opened it, seeing that unlike Javier's spell, this magick encompassed a lot more than their suite of rooms. Even though she was sure no one was awake to hear her, Sariah tiptoed down the stairs and headed back towards the kitchen. She snuck out the back door into the garden, and under the waning moon.

The Crow waited for her near a bunch of lavender plants. "My Lady. Thank you for coming." Sariah curtseyed, even though she was just wearing one of Javier's shirts. Luna landed on her shoulder and nuzzled her neck.

"Why did you call for me?" The Crow cocked her head as she was wont to do. She didn't sound angry, but genuinely sounded curious.

"I need to know how I died." Sariah had been thinking a lot about this. In order to effectively fight the man, and she had a feeling in her gut that it was a man who killed her, she'd need to be fully alert. Based on what The Crow had said about meeting her killer, she didn't know if she would be able to fight after seeing her own death.

The Crow nodded, and motioned for Sariah to step closer. As soon as she was able, The Crow reached out and gently tapped Sariah's forehead with one finger. Sariah felt herself falling, seeing images flash by her as she did.

Her arrival at Langton and meeting with Lord Darian. Her flirtation with him, and the first time they went to bed. Sneaking into his office and searching through his books. Seeing shipping manifests and plans to expand his trade routes. Sending a letter to Queen Elliana that was vague but succinct. "Got it. Will explain later. Coming home to you."

The images started slowing. A messenger handing the letter to Darian. His confronting her. The barely contained violence in his face and voice. He locked her in her room. She grabbed her weapons and climbed out the window. She ran from his lands.

Hiding out in the forest, trying to make her way back home. Staying off the road to avoid being seen. Hearing the patrols out looking for her. Pain at the back of her head.

She woke up on the floor of the cave. She felt completely sick. She knew what was going to happen to her. Knew that she was going to experience her own death.

She heard the footsteps, listened in horror as she realized it was Darian in the cave with her. Heard the page call out for him. Sariah tried to move, tried to struggle. Anything to make it stop. He pulled her up by her hair, and put his boot on her back. She saw the dagger coming. It was the one she got from Darian's man.

She saw the look on his face. She knew then that this man needed to be stopped. As he slit her throat, she felt no pain this time around. The Crow must have shielded her from that much. He wiped the blade on his pants before heading towards the mouth of the cave.

The Crow was standing there watching. Couldn't she see him? He turned just before he reached her, smiled at Sariah, and walked out of the cave. Sariah reached out to The Crow, beseeching her to make this stop. Bring her back. Her world went black.

In the garden behind Javier's manor, her body hit the ground with a thud, and she was completely still.

After this, Sariah would wake up for brief moments of time, seeing flashes of the world around her. Someone carrying her back to Javier's bed, The Crow kissing her brow. Javier waking with a start, and panicking when he can't wake her. Javier and The Crow arguing about her and what had been done.

Much of the time though, the world passed without her. She wondered how long she'd be stuck in these little slices of life, time passing, people moving on, and here she was, frozen. She was starting to get sick of it. She wasn't about to wait for The Crow to fix it.

Hell, she was no damsel in distress. She was a self-rescuing princess. With that thought in her mind, she started clawing her way out of the dark. Each time she saw a slice of life, she grabbed it, and refused to let go. And each time, her time awake got longer.

Javier was with her every second he could be. Talking to her, begging, praying, bribing. He even asked her to marry him. Promised her the world, babies, money, whatever she wanted if she'd just come back to him. Sariah's heart about burst from the love and sadness she was causing him. And she fought.

He held her in his arms every night. And she fought. The Crow was a regular visitor... usually when Javier was not around. He blamed The Crow for Sariah's state, and even though he had to know how dumb it was, he threatened her. The man threatened a goddess because he loved her.

She had no questions about it anymore. He loved her. She loved him. She would marry him as soon as she was able to fully wake up. How had she ever questioned it? Why did she ever fight it? She'd spend the rest of her life loving him, even if that life meant staying in service to The Crow. All she had to do was wake up.

"I need to help Lord Heath bring some goods to Langton soon. I know that you said your death had something to do with Lord Darian, but not trading with the man is just business lunacy. What do you think?" He paused, but continued quickly on, "He and

Queen Elliana have announced their engagement. While there are questions as to their happiness, it's a sound business move."

Sariah jerked in his arms. "Sariah? Can you hear me?" She sat up straight in bed, causing him to fall off in shock.

"What did you say?" Sariah was also shocked. Not that she was awake. She'd been becoming more and more awake as the days went on. She was shocked by the news Javier had just delivered, and wanted to make sure she had heard correctly.

"That I'm leaving with-" he didn't even get his sentence fully out before Sariah cut him off.

"No. About Queen Elliana. What did you say happened?" She was very intently looking at him.

"She and Lord Darian have announced their engagement. I guess he's been at Blackmore since we saw his men that day on the road." Sariah felt sick. There was no way that Elliana could marry that man. Hell, he probably planned to kill her shortly after the wedding and keep Blackmore as spoils.

"We need to go. Right away." Javier looked at her like she'd gone crazy. Sariah shook her head. "I'm alright, I promise. I'll explain it all later. But right now, we have to go to Blackmore. This wedding *cannot* happen." Sariah sounded so sincere, and she really looked like she was completely fine.

At his reluctance, Sariah took a good look at Javier. His skin was sallow, he had bags under his eyes, and she thought he even might have lost a bit of weight. She took her hands in his. "The hardest thing I've ever done is come back from death to you. I love you. And yes, I'll marry you."

Javier didn't hesitate. He leapt forward and took her lips. His passion was unmistakable. Sariah allowed herself and him to enjoy each other for a couple of moments before she pulled back. "Darian killed me. I was on a mission to get information about his dealings for Queen Elliana. He intercepted a letter I sent to her and misinterpreted it. He killed me with his own bare hands. And he *liked* it."

Javier's eyes were pure rage. "I'll kill him. I don't care how powerful he is. I'll cut out his heart and grill it up for his men." Sariah shook her head.

"It won't be up to you. The Crow said that my time was coming to face death and choose. For me, Darian *is* death. Literally. He took my life. The Crow brought me back, but he murdered me. I will be the one facing him down. And I need to choose. But choose what? To let him live? To take his life as he took mine?" Sariah had a feeling she knew what the choice would be.

Chapter Thirty-Four

After talking it out, Javier and Sariah decided that the best way to go about things would be to send a letter to Elliana, congratulating her on the engagement, and seeing if they could come visit for the engagement and the wedding. This way they weren't crashing the party, but should still allow Sariah access to Elliana in a way that would allow her to speak privately with her longtime friend.

Sariah was recovering from being indisposed for an extended period of time. She was up and about and able to do things a regular person could, but at night she and Javier would retreat to the practice area, where she would work on stretching and simple weight lifting. She found that she felt like she was coming back from an extended illness. The Crow had warned her that it would take a while for her to recover after experiencing her own death.

Sariah sent the letter to Elliana shortly after she woke, and she expected a response any day. Waiting was making her crazy. She wanted to just storm off to Blackmore and take care of her friend. But Javier cautioned her. She had no idea what the arrangements were between Elliana and Darian. She could be making things worse if she went unannounced. So Sariah waited, and practiced. She spent so much time with Javier during the day, and they made love at night.

Heath was a frequent visitor at the manor, wanting to avoid court as much as possible. "If I'm at court, Margaret will find a way to rope me into working. I work enough trading, thank you very much." He made a good switch in sparring partner for Sariah, and he, like Javier, never pulled his punches or gave any slack. Sariah wanted to be ready when Elliana's note came.

Sure enough, a few weeks later, a note came for Sariah inviting her to Elliana's Court. But it wasn't from Elliana. It was from Darian.

Sariah felt sick. She wanted to leave right away, but Javier cautioned her. They needed to come up with a gameplan.

Heath would not be able to come with them since he wasn't invited. It would be seen as an act of aggression, and could have Darian and Elliana declaring war on Belrick. Darian had phrased the invitation so that it sounded like it only was for Sariah, but since she and Javier were engaged, she would be able to bring him along with impunity.

Since Darian sent the invitation, Sariah had no idea what they would be walking into. He knew who Sariah was when she was at his court. The fact that she was sending Elliana a letter meant that she was obviously alive. To him that would seem an impossibility, since he, oh, you know, slit her throat and left her for dead in a remote cave.

"The man is charming. I hate to admit it, but he is." Sariah and Javier were laying in bed. It was very early in the morning, and they had been up most of the night trying to come up with ideas. "If he weren't charming, it wouldn't matter how much money he had- he'd never retain a following." Sariah rolled over on her belly and put her hands on Javier's chest. She put her chin on her hands, making it so that he wouldn't be uncomfortable as she laid on him.

He reached down and absently stroked her hair. "I've never met him or even seen him in person, but living in a country that borders his, it's not hard to learn about him. What really throws me is that his country *has* a king. Yet there's no question of who really rules. Why not just overthrow the monarchy?"

Sariah smiled. "I can answer that for you. We talked about it while I was at his court. It's too much work. He's not well liked by the common people, but with the nobility he's golden. In order to overthrow the monarchy, he'd have to use only mercenaries, as the soldiers would be honor-bound to fight for the king. He'd have to put up so much money and effort when he's basically already ruling in all but name." She let out a deep sigh. "Maybe he found a different way to rule."

Javier leaned forward and laid a kiss on her head. "We'll get there and do what we can if Elliana is really in trouble." He stroked her hair again.

"Are you not nervous at all? We're going to be there with zero backup." She turned her head to look at him.

"Well, not exactly. As long as Luc and Elliana's core guards are still there, they'll back you up." He smiled down at her.

"But will they?" Sariah bit her bottom lip. "When I left, everyone thought that Elliana banished me. That's... not exactly what happened."

Javier frowned. "What do you mean?"

Sariah looked down, not wanting to look at him. "Elliana and I went into that back room to talk. She realized I was in love with you before I did. She couldn't just let me go though. That wouldn't have been proper. Especially in the eyes of the court. She thought she would have need of me again someday, and frankly, she didn't want to lose me. We really care about each other." Sariah paused here for a moment, seeming to catch her breath a bit.

"She thought Lord Darian coming to her with a marriage proposal was still a good bet. She made the decision to 'banish' me so that she could later forgive me and have me back. She knows I'm dangerous as all of her Queen's Ladies are. What makes me nervous is that it's him writing the letter and not her. Why haven't the Queen's Ladies done anything?" Sariah frowned. She knew she needed to get back to Blackmore.

"Sariah, love. We'll get back to her. We'll figure out what's going on. I'm still worried about you facing him. I'd still like to kill him myself. But I know that The Crow has made it clear that you need to be the one to face him. It's part of your destiny to do so. And while she is not my favorite being right now, she may have a point."

Sariah looked up at Javier. "When do we leave?"

"I've informed the staff that we'll be leaving this afternoon. We can take our time getting back there. If we rush, they'll think something is wrong. We need to play this casual." He stopped and thought for a moment. "Do you think you'd be able to fake not knowing him, or what you two had?"

Sariah rolled her eyes. "Absolutely. The Queen's Ladies have been in place for years. We had to lie to keep who and what we were a secret. I think the defining factor will be if he can hold his rage."

Javier nodded. "Well, let's start getting around. How do you want to pack? Only for a couple of days in saddlebags, or do you want to take a trunk and a wagon?"

Sariah thought about it for a moment before responding. "Let's pack light for now. I'd hate to have to leave in a hurry and leave things behind. We can always say we're having stuff sent after us."

Javier nodded at this. "I prefer to travel light whenever I can. I like it. Alright. Our plan is made as far as it can be. I guess in the meantime we take things one day at a time."

Sariah pulled herself up to him and kissed him. She wanted to make love to him in their bed once more before they left. She hoped it would not be the last time.

Chapter Thirty-Five

As the sun came up over the trees, Javier and Sariah were on their horses and on the road. As they had ridden away from the manor, Sariah felt a sense of sadness. She had enjoyed such happiness there with Javier. If she did not best Darian, she would never see it again. Javier caught her attention. "No bad thoughts. We've got this. We'll be home soon, and then I'll make you my wife." He moved his horse closer to hers, took her hand and kissed it.

Sariah gave him what she hoped was a reassuring smile. "No bad thoughts."

As they came away from the manor's lane and moved onto the main road towards Blackmore, they realized they were being followed. Whoever it was, they were staying at a good distance. But Sariah and Javier were both on high alert, and so they heard the almost imperceptible noises a human and horse can't help but make.

Luna suddenly landed on Sariah's shoulder. Sariah drew comfort from her little friend as well as from the idea that The Crow was still with her.

The person followed them all day, stopping when they stopped, always keeping their distance. Sariah wondered if it was a simple brigand or if it was one of Darian's men. If it was the former, she had no fear that they could handle it. If it was the latter, they'd have to play very cautiously.

When they stopped for the night, Sariah took on her noble lady persona. She started referring to Javier as "husband," hoping he'd catch on. He did instantly, and played along. Sariah realized that they needed to draw their shadow out. If they kept traveling on high alert like this, they'd be exhausted when they reached Blackmore. They'd be in no shape to face Darian.

Javier built a small fire and Sariah set up some makeshift beds on the ground. They went about making dinner and chatting and laughing as any married couple traveling would. As they did this, Sariah heard the follower come through the trees and stay just out of sight. Whoever this was was good, but not as good as she or Javier.

As she moved towards the fire to sit and eat, she felt a twinge just above her left eye. Sharp pain had her closing her eyes for just a moment. When she opened them, she was no longer alone. She looked over at Javier and saw him watching her intently. He knew something had happened.

Sariah continued on as if nothing were amiss. Javier played along, although he watched Sariah a bit more now. While she could see the concern, he hid it under gazes of longing and sweet smiles. Yup. They were just a married couple in love, getting ready to go to sleep. Sariah made a big show of yawning. "Mmm. I'm exhausted. Are you ready for bed?"

Javier smiled at her, a little something extra in his grin. "I'm always ready to take you to bed my love." His bald innuendo made her blush.

"Well, come take me then." She tried to give it right back, but didn't feel as confident as he did flirting this way with an audience. He stood up and came to her quickly, drawing her to her feet, and taking her lips. His back was to their shadow.

He wrapped his arms around her, and once his hands were on her back, he started moving his fingers in standard military signals to help lay out his plan. While she had to guess sometimes based on context, the plan was for them to go to bed, and make it seem like they were going to make love. When they were "distracted," if the person following was a bandit, it would be the perfect time to attack. If they did not and just watched, then Sariah would separate herself from Javier a bit to take the person on one-on-one.

They moved towards the bed that Sariah had created and climbed under the covers. Faking making love was no difficult task. And sure enough, as soon as they got into the hot and heavy part of the show, the shadow emerged from the trees. Sariah flipped Javier over so she was on top, hoping that the assailant would go for her, thinking she was easy prey.

They took the bait and grabbed Sariah from behind, pulling her off of Javier, and into the clearing. She was being held by her hair, her neck bent at an uncomfortable angle. She let out some sounds of distress, knowing that the man who held her not only expected it, he wanted it. "Come now, mate. You wouldn't want anything bad to happen to your pretty young wife, would you?" The man spoke with a slight accent, and he sneered at Javier, who had started to get up, but at his words sat back down.

"That's right. Now, I want whatever valuables you have. All of them. Wealthy couple such as yourselves are sure to be traveling with some trinkets. And gold. I bet you have lots of gold coins." The man nodded quickly, as if assuring himself of this fact. He seemed a bit twitchy and unsure of himself. He definitely wasn't a seasoned pro. Sariah rolled her eyes once she was sure that the man wouldn't see it.

"While you're doing that, I think I'm going to take your wife right over to those trees and entertain her." He slid his free hand down until he groped her breast. Sariah let out a little whimper. "Don't worry, pet. I guarantee you'll love it." Letting go of her breast, he reached down and grabbed his crotch, shifting his hips towards her.

The look of pure rage on Javier's face was not play at all. He was ready to kill this man for having touched her. Sariah tried to motion to him with her hand to stand down. He must have seen it, because he did not jump up and take the guy's head off with his bare hands.

Sariah let the man lead her a little ways away from the campsite. He told her to turn around and face away from him, and to pull down her pants and bend over. She could hear him rubbing himself already. Not wanting this to go any further, Sariah suddenly felt the sword coalesce in her hand.

In one swift move, she swung around, bringing the blade level with her shoulders. Never losing her momentum, she swung the blade across the man's throat. He looked at her in shock before falling forward to the ground. Javier was right behind him, watching her, as The Crow stepped out of her. Rather than what she did before, The Crow turned and kissed Sariah on the brow.

When she stepped away, Sariah had the imprint of a small crescent moon just below her hairline. Laying on its back, the points of the moon pointed to her hairline, and the rounded part pointed down towards her face. Sariah reached up and touched the spot. It had burned for a quick second when The Crow kissed her. Now it felt nice and cool.

The Crow smiled at her before turning to tend to the remains at Sariah's feet. As she walked away, Sariah moved to where Javier was standing. He reached out when she got to him and touched the small moon. "What is it? It felt like a brand, but now I don't feel anything." Sariah reached her hand up to his.

"It's a small crescent moon. It's very beautiful on you." He leaned forward and kissed the spot, and then kissed her lips. "My warrior goddess."

Chapter Thirty-Six

The next morning they backtracked a bit and found the bandit's horse tied to a tree just off the road. The man was smart and didn't tie the horse tight, allowing it the ability to escape if it needed to. It was a very docile horse though, who nickered in pleasure at seeing some people. Sariah laid some oats down for it and gave it some water.

They let the horse have her fill before tying her to Sariah's mare. The two horses seemed completely content at traveling together. Sariah and Javier decided to offer the horse to Elliana as an engagement present. Maybe be able to build some good will.

They were close enough now that if they pushed through the day, they could make the castle by nightfall. They did not like the idea though of coming into an unknown situation in the dark. They made the decision to find somewhere to stay in or near the village, and to approach the castle in the morning.

Sariah initially thought about staying with a contact in the village, but quickly nixed that idea. She didn't know what kind of reception she'd get, especially since she didn't know the situation at the castle. As much as she wanted to push through and get there, she knew that their plan was a solid one. She needed to wait.

They camped down in the forest a ways from the village. Not wanting to be seen, they didn't light any fire, and they tied their horses off a ways from where they slept. Neither one slept well, as they were both on high alert due to the proximity of the castle.

As soon as it was light enough out to see, they set off. They approached the village as they had left it- through the farmlands. As they rode past fields of crops, Sariah noticed that many of the fields had people working them, which was not uncommon. What was strange, was the fact that these people wore manacles and chains. There was a guard at every field as well, but they were not guards she recognized.

The people working the fields were dressed in the grey common uniform of the prison. They were convicts. Sariah slowed her horse. This was not anything she'd seen in Blackmore before. One of the female prisoners looked up at the road.

Sariah jumped off of her horse and ran to the woman. She hugged her fiercely as they both dropped to their knees. The guard for the field looked over, but since the woman wasn't trying to run away, and neither were attacking him, he turned away again, bored.

Javier pulled closer to the field, but didn't dismount. Sariah looked back at him and thought this was wise. His appearance in the field could cause the guard to come investigate. Sariah saw the moment that he realized why she had run into the field. While he had not recognized her at first, Sariah would always know her friend.

Sariah pulled back and held Lara at arms length. "Lara! What happened? How are you here?" Then, lowering her voice, "are you on a mission? Where is Luc?"

At the mention of her husband's name, Lara's eyes filled with tears. "He's gone. They're all gone. When Darian came..." Lara let out a sob. "He started changing things right away. Elliana said *nothing* against him. She just let him make the changes. Luc and the guards loyal to Elliana and the crown got together to revolt... oh Sariah. It was awful. Darian's mercenaries quelled the revolt quickly. All involved were arrested. The wives of the guards as well, even though we didn't take part. We were all dragged out to the town square. The men..." Lara collapsed in tears. She couldn't continue.

Sariah held her friend and just let her cry. When she could shed no more tears, she continued. "Elliana finally stood up against Darian. She didn't want her Ladies to suffer the same fate as their husbands. She did it publicly, there in the square. He smacked her.

Hard. Split her lip. And then he punched her in the stomach. As she lay there on the floor, doubled over in pain, Darian declared that we were to spend the rest of our days in prison, and working in the fields to earn our keep. Oh, Sariah..."

The more she heard, the more her rage built. She had no doubt what Lara meant by "gone." Luc and all of the core of Elliana's guard had been executed. In front of their wives by the sound of it. And from her inability to speak from it, Darian had made sure they had suffered.

Sariah looked up the road bank to Javier. She was not about to leave Lara here to die at the hands of that madman. He saw the determined look on her face and cursed under his breath. It looks like plans had changed. He took a deep breath and then made a complex hand movement.

Sariah saw as soon as the spell took hold. The guard and all the prisoners but Lara were frozen. She grabbed Lara's hand and made a run for the road. Lara's manacles and chains were thankfully loose enough to allow for fieldwork, which also allowed her to hold the reins and ride a horse.

Sariah got her up onto the extra mare, and mounted her own horse as quickly as she could. "We need to go back. We cannot stay here." Javier didn't bother asking questions, just cut the tie that held the mares together, and kicked his horse's flanks to get it moving. The ladies followed suit, and rode off like they were being pursued. As soon as Javier's spell failed, they most likely would be.

They rode hard away from the village, but soon slowed their pace. They knew that riding through the night was going to be their best bet. They could reach Belrick Manor by the next evening if they rode straight through.

In addition to rage, Sariah had sorrow ripping through her. She thought of Luc and the times they had spent together. She had loved him like a brother, and now she'd never get to see him again. To speak to him again. She took a deep breath to stave off her tears. She couldn't break down yet. Once they were home, she'd be able to break down. But right now? She had to stay strong.

She looked over at Lara. Her friend was so strong. She was obviously grieving, and exhausted, but she held on. Sariah looked at Javier ahead of her and flicked the reins so that she could draw level. "We need to talk. And we need help. We're not going to be able to do this on our own."

Javier looked over at Sariah. "I've been thinking about it. Once we get back to the Manor, I'm going to ride up to the castle. You see to Lara. I'm going to petition Lady Margaret. She's a trade partner with Darian, but she also believes in doing things fairly. If I can win her to our side, we'll have an army at our disposal. If I can't, well, I have money. I'll start hiring any mercenaries I can. We won't let this go unpunished." Javier's face was angry, but also concerned.

Sariah nodded. "It's a solid plan. How extensive is your herb garden? I want to make a special tea that will help Lara sleep. And ease some of her pain."

Javier thought about her question for a moment. "We have most of the common herbs used in cooking and medicine. However, the castle's garden is much more extensive than mine. If I don't have it, I will get it for you." He reached out for her hand and kissed it. Behind them, they heard Lara start to cry. Sariah looked at him with sad eyes before dropping back to ride even with Lara.

Chapter Thirty-Seven

Back at the manor, Sariah got Lara settled into a very nicely appointed guest room. It was very close to her and Javier's room, which is why she picked the one she did. As she stayed with Lara, and Javier went to the castle, Sariah started second guessing their plan. If they declared war, so many lives could and would be lost. It would tear the nations apart. Sariah laid on the bed with Lara, just holding her and stroking her hair, as one would do with a child. Sariah had a feeling that Lara had not had a chance to grieve since she was immediately thrown into jail and subjected to hard labor.

The fact that the other Queen's Ladies were also working the fields right now made Sariah crazy. She wanted to rush right back and liberate them all. But she knew that this was an impractical desire. Sariah would leave Lara only briefly to clean up, or bring food. She had the maids bring some clothes for Lara, so that she would not have to stay in that horrible prisoner's dress.

Late that evening, Javier poked his head into the room. Sariah saw him, and, seeing that Lara was sleeping, she slid off the bed very gently, and walked quietly out of the room. Shutting the door gently behind her, she went to Javier, and hugged him. He stroked her hair back and kissed the top of her head. "It's done. Lady Margaret is prepared to march against Lord Darian. It didn't take much convincing once I relayed what Lara had told us."

Sariah looked up at Javier. "Are we doing the right thing? A war has just so much risk and cost." She bit her bottom lip.

Javier tilted her chin up with a finger so that she was looking at him. "This is our only chance. He took the best and most dangerous men and women in Elliana's court, and he executed them or made them criminals. There's no way we could face them on our own.

And I could hire mercenaries, but it would bankrupt us. I would be willing to do it for you if Margaret had not been willing, but since she is, I think it's the best and smartest thing to take her up on it." Javier gently kissed her lips. "I need to head back up to the castle. I'm going to be gone at least overnight. Will you be alright here?"

Sariah nodded. "I have Lara to take care of. I would like to say that it won't make me miss you, but I try not to lie to you anymore." Sariah smiled up at Javier with a twinkle in her eye, and then stood on her tiptoes to kiss him again.

"I'll be back in a couple of days at the latest. Send someone to the castle if you need me. I'll be home as quickly as possible." He kissed her again, this time very passionately. Then he put his forehead to hers. "I love you."

Sariah's heart skipped a beat again. Anytime he said it to her, it did. "I love you too." Javier held her hand until their fingers slipped apart as he walked away. He headed into their suite, most likely grabbing a change or two of clothes before leaving to head back to the castle. Luna flew down to Sariah's shoulder as she watched Javier walk down the hall.

"I need her." Sariah said very quietly to Luna while stroking her head. She needed to make sure that Javier would not hear this, or he might be worried enough to stay. He still wasn't overly fond of The Crow, and there would be no way that he would want Sariah to see her alone. Luna nuzzled Sariah with her beak before taking off again.

Sariah turned and went back into the room with Lara. Lara was still sleeping, and Sariah crawled up on the bed behind her, and wrapped her arms around Lara's waist. "I promise you. I will avenge him. I will take the cost of your labor out of his hide as well. Darian will feel my wrath." Sariah had felt the anger rising in her since she had heard Lara describing what had happened to herself, Luc, the other Ladies, and Elliana. Sariah knew that The Crow had cautioned her about taking vengeance against Darian, but Sariah had so much rage now, she didn't know if she could just give him over to justice.

The Crow appeared in the room, Luna perched on her hand. "I know why you called me forth. I cannot recommend this path that you're on. However, as I told you in our first conversation, there are always choices to be made."

Sariah looked at her with determined eyes. "Can I beat him? One on one? I've seen my death. I know he's the cause." Sariah waited with baited breath.

"You can, yes. But there are several circumstances that would need to be met for you to succeed. I cannot see what these are, but I know they are there."

Sariah nodded, and looked down, thinking. If she could go and end this herself. Stop a war, even if it cost her her existence... should she? Could she? She looked over at Lara, who looked defeated and sad even in sleep. She thought of Javier and the life that they could share. She looked up at The Crow intently. "Can I...." she swallowed. "With my death I mean, can I have children?"

The Crow cocked her head to one side. "I cannot say for sure. Life and Birth are not my purview. I am a mistress of war and death. I don't see why you couldn't though."

Sariah nodded at that. She wasn't sure if she could have them, and she had a feeling that Javier would want children. Once he was married, he'd want to settle down, and plant roots. He'd still have somewhat of an adventurous spirit, and would expect his wife to as well, but, yes, he would want children. He would want to carry on his legacy. Sariah wondered if she really was the right woman for Javier. She wanted him to be happy, and she didn't know if he would really be able to be happy with her.

Regardless of what she decided to do, in order for him to be happy, with or without her, she was going to need to take care of Darian. "I need my people to be happy. Right now they are suffering, needlessly. I can take care of the cause of their suffering. I can make their lives better."

The Crow nodded at Sariah. "So, you've chosen then?"

Sariah nodded back at The Crow. "Yes, my lady. I have chosen."

The Crow looked at Sariah for a moment. "So be it." And then she disappeared, taking Luna with her.

Chapter Thirty-Eight

Sariah waited until most of the house had gone to sleep. The maid had brewed an herbal tea for Lara to help her sleep, so Sariah wasn't afraid of her friend waking up and stopping her. She had seen Javier head out for the castle earlier in the evening, so she knew he would not try and stop her either. She walked back into their suite and found some paper and a pen. She wrote a short note and sealed it, putting his name on it. She kissed it as she put it on the bed where he was sure to find it once she had left.

She walked over to the wardrobe and grabbed one of the small packs that Javier kept there for his travels. She loaded up a few pairs of clothes and one gown into the bag. She armed herself with her weapons, putting the dagger she took from Darian's man into the pack. She took one last look around the room. She hoped with all of her heart that she'd be able to come back. Thinking of The Crow, she walked into the bathroom to look in the looking glass. She saw that The Crow's brand was still on her brow. She felt more confident seeing it there. Even though she had taken Luna, The Crow had not completely forsaken her.

She slung the pack over her back, and walked out of the room. Looking back one more time and thinking of the life she was leaving behind, she shut the door on their suite. She fought back tears as she moved through the castle, heading for the front door. No one tried to stop her. No one was awake or around who would even realize she was gone. She opened the door to the manor, letting her tears fall freely now. She wished they could have had more time together. She closed the door on the manor, and set out on the lane.

As she walked, she steeled herself against the feelings of loss and longing. She could not go into this mission with those or she was sure to fail. That's how she looked at this- a mission. She didn't try and plan, she knew that would be foolish. While she had an idea of what was going on in Blackmore, since they took Lara away, things could have totally changed. Sariah hoped that Elliana was still alive.

She heard hoofbeats on the road, and immediately dashed into the undergrowth of the forest. She flattened herself on the ground, and held utterly still. Originally thinking Javier or his men were pursuing her, she soon realized that this was not the case. Soon the lone rider and horse had passed her in a flurry of staccato beats, and she was able to come out of hiding.

The moon was not in the sky tonight, which was good for her. She knew the way to Blackmore, and it would be harder for someone to spot her on the road. She was not worried about the distance. She had always liked walking and running, and this was just an extra long walk for her. She knew it would take her several days to get to Blackmore walking, but she knew she needed to be as far from Belrick as possible when Javier returned to the manor.

Sariah found herself needing to duck and cover a few more times as she walked that night. The road though was mostly deserted. As the sky started to lighten, she was trying to decide how much further she should go before she made camp. Her camp would be a very simple one, just her laying on the ground and using her pack as a pillow. She would sleep armed, and she knew that she would not sleep fitfully, since she would need to be on alert the whole time. She decided to go as far as her body would let her.

Looking around as she walked, she also knew that she would not pass up a good hiding spot for the day if she came across one. As the sky lightened more, she left the road to walk in the forest, parallel to the road. She did not want to be seen if she could avoid it. She tried not to think of Javier as she walked, but, having been on two journeys with him recently, she could not avoid him. She thought about their meeting, how she rode ahead of him on the way back to Blackmore.

She thought of their journey to Belrick, and how he tried to seduce her on the side of the road. This trip, walking along this road, she never felt more alone.

Sariah found a place to pass the day, and it passed uneventfully. In fact, the next few days passed uneventfully, and she made her way to the outskirts of Blackmore Village. She smelled smoke, and got a sick feeling in the pit of her stomach. She quickened her pace, suddenly not worrying about being seen. As she came to the first farmhouse, she saw that it was burned. Burned beyond recognition. She saw that the fire was fresh, it had only recently burned out, and it looked like it had burned for at least a day. Parts of the frame of the house stood, and Sariah carefully approached the structure, pulling her shirt up to cover her mouth.

She walked up to the door of the farmhouse and immediately had to drop her shirt, lean over and vomit. There was a chain and lock on the door. There was only one reason to lock the door of a burning home... to make sure that those inside could not escape. Sariah still felt sick, although she had thrown up the small amount of food she had eaten recently. She was sure that this was revenge upon the village for her and Javier freeing Lara from her predicament.

She thought of examining the remains of the home, but realized that there was nothing she could do. As long as Darian was in power over Blackmore, sights like this would become common. Tears filled Sariah's eyes again while her heart hardened towards the man further.

Since she had entered the farmlands, there were not really any good places for her to hide, so she stuck to the road as much as possible, taking the ease of travel over trying to slink through the crop fields. Darian had left the crops of course, having the means to work them with his own people. Why waste a profit? Ugh. The idea of it made Sariah see red. She was going to kill that man. She wanted him to suffer while she did so.

Sariah came across other farmhouses, all of them burned. She stuck to the road and didn't move closer, knowing that she'd come across the same scene she had seen at the first farm. As she came up on the outskirts of the village proper, her heart broke in two. She saw Mistress Eleanor's home. While she had hoped with all of her heart that the homes closer to the village had been spared, their farm had been quite profitable, and she saw that their home too, was burned to a shell.

Sariah thought of that little girl looking up at her, the one that she saved from the fate her mother had given her. She hoped that the family did not suffer, but at the same time knew that was an unlikely scenario. She clenched and released her fists as she walked. She was beyond hiding now. She had it in her mind to walk straight up to the castle and demand to be seen. Hell, she had an invitation from Lord Darian himself. What were the guards going to do, deny her entry?

This thought steeled her resolve. She started walking up the road towards the castle. The homes in the village itself seemed to have escaped Darian's wrath. She was glad to see this, but she noticed that there was no one out on the street, and the feeling of happiness that the village normally had was gone. The windows were all shuttered, and the village appeared to be a ghost town. As she came to the square, she saw that the scaffold was still erected, and fresh rope had been hung. Darian had been a busy man, exacting his revenge. Sariah kept going, not looking too close at the place where her good friend had met his maker.

Chapter Thirty-Nine

At last, Sariah found herself facing the castle. She stood a good distance from it, looking up at the stone walls and the thick wooden door that was the only thing standing between her and the woman she had come to consider like a sister. She was deciding just what to do when the door opened, and a single guard strolled out towards her. He wore Elliana's colors, but he was not anyone that Sariah had recognized… until he got closer.

Sariah suddenly realized that this was the man she took the dagger from. She gritted her teeth as he moved closer to her. "Lady Sariah!" he called out. Well, clearly someone in the castle knew who she still was. She'd only seen this man a few times, even at Darian's court, and yet he was able to recognize her by sight?

"Sir." She kept her voice low, and did not make any sort of bow or acknowledgement of his station. He smirked at this pointed slight, and held his hands out to each side of his body. He was showing her that he was not armed at all, and that he was approaching her as a measure of good faith. Sariah wanted nothing more than to run him through.

"You have been long expected and awaited by your beloved friend, Queen Elliana, as well as her betrothed, Lord Darian. Would you allow me to escort you to them?" While it was phrased as a question, it really was not one. She knew that whether she liked it or not, he would be escorting her into the castle.

Sariah had a moment of panic at the thought of going into the castle and being trapped, but this is what she came here for. She needed to face Darian herself, and she needed to be the one to decide what happened to him. Sariah gave the tiniest nod of her head, acquiescing to this request.

Without another thought, the guard turned his back to her and started walking back into the castle. As she got a bit closer, she saw that every archer on the wall had bows trained on her. She would not have made it out alive if she had shown any hint of violence. Her stomach tightened in pain. She took a deep breath as she walked, realizing that she would never be able to get back home to Javier and Lara. She begged forgiveness of him to the universe or whomever was listening before she crossed the threshold of the castle.

Sariah was taken to her old room in the castle. It was exactly the way she had left it- trunk sitting partially packed on the bed and all. Unlike before though, when her "escort" closed the door behind her, she heard the snick of a key turning in a lock. She tried the door handle, but sure enough, she was locked in.

She walked over to her window, and tried opening it. It opened only a crack, whereas before, she was able to open it all the way. They didn't search her or take her pack, so they clearly weren't worried about her carrying weapons. The whole situation seemed odd to her, but she figured that if they were going to let her keep her weapons, she wouldn't argue.

Not knowing when she would be called for, or if anyone would come into her room, she very quickly used the wash basin to clean off some of the dirt from the road, and changed out of her riding clothes into one of her gowns. Since all of her things were still in her room, she chose one of her favorite gowns, a blood red one. She figured this fit her mood far better than the navy blue gown that she brought with her.

Since she had nothing better to do, and she really was exhausted from her trip, she decided to try and nap. Before she laid down, she moved her trunk into the corner of her room, and moved any weapons that she couldn't carry on her to the secret compartment in her wardrobe.

She climbed onto her bed, thinking of Javier and the last time they shared it. She had hoped to come back here with him one day, and to share it again, but she had a feeling she wasn't going to make it out of this mission alive. She closed her eyes and tried to sleep.

A sound woke her, but she wasn't sure what. She sat up in her bed and looked around before turning her gaze to the window. The sun was setting, and the light was turning golden, giving her room a pleasant glow. When she went to lay back down, she caught movement out of the corner of her eye.

Turning her head in that direction, she found herself face to face with The Crow. Rather than being in her human guise, she was in her corvid form. She turned her head so that she could clearly see Sariah out of one of her eyes and cocked her head.

"I have no idea what I'm doing here. I've been locked in my room since I got here. Unless you're planning on bestowing me some of your amazing powers, I'm stuck here until someone decides to let me out." She knew that antagonizing a goddess was not a good idea, but at this point, she didn't really care.

The Crow turned her head towards the bedroom door. Sariah followed suit, and sure enough, a key in the lock signaled that someone was there to let her out. Rather than open her door and barge in, they politely knocked, and waited for a response. Sariah turned to look at The Crow with incredulity - they were still observing some niceties even though they had her locked in?- but The Crow was no longer there.

"Go figure." Sariah muttered under her breath before calling out more loudly, "Yes?"

"Lady Sariah, your presence is requested in the main hall for dinner." The voice was a young man's, which was odd, since before, Elliana didn't let men wait on her Ladies. But, as Sariah knew, things had changed. "Do you need me to wait while you change?"

Sariah stood up and walked to the door. She opened the door to see a pleasant young man in livery standing at a polite distance from her door. She raised an eyebrow at him. "No, I'm quite ready." She ran her hands down her gown to smooth out any wrinkles before following the servant to the main hall.

Sariah wasn't sure what to expect in the main hall, but it looked like any other dinner service. She didn't recognize anyone at the tables other than Queen Elliana, Lord Darian, and a few faces at the table where the Ladies used to sit. Instead of Ladies though, it was filled with men, all of which she recognized from Darian's court.

At her entrance, the attention of the two main tables turned. She wasn't exactly blending in with her bright red dress. Most everyone else in the main hall was wearing shades of brown, grey, or black, including Queen Elliana. Well, she wanted to make a statement, and she was indeed making one.

Darian frowned at her, and Elliana hid a smile. That one small smile told Sariah everything she needed to know. Her friend was still there. She was just being held down with a boot on her neck. The boot of the man sitting next to her. Sariah did the only thing she knew that would work, she put on her most pleasant smile and her most elegant demeanor.

She walked into that room every bit the Lady she had trained to be. She kept her head up and her smile on, even as she approached the Queen's table. She saw that a place had been made right next to Lord Darian. Well, if they could play the game, so could she. She went down into a low curtsey before the raised table.

"Forgive my tardiness, Highness. I was unaware how late it was. I was resting after my long journey." Sariah addressed only Queen Elliana, but was not surprised at all when it was Darian who responded.

"Lady Sariah. So lovely to finally meet you. Queen Elliana has spoken much of your beauty, grace, and *loyalty*." This last was said with some disdain. It was his questioning her loyalty to him that cost her her life in the first place.

Sariah turned icy eyes on Darian. "Forgive me, sir, for not including my congratulations on your upcoming nuptials. I was so *happy* to hear that Queen Elliana had finally found someone she wished to spend the rest of her life with." Sariah noticed right away how Elliana looked down at her plate and refused to join in the conversation or corroborate anything Sariah was saying.

Sariah didn't need to get Elliana alone anymore. What she and Javier had feared was coming true. Darian had found a way to legitimate rule, and he was taking it with an iron fist. Sariah's hand itched for a blade. She could hit his eye with one of her throwing knives, and then it would all be over. But it wasn't good enough for him. He needed to suffer for what he had done.

Lord Darian motioned her up to the spot next to him and talk resumed in the hall. Once she had been seated and food began to come out of the kitchens, Darian leaned over towards Sariah and said very quietly so that no one else could hear, "You're supposed to be dead! How is it that you're not?" His voice was outraged.

"Sir?" Sariah turned to him as if she had no idea what he meant. She picked up her knife to start eating her dinner, and it was like the world paused. She felt the handle of the knife in her palm. She saw the edge of the blade, and knew that it could handle one slice. She looked over at Darian and just pictured herself jumping up and slashing the knife across his throat.

If she did that here, in front of this many people, she knew she was dead. She'd never make it out the door. And then Elliana and the other Ladies would end up suffering the consequences. So, she picked up her fork, and started eating her dinner. Darian had no idea just how close to death he came in those moments.

He scoffed at Sariah's feigned innocence, and turned to Elliana. Sariah ate her dinner in silence, glad that for now, Darian had turned

THE QUEEN'S LADY

his attention elsewhere. Sariah looked over at Elliana often through dinner, hoping to catch her eye, and maybe figure out a way to get her alone. However, it seemed that Elliana was very carefully not looking at Sariah.

Sariah thought about the fact that Javier would have gotten home by now. He would have read her note, and most likely cursed her name over and over. She really hoped that he would at least heed her advice, and stay in Belrick. She didn't want a war in her name, and she was doing anything that she could to avoid it.

Once dinner had ended, the main hall started emptying of people. Sariah watched them go, and unlike how things were before, realized that they were all going their own way instead of heading over to the theater for evening entertainment. While a lot of things had surprised Sariah with the changes, this surprised her the most. Elliana had loved all of the arts; dance, theater, music. It would take *a lot* for her to give them up. In her surprise, Sariah turned to Lord Darian, "Will there be no evening entertainment?"

Darian turned to her, annoyed at being addressed, and said, "No. Queen Elliana stopped evening entertainment shortly after you left. As much as I, too, love the arts, I will not put my future bride through misery sitting through performances that she can no longer abide."

Sariah frowned. Had she been the cause of Elliana discontinuing evening performances, really? She looked over at Elliana, but the Queen was still staring at her plate. It hurt Sariah deeply to see bright and bubbly Elliana being so withdrawn. She saw no physical marks on the queen, but knew that Elliana must have been beaten into submission, physically or mentally. She vowed again that she would make Darian pay. She just had to bide her time.

She stood once she had finished, and curtseyed before Darian and Elliana. "I will take my leave if I may?" She hated putting herself in a position of vulnerability around him. His grin showed that he knew just how much it bothered her.

"Of course, Lady Sariah. If I may, I would like to visit you in your room later this evening? It has been a while since we've seen each other, and I would love a chance to catch up with you?" It was the first time that Elliana had spoken since dinner had started.

Sariah smiled warmly at Elliana, not missing the Dark look on Darian's face. "Of course, Highness. If you'd like, you can come with me now, and we can chat on the way back to my room as well?" Sariah hoped to spare whatever punishment Darian had been thinking of doling out to Elliana.

Elliana nodded, and stood. Darian's hand shot out and grabbed Elliana's wrist. The motion was abrupt enough that those still in the hall turned to see what was happening on the front table. Realizing he had an audience, he covered by kissing Elliana's hand. "Hurry back, my sweet. I wouldn't want to miss you too dearly."

Elliana nodded, her lips firmly pressed together, and signs of stress around her eyes. Sariah held out her arm for the Queen, and the two ladies walked off, leaving Darian to stew. As soon as they were out of the hall, Sariah noticed that they picked up a tail. A different guard than the one that escorted Sariah before, it was very clear that he was still there to keep an eye on the ladies.

"So much has happened since I left." Sariah decided to keep things light as she could, since the guard would most likely report everything back to Darian. "I am engaged to Sir Javier. He is an amazing man, and I can hardly believe my luck in the match." Yup, just two girls chatting about romance. Nothing to see here.

"Oh, Sariah! I am so very pleased. I saw how well suited you were when you were here. Have you picked out your wedding clothes yet? I would love to hear about your gown!" Elliana smirked in Sariah's direction, letting her know that she was happy to play along.

Sariah slowed her pace some, hoping to bore the guard into a stupor. "Oh, I have, and you would not believe the intricacy of this gown…"

Chapter Forty

By the time the two ladies made it to Sariah's room, the guard was yawning with boredom. Since Elliana was still Queen in her own right, she turned to him, "Thank you, Sir Bryce. You may return to Lord Darian. I will call someone to escort me when I have finished visiting with my friend. Bryce's mouth opened in shock. He wasn't sure what to do. "That will be all." Turning away from him, Elliana went into Sariah's room.

Sariah looked at the young guard with a bit of sympathy. She knew that if he went back to Darian prematurely, he was going to face the Lord's wrath. However, if he stayed, he would be defying orders of the Queen of Blackmore. She smiled at Sir Bryce and turned into her room, closing the door behind her.

Sariah turned to her old friend, and embraced her warmly. "Oh, Elliana. I am so sorry." She pulled back from the queen with tears in her eyes. "Lara told me what has been happening since I've been gone, and I feel like it is all my fault."

Elliana shook her head. "No. It is not your fault. I invited Darian here, knowing his reputation. I just had thought maybe it was over exaggerated, or he was misunderstood. I know better now. I have been stuck. If I speak out against him, he retaliates. All of my best men are gone. After Lara escaped, he sent the rest of my Ladies to Langton, where who knows what awaits them there. Hearing that you were wanting to come, oh, it lifted my heart." Elliana paused here, and a strange look came over her face.

"When he read your letter, all of the blood drained out of his face. He looked at the date several times before demanding to know who you were, and how this trickery came about. He said he killed you."

Sariah opened her mouth and shut it again. She didn't know he'd have told anyone that. "Umm. Yeah. He is the reason I lost my memory. Apparently it was too traumatic for me to process at first. He left me in the woods, and he thought I had died. I didn't though. He didn't hurt me as badly as he thought he did. That's why I came back covered in blood." Sariah knew that her excuse sounded half-formed, even to herself. But what was she supposed to do, tell Elliana the truth? Ha.

Elliana's face got dark. "Oh, Sariah. I'm so very sorry. When did you remember this?"

"Right before I came back here. Elliana, the things he's done. They're unpardonable. Beyond killing friends that I considered family, he's killed off all of the farming families. Locked them in their homes and then set the buildings ablaze. He has to be stopped."

Elliana's eyes filled with tears. "He's too powerful. He walked right into Blackmore and just took over. I and my people didn't stand a chance. If you had been here, you too would be in Langton, or dead."

Sariah embraced her friend. She was not sure of what she really could say to reassure her. She wanted to say that it would all be alright, and that she had plans to off Darian, but she didn't know who was listening. So instead she just held her friend for a while and told her it would all be okay.

After Elliana left Sariah's room, Sariah didn't hear the door lock again. She wished she had a way to get a message to Javier about the other Ladies. To let him know that they were in Langton, and that Darian was in total power here. She paced the floor of her room a bit, opening her window the crack she was allowed to, and looked out into the night.

She felt so lonely here. The only friend she had was Elliana, and there was no chance that Darian would let her go. Sariah turned away from the window, wondering just what the hell she had gotten herself into. How was she going to fix this?

She heard a clicking noise and turned around. The Crow was sitting in her window. Not on her window sill, but physically part of her was *IN* the glass panes of the window. Sariah's mouth dropped open. "I guess you really can't keep a goddess out when she wants to go somewhere."

The Crow cawed before hopping into the room. She hopped towards Sariah. One moment she hopped into the air as a corvid, and the next, the woman was standing before her.

"You have a choice to make, Sariah. And you're running out of time. Rather than heed your advice, Javier has decided that he was not going to live without you. He gathered what few men and supplies that Margaret could give him on short notice, and is headed this way." The Crow was completely calm saying this, as if she didn't just shatter Sariah's world.

"*No!*" Sariah gasped. He couldn't. He would get killed. This was *not* what Sariah wanted.

"I told you he loved you... he is a good man and his love is pure. He would do anything for you, even if that means giving up his life." The Crow stepped closer to Sariah and held out her hand, fingers pointing towards Sariah, thumb pointing up, as if she were wanting to shake hands.

Sariah looked at The Crow's outstretched hand for a moment before reaching out and grasping it with her own. "*Choose.*" Sariah felt the mark on her forehead burning. The ground dropped out from under her, and she was in a world of white.

Would she give up her life for Javier? Absolutely. Could she walk away from killing Darian to go back to him? She paused. She couldn't. She needed to stop this. This was bigger than herself. Bigger than her love for Javier. If left unchecked, Darian's rage and anger would spread across the world. So many people would die.

THE QUEEN'S LADY

Sariah thought of Luc, of the families in the farmhouses who had perished, the guards she knew as friends, the Ladies who were suffering in Langton. No. Darian would not get away with the atrocities he had committed. The scar on her throat began to burn as rage built inside of her. The moon brand on her forehead also burned more intensely.

The Crow appeared before Sariah in her human form in the world of white. "*You must choose.*" Her voice seemed to come from everywhere and nowhere at once. Sariah felt an immense pressure building, squeezing her body, making her bones groan under the pressure.

She cried out in pain. She couldn't take much more of this. "*CHOOSE!*" The Crow's voice was almost a scream in her head. Sariah felt her pain, her rage, and anguish peak. The pressure became unbearable. She reached out, and her hand clasped on the hilt of a sword. The pain stopped immediately. Before her world went black, she heard The Crow say, "The choice has been made."

Chapter Forty-One

When Sariah came to, she was splayed out on the floor of her room. Her head was pounding, and she felt like she had taken the worst beating of her life. The brand on her forehead still burned, and her throat was sore, but other than some pain, she didn't think anything was wrong with her.

She thought about what had happened- what The Crow said. Sariah wasn't sure what choice she had made, although the goddess apparently knew. Then she remembered the other part of what The Crow had said and she sat up. She held a hand to her head as the room spun, but she was able to stay upright, and she didn't vomit.

She had to take action. She had to figure out a plan so that she could have things in hand again when Javier arrived. She wouldn't risk him. Sariah stood up. The room wavered a bit, but didn't spin. Good. She was making progress.

She walked over to her wardrobe and pulled out the only thing that was in there- a black leather set of breeches, a tight black satin shirt that was part corset part vest, black bracers, black gloves, and finally, black knee-high boots. She knew this hadn't been in there the day before. She pulled on the breeches and started to put on the vest when she stopped to look at her arms.

Her once pale, toned arms were now covered in black tattoos. Starting at her shoulder and going down to her wrist, she had crows and runes, Celtic knots and words she couldn't read. She wondered in amazement at her arms for a moment before pulling the vest on over her head. The vest was sleeveless, showing off her arms. She tightened up the laces on the vest, noticing that it fit her like a glove.

She pulled on her boots and then opened her weapon stash. She stopped. All of her weapons were gone but one. A long handle with criss-crossed black leather over snow white, the guard of the sword was also black. The blade was slightly curved, and only sharpened on one edge. The tip was extremely sharp. There was no question what this weapon was for. It screamed violence.

Sariah walked over to the looking glass. She didn't know the woman looking back at her. Her once bright gray eyes were now black as night. Her moon brand had a slight blue ethereal glow about it. Her once long beautiful black hair was shorn off, cropped close to her head on the sides, and sticking up somewhat- slightly spiky on the top.

She slid her braces onto her forearms and laced them up tight. Finally, she pulled the black gloves on. She paused as she did so, noticing that her nails were longer and pointed, almost like claws. She flexed her hands a bit after she had pulled the gloves on, making sure that they would not impede her flexibility. She gave a couple of kicks in the new pants and boots as well, testing for the same thing.

Turning her gaze to the window, she saw that the sky was lightening with the dawn. She knew it was time to act. She walked over to the door of her room, and tried the handle. Locked, she growled in anger, and the door clicked as if a key had opened it.

She pushed the door open and stepped into the hall. Seeing as she didn't plan on coming back to her room, she left the door open and started down the hall. She was not walking so much as strutting or stalking. Each step she took made her hips sway, and her body had a sense of fluidity to it that she hadn't had before. Her body didn't feel sore anymore. In fact, she felt energized.

She didn't know where in the castle Darian was staying, but it didn't really matter. She was a predator stalking her prey. She knew she'd find him eventually.

The first guard she came to ordered her to halt. She cocked her head to one side studying him, wondering who *he* was to command *her*. She flicked her fingers out in a shooing motion. A blackish mist shot from her fingers, and the guard flew through the air and backwards, as if a very large force pushed him out of her way. Sariah smiled at the terrified look on the guard's face before he turned and ran away.

His armor striking the stone floor had caused a lot of noise. As she continued down the hallway, more guards came running towards her. She gave a flick of her fingers in their direction, and they flew into the walls, held there for a moment as she passed. She heard them hit the floor with a thud before they too, got up and ran off.

While amused at their fear, Sariah was not doing anything to outright harm the guards. She could if she needed to, but as long as they offered her no resistance as they fled in fear, she didn't need to harm them. She was after much bigger prey. She put her hand on the long hilt of her curved sword, which she had tied to her waist with a black satin ribbon. The feel of the hilt gave her comfort, and reminded her what she was doing this for.

While the guards kept coming for Sariah, she was able to dispatch them quickly, and without bloodshed. These men had families, and had really done nothing except bend to the will of a man they knew that they could not defeat. She meant them no ill will, and hoped that as she righted these wrongs, they'd turn back to a righteous path.

Sariah headed towards the Queen's Chambers. If Darian thought like she believed he did, she'd find him there- the heart of the castle. The center of its power. When she began seeing mercenaries, she knew she was on the right path.

The mercenaries did not scare as easily as the guards did. They were being paid, very well, to protect Lord Darian. Sariah had something bigger on her side though.

She curled her fingers into a clawed hand, and dragged it through the air, as if she were scratching something. The mercenaries shouted and one ripped open his shirt. Five long red welts were on his chest, as if Sariah had indeed reached out and scratched him. Another had welts down his face, and another his arm.

The men looked at each other and then growled at Sariah. They took off in a run towards her. She flicked her fingers to knock them back, and made the scratching motion in the air again. This time when the man with the open shirt looked down, he saw the welts had started bleeding. They burned as if hot. He cried out, and looked at Sariah with horror.

When the other men realized what had happened, they too turned scared faces towards the single woman standing across from them. She arched one brow at them and quirked her lips into a smile. The men's faces paled before they turned and ran from her.

Soon, the hallways were empty, Darian's men not willing to risk a confrontation with The Dark Lady. A few had run to the Queen's Chambers ahead of her to warn Lord Darian what was coming, and to urge him to leave the castle grounds. He refused, saying that a little bitch wouldn't chase him away from his spoils.

As Sariah walked down the hallway towards the chambers, she found no resistance. All of Darian's men had cleared out, including the ones who had come to warn him what was happening. Sariah lifted one booted foot and kicked the door in to the Queen's personal receiving room.

Stepping into the receiving room, Sariah cocked her head this way and that, observing the situation before her. The room was in complete disarray, the Queen's beloved couches overturned and broken, her books scattered all about the room, the lush rugs on the floor bunched and torn.

He had quite a temper on him did Lord Darian. She saw shattered pottery against the walls of the room where he had smashed mugs and dishes as things didn't go his way. Sariah raised an eyebrow at the room, observing it clinically. Something wasn't quite right about the state of the room, but she couldn't figure out exactly what it was.

She turned towards the door that led to the Queen's bedroom. This was somewhere that Sariah and the other Ladies had never been before. The Queen always met them in the outer room. She gently pushed open the door, not sure what she would find.

Stepping into the bedroom she found a large room with tastefully appointed furniture. But she smelled something not quite right. When she registered the smell, the image before her eyes flickered.

Sariah closed her eyes and took a deep breath, smelling sweat, blood, and fear. She opened her eyes to a completely different scene. The room was empty of furniture, but there were manacles and chains along the wall. The center of the room held racks of various weapons, and there were dark stains all over the floor.

Sariah clenched her jaw in anger. Several people were chained to the wall, male and female. They were completely nude, and they bore the marks of torture. She recognized two of her fellow Ladies, as well as one of the Queen's core guards. None of them were breathing. They had finally succumbed to the pain and suffering that had been inflicted upon them and they were finally free.

Sariah kicked over one of the racks of weapons, letting out an enraged scream. With her injured throat, the sound came out as something one would expect to hear beyond the grave. She whipped around and ran out of the torture chamber, having realized what bothered her about the receiving room.

She stalked the castle, checking every room, and finding it empty, or finding the remnants of the mercenaries' depravities. Sariah screamed in frustration as she stalked to the front of the castle. Walking through the front gates, she turned around and held both hands out. She swooped them down and then back up, as if she were scooping something up.

Soon, smoke appeared out of several of the castle's windows. Flames began to be visible in various parts of the castle as well. Sariah sat down hard on the ground, pulling her knees up in front of her. She sat there, prepared to wait as long as it took to watch the castle burn to the ground. She felt a gentle hand come down on her shoulder, and placed her hand on top of it.

That's how Javier found her that evening. She was sitting outside of the castle, now a smouldering pile of rubble, with The Crow standing just behind her, a hand on her shoulder.

Chapter Forty-Two

Hearing him approach, The Crow disappeared, and Sariah stood up, turning to face him. Javier stopped for a moment to take in her changed appearance before continuing forward. He took her face in his hands, and he kissed her.

Whatever Sariah had been expecting from him it certainly wasn't that. Tears sprung to her eyes as she returned his kiss with passion, wrapping her arms around him. Javier dropped his arms from her face, and pulled her to him, feeding all of his fear and anger into that kiss.

Sariah pulled back just a bit to look at him. She said nothing at first, just rubbed her hand across his brow and down his cheek. "I'm sorry."

He kissed her very gently, and then turned them away from the castle ruins. "Is it over?" The hope in his voice broke her a little bit.

She looked up at the men who had ridden with him on what turned out to be a fool's errand. She turned to Javier. "We have been deceived. We need to prepare for war. Let's go home, and I'll explain it all."

Javier nodded slowly at his warrior goddess before leading her to his horse. As was their custom, he mounted first and then helped her onto the horse. Unlike before though, this time she rode behind him with her arms around him. She wanted him to be able to hear all that she needed to say to him. "I don't know what way you came in, but leave by way of the farmlands. They're part of my tale."

Javier turned his horse in that direction, looking behind him to see that his generals followed suit.

The size of the small army surprised Sariah. She hadn't realized how big of a standing army Belrick had. But Lady Margaret was no fool. She had been reading between the lines for some time, and had been shoring up her defenses in case trouble came knocking.

Sariah began her telling with her thoughts as she left the manor, finishing with Javier finding her watching the remains of the castle burn. By the end he was stiff with anger. Sariah had a feeling some of that anger was directed at her, while a majority of it was directed at the guilty parties.

Javier informed her that they were going to head straight to the castle to meet with Lady Margaret so that she could be apprised of the situation and adjust her battle plans accordingly. Sariah nodded into his back, and then leaned her forehead into him, taking slow deep breaths so that she could revel in his scent.

She had never again expected to meet him in this life, so having her arms around him and being surrounded by his scent were a type of heaven for her.

As they rode, Sariah began thinking about what Lara had told her. Something didn't quite fit with the evidence that Sariah had just found. "We need to go to the Manor before the castle. I need to speak with Lara. It won't take long, I promise. I just need to get something clarified about what she told me."

When Javier and Sariah reached the manor, Sariah dismounted right away and told Javier to go ahead to the castle. She'd walk or take a different horse. Javier didn't like it, so, he sent the rest of the men on to the castle and he went inside with Sariah.

Sariah found Lara much as she had left her only a few days before. Still shocky, Lara at least was happy to see her friend back, since she thought that Sariah would die facing down Lord Darian. Sariah embraced her friend and sat down on the bed with her. Javier leaned against the wall near the door, not wanting to be in the way.

"Lara, I wanted to ask you some things about your account of what happened in Blackmore. Having just been there myself, some of what you said doesn't match what I found." When fear filled Lara's eyes, Sariah was quick to reassure her. "I don't believe you lied, do not fear that. I just don't know that I knew what to ask before."

Lara relaxed some, and waited for Sariah's questions. "You said that you were all arrested, and that the men who had led the revolt were executed. Did you see the executions?"

Lara shook her head in the negative. "We were immediately separated from the men. Myself and two of the Ladies were taken to one part of the castle and locked in a room. I don't know what happened to the other two. I just assumed the same. Later, we were taken out to the square. There were several men on the scaffolding, hanging... I turned away instantly. I didn't want to see Luc like that." Lara put her face in her hands and started crying softly.

Sariah put her arm around Lara, and leaned in closer. "Lara, I'm so sorry. I have one more question for you. Did you see how many men were in the square? This is very important." Sariah waited, not sure that Lara had heard her question.

"...Yes. There were four men hanging, and six already taken off the scaffolding, stacked up near it on the ground." She paused, realizing where Sariah was going with this. "They didn't bring anyone else out while we were in the square. If only ten had been executed, where did the other six guards go?"

The Queen had sixteen guards she assigned to her personal protection detail. They rotated in eight hour shifts, four guards on at a time. If Darian had only executed ten of Elliana's men, what did happen to the rest? She intended to find out.

Sariah turned to Javier and gave him a very serious look. They didn't know who had been executed and who was still alive. She turned back to her friend. "Lara, I cannot give you hope. I have a feeling that the guards who were not executed turned against you all. Luc was an honorable man. It is more likely that he is dead than turned traitor."

Lara nodded sadly. "He would never turn against me or his brother guards. He'd have come for me if he were still alive and able. I'm not counting on you finding him with the others."

Sariah hugged Lara and whispered in her ear, "I will avenge him for you." Lara hugged Sariah back very tightly. Sariah looked up at Javier with determination in her eyes.

Chapter Forty-Three

Javier and Sariah left Lara to sleep, and headed back out front where the horse was tethered. He was about to help her mount when he stopped. They had hardly gotten a moment alone since he found her near the rubble. He ran his fingers through her short hair. She rubbed her hand on the back of her neck, a little bit embarrassed. "I'm not sure how this happened. I woke up after dealing with The Crow, and found that my hair had been shorn. It will grow. I know it's not very elegant..."

Javier kissed her very passionately. "You are amazing. You are beautiful, and sexy, and I will never *not* want you. You are my warrior goddess, and I love you." He kissed her again, a bit longer this time. When they pulled away, they were both out of breath. "Now, let's go take care of this problem so that I can marry you and take you back to my bed." He gave her his evil grin, and she smiled back at him.

He cupped his hands, and she put her foot into it. He boosted her up onto the horse and climbed up behind her. She wanted his arms around her. She knew that she was more than capable of taking care of herself, especially with her new abilities, but it still felt good to be wanted.

Sariah looked up at the castle as they approached it. Where Blackmore castle had seemed forbidding, Castle Belrick was a fortress. It wasn't forbidding per se, but it was certainly imposing. The stone used to build it was so dark that it was almost black. And where Blackmore castle had sprawled, Castle Belrick towered. It was fairly narrow but extremely tall. It must have been at least fifteen floors to Blackmore's three.

The large wooden doors were at least two floors tall. They were banded with black iron, and they were stained almost black. "Well,

THE QUEEN'S LADY

Lady Margaret surely is making a statement, isn't she?" Sariah said sardonically.

Javier chuckled behind her. "She wasn't the one who built it to look like this, but she also hasn't changed it. Intimidation is a great mind game." Javier waved a hand to the left of the door, and the doors slowly started opening. She imagined that it took a lot of work and manpower to make those doors move.

Once the doors opened, Javier rode them through the entryway. Men called out to Javier in greeting as they moved through the courtyard. Near some stone steps at the entrance to the castle, Javier dismounted and held his arms out to Sariah to help her dismount as well. She let him help her down as she looked around at the small courtyard. Much like Blackmore castle, Castle Belrick had a small stable that could temporarily house mounts. He saw her looking at it and said, "The larger stable is around the side of the castle, in the woods. The horses that are bred here are things of beauty." Sariah smiled at Javier. He held out his arm to her and she took it. They strolled into the castle calmly, even though they both knew that the calm wouldn't last.

Sariah looked around as they walked through the castle. It reminded her a lot of Blackmore castle, but she imagined most stone castles looked similar. Javier occasionally looked over at Sariah as they walked, although he didn't speak. Sariah knew that they had a mission, and she knew that they were getting ready to meet with Lady Margaret to set the plan in motion. He turned towards a pair of double doors on their right and nodded to the guards on either side of the frame. When the door opened to a full court with Margaret and Heath sitting on silver thrones at the front of the room, she knew that there was no going back.

Sariah took a deep breath. "Ready?" Javier asked her.

She let the breath out slowly. "Ready." She held her head up regally as they walked through the throng of people sitting and standing in the room, looking at them as they passed. The walkway felt like it took forever, and at the same time felt like it took only moments. When they got to the front of the room, Sariah dropped to one knee, bowing her head. Javier stood behind her still. Luna fluttered down and sat on her shoulder, causing some gasps and exclamations from the crowd. No one was sure where the bird had come from.

"Please rise." Lady Margaret had a pleasant deep alto voice. She was indeed tall and slim, and where her brother was light, she was dark. Her hair was a dark mahogany, almost black, and her skin was tanned, almost the color of Javier's, but not quite. She had the same emerald green eyes of her brother though. And they were looking kindly upon Sariah.

"Lady Margaret. I thank you for offering your assistance in stopping the travesties that Lord Darian and Queen Elliana have unleashed on these lands." Sariah saw both Lord Heath and Lady Margaret start a bit at this. They had known the part that Lord Darian had played, but other than Sariah, Javier was the only one until this moment privy to the fact that Queen Elliana was only playing the part of the victim.

"Queen Elliana?" Margaret's voice was sharp, but not angry. Sariah had a feeling that she did not like being caught by surprise, and this indeed was a surprise.

"Yes. I had thought her to be a friend, and to be innocent in all of this. However, as I discovered yesterday when I entered the Queen's chambers in pursuit of Lord Darian that Elliana has not only been complicit in his doings, she has been orchestrating quite a few of the incidents herself. Her bedroom was a torture chamber, where she had taken the lives of two of her Ladies and one of her guards. There was much old blood underneath the fresh, so these are not the first lives lost at her hands." Sariah paused, still upset at seeing former friends treated with such disregard of human life.

She opened her mouth but stopped. What she was about to say was going to irrevocably change the world as they all knew it. She looked down for a moment, gathering her thoughts. When she looked back up, she saw that the entire room was frozen, including Javier. The Crow walked out from behind Margaret and Heath's thrones.

"You carry my mark and my blade. You do not need this war. You and Javier can take care of Elliana and Darian yourselves. You can save the lives of so many." The Crow had perched herself with an arm draped over the top of one of the thrones, thrusting her hip out. "You are above the doings of man, as the scion of a goddess. Javier has given himself to me as your protector and companion. He is not without skill, and if you ask it of me, I will grant him additional powers as well."

Sariah frowned, her brow wrinkling. "At what cost did he offer himself? And at what cost will you give the additional powers? Morrigan, you have done nothing but move me as if I were your pawn on a chessboard. Why should I listen to you? Why should I trust you?" She was angry at The Crow. So very angry.

The Crow smiled at her, but it was more of a flash of teeth than a pleasant smile. "Careful, girl. You walk a thin line with me."

Sariah waved her hand in dismissal of what The Crow had said. "What are you going to do, kill me? I was already dead! You pulled me from death and brought me back to a world crumbling with violence. You then had me relive my death so I could what? Become a stronger *plaything* for you?"

The Crow stalked forward and slapped Sariah's face. Sariah just whipped her head back towards The Crow, even angrier than before. "You deserved that and you know it. Yes, I could do a lot worse, but why? You are my link here to the mortal world. You *never* have been a 'plaything' for me. In fact, I really only want your happiness. The happier you are, the longer we have to bond. The more that we bond, the longer that I get to stay in the mortal world."

Sariah's voice cracked, and tears filled her eyes. "Why did it have to be me? Why do I have to be the one to have lost friends and have seen such atrocities?" She fell to her knees, her hands up on her thighs almost as in supplication.

"Oh, my dear. There has always been evil in the world, and there always will be. It's only good people like you who cannot bear to see injustice, and who stand up for right in the face of evil that the world still turns." The Crow gently placed her hand on the top of Sariah's head. "You need to decide how you want to handle this. If you want to manage it yourself, just take Javier's hand, and he will unfreeze with you. Then you two can leave, and go after Darian and Elliana. If you wish to still involve the armies of Belrick, I cannot stop you, and I won't. Just wait a few moments after I leave, and the room will unfreeze as a whole. I will be watching your choice, so that I can keep the room frozen if you choose to handle things on your own. You will need to decide quickly, so…" and with that, The Crow disappeared.

Sariah quickly dried her eyes, stood up, and took Javier's hand. He unfroze and looked around him before raising a brow in question at Sariah. She just shook her head, and pulled him towards the door. He went with her without a fight, showing her just how much he trusted her. "Change of plans, then?" He asked her as she raced back through the castle, trying to get to the entrance and back to their horse.

"Well, I'd say yes, but since I've never really had a plan, I can't say that it's ever changed." He snorted at her quip and just followed her out of the castle and to their horse.

"Well, I take it we're not starting a war today." He climbed up on the horse, and helped pull her up behind him.

"No. While we were in there, The Crow came to me. She reminded me of who I am, and that I do not need the assistance of 'mere humans.'" she put emphasis on those last two words, also affecting an upper-crust accent to go with it. "She said that as her scion, with your help, I should have no problem taking care of them myself." She tucked her head against his back. "I, uh, well, she smacked me at one point too."

Javier pulled up on the reins sharply and turned to look at Sariah. "What did you do to piss her off that badly?" The look on his face was one of both horror and pride in equal measure.

"I may have insinuated... well, no. I need to be honest, I blatantly accused her of treating us like her playthings. She told me I was walking a thin line, and so I mouthed off some more. She wasn't fond of that." Sariah hid her grin in his back, but she couldn't hide the sound of it from her voice.

He laughed, and started the horse back on the road. "She told you then, didn't she? What I am to you now?" He sounded almost uncertain, as if he was afraid of Sariah's reaction.

"She did. And I thank you sincerely for that, as I assume it gives you similar longevity to me, but, what did you give up for it? She said she asked nothing of you, but I find that hard to believe. Gods are fond of bargains." She really wanted to believe that The Crow told the truth, but she was having a hard time with that thought.

"Nothing. And she didn't offer it. I had to convince her of it. I cursed her name up and down until she came to me after you left for Blackmore. I told her I was going after you and that you were mine. She knows how we feel about each other, and told me that she thought two bull-headed people such as us are perfect for each other. Then I told her I wanted to be with you always, and if she did not allow me to be, I would take you from her. I was not joking, and she saw that. So, she came around to my idea, and made me your companion and protector. Now you can't get away from me." Just like she had, he was putting humor into his story. She had a feeling that if they didn't, their brains would catch up with the fact that they were angering a god and they would curl up into little balls sucking their thumbs.

Chapter Forty-Four

Sariah felt a sense of foreboding as they rode closer to Langton. They had a goddess on their side, but they were facing evil- The Crow confirmed it. She put her hand on the hilt of the blade the goddess had gifted her. She knew that there was something special about this blade. She also knew that she needed to wield it with justice in mind, and not vengeance. She needed to stay level-headed, and do her job. Her anger would be her enemy.

She and Javier were quiet as they rode, both deep in their own heads. Sariah didn't want to overthink what she was about to do, but at the same point in time, she felt that she needed some type of plan. She knew that Elliana and Darian would be expecting an army, and when it was just the two of them that showed up, they would become overconfident.

As they got closer to Langton, they began to smell smoke. They looked at each other with concern on their faces. A short time later they were able to see smoke in the sky. So much smoke that the sky over Langton looked black. Sariah thought back to the farmhouses in Blackmore and had a bad feeling in the pit of her stomach.

When they crossed the border into Langton, they were in lush forests, but the air was thick with the smell of burning. The air started turning hazy the closer they got to the castle, and Darian's seat of power. Sure enough, as they started passing buildings, everyone that they came to was burning. "They are burning all the buildings and crops so that our army can't use them against them. They don't think they can win against us...." Javier's voice trailed off as he saw the scene at the first farmhouse they came across. Darian's men had definitely been there and burned the home and outbuildings. They also left no survivors, animal or human. There was carnage spread across the lawn for all to see.

"They're mad! Anyone who could sanction this to anyone, much less their own citizens..." Sariah's voice trailed off, thinking of the farmhouses again. "No. This wasn't Darian. This was Elliana. She is the one who sanctioned these killings. She's taking over his land with raw power. The mercenaries have become hers now."

Javier didn't argue her point. She was so sure of what she was saying, and she had been at Blackmore those last few days. She knew what was going on here. She looked away from the scene at the farmhouse, and from there on out, kept her face forward. Javier would slow a bit at each homestead they came to, in hopes that they would hear someone call out that they could potentially help, but there was no one alive to call out.

Langton was a very large country, about the size of Belrick and Blackmore combined. It was long, but not very wide. Unfortunately for Javier and Sariah, the castle lay at the point furthest south, along a sea coast. It was an easily defensible position, and one that had not been breached in recent memory.

As they got deeper into the country, they did begin to see signs of life, which was a good thing. If Elliana had burned all of the homesteads, there would be no one left for the mad couple to rule. The smoke was still heavy even though homes had not been burned, since the mercenaries and what was left of Elliana's army were still burning the fields.

Sariah and Javier decided to test the new abilities that The Crow gave them by not stopping to rest. And sure enough, they didn't feel the need to. The exhaustion that would have plagued them before never seemed to set in, even as they rode deep into the night.

The night was particularly treacherous for the pair since the milky air became opaque in the dark, and allowed for almost no sight beyond a few inches in front of, behind, or to the side of the horse they rode on. Since Javier was steering the horse, Sariah had her hand on the hilt of her sword, waiting to wield it at any threat directed against them. The only good part about the smoke was that snipers and bowmen would likewise be afflicted by the limited visibility.

Sariah heard something in the smoke just behind the horse. She tapped Javier to the lower right side of his back, letting him know that there was something following them to their right flank. She could not see whoever or whatever it was, but she could tell it was there. When she heard the growl, she relaxed. Wolves were no threat to her and Javier, and she knew they were out scavenging the dead.

She did not let down her guard, even knowing that it was just a wolf following her, and she was glad she didn't. It allowed her to bat the throwing knife out of the air that would have otherwise sunk deep into her shoulder. She jumped off of the horse, and crouched down, quickly moving towards the direction the knife was thrown from. She didn't know if Javier had stopped or if he was following her, but she knew that she could not let this violence slide.

She pulled her sword free of her belt, and stopped where she was, listening. While the person who threw the knife was quiet, they were not the only one of the party, and someone rustled the grass where they had camped down. Sariah inched her way in that direction, and when she was close enough that she could make out their forms in the smoke, she took a breath and swung her sword out, feeling it connect with flesh, but slice through like butter. A scream of pain was quickly cut off with another swing of the blade. The last man there was on his knees whimpering, praying that whatever demon had come for them would let him live. If she had not recognized him from the mercenaries she had seen in the main hall of Blackmore, she might have granted his prayer. Instead, she made quick work of him, exacting justice on the trio for the blood spilled in Blackmore.

Sariah quickly turned back towards where she had left Javier. She heard a gentle tapping noise, and realized that he was tapping his fingers on the saddle horn, giving her a direction in case she got lost in the smoke. Once she was far enough away from the remains, she heard growling and tearing. The wolves would feast tonight.

Chapter Forty-Five

When Sariah reached Javier, he didn't speak, just reached a hand down to help pull her up behind him. They rode on through the night with few other interruptions. Come morning, the smoke seemed to have lessened some. Javier thought he remembered from maps he'd seen of the country that the closer one got to the castle and coast, the fewer farms there were. Sariah thought that must be right, since it had been a while since she'd seen the glow of flames, and the breeze was much more prevalent here.

They were a bit concerned that as the smoke cleared they'd become easier targets for anyone looking for them, but since Sariah had only met that one small group of mercenaries, they thought that maybe Elliana and Darian were concentrating their forces at the castle. Sariah knew that she was capable of handling multiple assailants, but she had no idea what Javier's new abilities would allow him to do. Since they were so exposed and vulnerable she didn't want to ask him. But in order to accurately make a plan, they would need to have some idea of what the other was capable of.

Sariah leaned forward as if she were tired, and needing to rest against Javier. She tilted her head so that anyone looking at her would not be able to tell she was speaking. Keeping her voice extremely low, she asked, "I believe The Crow gave you some new abilities as we left Castle Belrick. I don't know if you had received any previously. Would you have any idea what these could be or what they would allow you to do?"

Javier hmmed as if enjoying having his lady leaning against him. He bumped his shoulder gently before saying, "Come now, love. We'll be there soon, and I'm not sure that I know all of the customs of the locals. A pretty face is sure to help us along." Parsing what he said, the best Sariah could figure was that he wasn't sure what he would be able to do, and he also wasn't sure what exactly she would be able to do. Well, great. Once again, they were going to manage this by the seat of their pants. Sariah mentally shrugged. Oh well, at least that had worked out for them so far.

As the sun started to set, Sariah got her first whiff of what she assumed was ocean air. She smelled wet, and fish, and salt. Having grown up on the banks of a lake, she knew the first two. The last she supposed, is what made the difference in enjoying a sea coast to a lake. The breeze had also picked up, and cleared away the last of the smoke. The land was getting rockier and somewhat hillier, and the ground was sandier with longer and sharper grasses. Sariah knew that they had to be very close now.

Javier reached a hand back and squeezed her thigh. She perked up at this, looking around. At first she saw nothing, but as they crested a ridge, she saw what had caused him to get her attention. They were headed into a very small fishing village. The streets were empty, and it looked quite deserted. However, they heard the bark of a dog which was quickly cut off, and they heard a door slam shut. There were people in the village, but they were staying put. Sariah wondered what lies had been spread through the village about them, and if they were walking into an ambush. She saw where she would have mercenaries hiding if she were Elliana and Darian, and yet they had done nothing that Sariah or Javier had expected so far.

Sariah leaned in close to Javier, "I don't know if they'll do it, but I would put mercenaries in the tavern for sure. Maybe the chapel up the way as well." She was barely whispering. He nodded his head slowly, as if he was just plodding along with his horse. He saw and agreed. Sariah closed her eyes, trying to listen for anything that might give away an ambush. She heard nothing, but the village was too still, too calm. Something wasn't right.

She cried out to Javier just as she saw the razor wire come up. He was able to duck his head, catching just a bit of his temple on it. Blood ran down his face from the cut. Sariah got extremely angry at seeing that blood. Her vision turned red, and she jumped off the horse, headed towards the side of the wire closest to her. She found a single man there, and dealt with him swiftly, throat punching him and cutting off his oxygen. Turning to look at the other side of the street, she saw that the wire was tied off, and there was no one on the other side. His eyes rolled to the left, looking for help, which is what she had been waiting for. She stabbed him with her sword, and moved on.

Javier had hopped off the horse as well, and was crouching near a building, holding some cloth to his head to stop the bleeding. She motioned that she was moving ahead and to the left, and he nodded, staying where he was. Sariah was in an alley, and she pressed her back against the building she was using for cover. She inched forward, thanking The Crow for providing her with quiet boots. She ducked under a window, wishing it had been open to see if anyone was inside. But it was shuttered tightly, and so she was forced to move on. She was breathing slowly and evenly, keeping her calm.

She saw that the alley ended a few steps ahead, and she had a decision to make. She could either turn to see if they were holed up in the building she was leaning against, or, she would be vulnerable in the street. She took a quiet deep breath and let it out slowly. She licked her lips, stalling a bit to ready herself. She quickly rounded the corner to her right, spotting the door of the building and kicking it in. She chose wisely, as she found ten or more armed men inside the building drinking and laying about. Quickly pulling her arms back to her shoulders, she flung them forward, flicking her fingers as they outstretched.

Grey smoke shot from her palms, filling the room, and pressing the men to their chairs or the floor, wherever they had been resting.

Sariah took in the men in front of her, recognizing mercenaries and some of Elliana's soldiers. The men were unable to move their bodies but rolled their eyes in her direction in terror. She had moments to decide what to do with them. Since she didn't recognize any of them, she gave a flick of their wrist, and their heads smacked firmly into tables and floors, knocking them all unconscious. She would not condemn men for the company they kept if she had no proof of their wrongdoing.

She stuck around a moment to make sure no one was still awake before heading out of the door. She stuck close to buildings, peeking her head around corners as she made her way back to Javier. She was very close to getting back to him when, coming around a corner, she came very close to having her head taken off. A large axe swung in her direction, burying its blade deep into the side of the building she was leaning against. She quickly rolled forward, taking out the legs of the man wielding the weapon.

Even though the man was huge, probably the biggest man she'd ever seen, he managed to avoid her leg swipe, and landed a blow to her head with one of his large fists. She felt like she'd been kicked in the head by a horse! She knew that many more hits from him would disable her, so she quickly scrambled away and got to her feet.

She was glancing around quickly, to make sure no one else was coming at her, and, seeing no one, she flicked her wrist at the hulking form before her. He went flying into a building, smacking his head hard on the ground when he landed. He didn't get up, and she didn't move closer to check on him.

Hearing the commotion so close, Javier rounded the corner, alleviating her need to continue searching for him. He looked from the prone form to Sariah and raised an eyebrow but said nothing. The bleeding on his head had stopped she was grateful to see. "We need to get out of this death trap." She sounded somewhat winded, and had a sheen of sweat on her brow.

"Oh, come now, it's not all that bad. I thought we could return here for our honeymoon." He gave her one of his wicked grins as he swung his leg over the horse and settled into the saddle. Reaching down for her hand, he winked at her and said, "wouldn't it be fun to relive such great times?" she groaned at him in exasperation as he kicked his heels and they quickly rode out of the fishing village.

Chapter Forty-Six

They could see the castle from the road. It was built up into a rocky hillside that led straight down to the sea. When Javier had said it was a good defendable position, she hadn't pictured this. Approaching the castle from the road would be suicide. They'd be prime targets for archers, and could easily be flanked from the fishing village.

To approach it from any direction was really going to be a nightmare, but the best chance they'd have is to lose the horse, and come in from the west where there was some vegetation that they could use as cover. Sariah was suddenly thankful for the leather gloves she had with her. She didn't mind climbing, as long as she wasn't going to cut her fingers and hands up in the process.

"The West?" She asked Javier, wondering if he had spotted something she hadn't.

He sighed. "The West." He was muttering something under his breath that she couldn't quite catch. She left it alone, figuring that if it were really important, he'd tell her what she needed to know.

They headed west and very loosely tied the horse to a tree. It would let the horse know that they wanted it to stay there, but if it needed to go for some reason, one good pull and the horse would be free. Sariah took one last look at the horse, the only tie to their life back in Belrick, and turned towards the castle.

Knowing that they were expected (they had seen a messenger from the village head up to the castle), they were quickly and stealthily making their way across the field towards the castle. With the constant breeze, they were able to get down on their bellies and crawl through the grass like snakes. The breeze would hide any movement they would create.

With her sleeveless shirt, Sariah's arms were scratched and bleeding in several places by the time they reached the rocks. She frowned at the scratches, and then turned to the task at hand.

The side of the castle they chose had a rock face about three times the height of Javier. Not impossible, but not easy, either. The rocks were craggy and good for climbing, but the breeze that hid them in the grass was much stronger this close to the castle.

Sariah looked nervously at the rocky waves over the side of the cliff before taking a deep breath and jumping in place a few times. She pulled on her gloves and looked over at Javier who gave her a weak thumbs up before turning to the rock face himself.

Sariah lost herself in the climb. It was a short climb, but with the wind pushing her around, and the potential fall if she slipped wrong, she wanted all of her concentration on what she was doing.

After what seemed like an eternity, she pulled herself up over a narrow ledge to the wall of the castle. She looked down and saw that Javier was right behind her. He was sweating profusely and had a green tinge to his normally dusky coloring.

As soon as he lifted himself onto the ledge, he leaned over and vomited. "Are you alright?" Sariah was very concerned for Javier.

"Heights. It had to be heights." Sariah chuckled, leaned over and kissed his cheek.

"You'll be fine in a few moments. You made it. Now all we have to do is break down the front door, and we're in." She said this with far more confidence than she felt. The task seemed monumental. But she needed to do it. She looked up at the sky and saw a crow flying nearby. Knowing that The Crow was with them made her feel a lot better.

They rested just for a moment before making their way around the castle wall on the narrow ledge. Both Sariah and Javier looked up regularly to make sure they hadn't been spotted by any archers. The castle wall was round, something Sariah had never experienced before but was extremely grateful for. There were no corners to manage.

They finally reached the edge of the road leading to the castle doors. Sariah saw the small windows archers usually aimed out of, but she didn't see any signs of any archers. Just in case, she flicked her fingers towards the windows, hoping that she could knock any archers back that could be hiding. Hearing nothing and seeing no arrows being shot at them, they quickly moved to the doors.

The doors were made to open outwards, and there were no handles or anything to grab onto to pull the doors open. Sariah was pondering their next move when Javier stepped back a few paces, and looked up at the doors.

He threw an arm out, his hand closed as if he were grasping something. Sariah saw translucent grey smoky ropes going into the doors. He held the ends of these ropes in one hand, and as he pulled, the door shuddered. He leaned back a little, pulling harder, the muscles in his arm flexing and straining as he pulled the smoke ropes. The door finally gave way, but he was going to have to hold it open while she slipped in to see if she could find a way to get him inside.

As soon as she was inside, the smoke ropes snapped, and the door closed behind her. She looked at the door to see if there was any way to open it from her side when she heard the creak of a bowstring being pulled back. Sariah suddenly knew why there had been no archers on the walls- they were all waiting for her in the entryway of the courtyard just beyond the door.

They had hoped to trap her and threaten her into submission. She arched a brow at them, but held still, not giving an inch. Some of the archers started shifting nervously, wondering why she didn't surrender. They had no idea who they were dealing with.

Chapter Forty-Seven

In a move that was almost becoming second nature to her, Sariah tossed her arms out, flicking her fingers in the direction of the archers. All of their bows flew out of their hands, splintering into tiny fragments of wood that landed behind them. Another flick, and not an arrow was left for them to use. "You can run away now." She said in a bored tone.

By the time the first man rushed her, she had her blade out and was swinging it with deadly accuracy. His body landed on the floor just past her, his momentum carrying him to rest on the courtyard floor in front of the door.

Sariah felt her brand burning, and knew that she wasn't alone. Three men rushed her at once, daggers drawn, but she made quick work of them, her blade flashing so fast it was hard to see. They joined their brother on the floor in eternal sleep.

Sariah turned her eyes on the last couple of archers, her patience worn thin. "*WHERE ARE THEY?!*" The two archers jumped at her bellow and pointed towards the doors leading into the castle itself. "Let my companion in and tell him where I've gone. Then you may leave. I have no quarrel with you as long as you show me no violence." The men nodded vigorously, and rushed to do as she had bid.

Knowing it would take them a while to get the doors open, Sariah strode to the doors that would take her into the castle, her blade still unsheathed. These doors pushed inward, which could allow someone to hide behind them and ambush her. Her lips quirked in a smile at the idea. She was just getting warmed up.

She kicked the doors with the full force of her fury, and they slammed open, smacking the men behind them into the stone walls. She pushed her hands backwards towards the doors, and heard the men groan under the pressure of the wood pushing them into stone. Making sure the doors would hold like that, Sariah moved deeper into the castle.

She had no idea where she would find Darian and Elliana, she headed towards where she believed the main hall or great hall should be. She knew them well enough to know that anything they staged and any standoff they'd planned would be a showy and dramatic one. The main or great hall would create the perfect stage for them.

Sariah encountered zero resistance as she stalked through the maze of hallways. Either word of her new abilities were making the rounds, or her prey stacked their last line of defense at the scene of their final stand. She was betting on the latter. More dramatic that way.

As she turned a corner, she found herself facing a hallway with several barricades strewn about it. Made of broken furniture from the castle, Sariah assumed that they were supposed to slow her down in case she were to be ambushed. She scoffed at the feeble attempt to keep her away from her target.

She made a shooing motion with her hands, and the wooden barricades shot up into the air and held at the ceiling. The men who had been hiding behind them looked up at the items in fright before turning wide eyes to her. "Boo." She said in a completely deadpan voice. The guards took off, running around her and not looking back.

She walked up to the doors of the great hall. Their handles were perfectly spaced for her to grab them and throw the doors open so that she could stalk in. Sure enough, Darian and Elliana had set quite the scene. She was on a raised dais sitting upon a golden throne. They wore crowns of golden bones. Blood dripped from the dais onto the floor.

At the base of the dais lay Luc. Darian stood over him with a knife, slicing shallow cuts across Luc's exposed skin. He was chained up naked, so there was a lot of room for Darian to work with. Sariah's vision turned red.

"Bow before your queen!" Sariah turned her eyes on Elliana. The Queen flinched, and Sariah smiled, showing her teeth. Realizing what she had done, Elliana stood up before her throne, and looked down upon Sariah, smirking. She felt she had won, since she made herself taller and better able to look down on those beneath her.

Sariah rushed forward and swung her blade, taking Darian's head off in one smooth stroke. Using the momentum from her charge, she leapt onto the dais and started towards Elliana.

Elliana started backing away, seeing for the first time just how much Sariah had changed. Sariah followed her, keeping her eyes on Elliana's every move. Stalking her. "What's the matter, Elliana?" Sariah's tone was mocking. "You trained us to be perfect killers. You sent us out on missions for you, making us believe that we were in the right when we needed to take a life. Are you unable to face what you've *created*?!" The last word roared out of Sariah's mouth.

Elliana made a small sound of distress in her throat. It fueled Sariah's rage. All of a sudden, Javier rushed through the door. Seeing the state Luc was in, he rushed over to him, ripping his shirt off, and applying pressure to the cuts that were bleeding the worst. Sariah looked at her love for a moment before turning back to Elliana.

"You almost cost me *everything*!" Elliana flinched again at the venom in Sariah's voice. Sariah held up her blade, pointing it in Elliana's direction. Liquid smoke dripped from the blade of the sword, seemingly fueled by the anger and hatred that Sariah held for this woman that she thought of once almost as a sister.

The Crow popped into existence behind the Queen. "*Choose.*" Sariah growled at the goddess. "*You must choose.*"

Sariah stopped moving forward, and looked over at Javier and Luc. Javier looked at Sariah very solemnly. He would not make this choice for her. It was hers to make.

Sariah thought of all the lives lost because of this woman. All of the trauma that she caused. She lifted her blade and growled. "*You must choose.*" The goddess said again behind the Queen.

Sariah thought of the gardens at Belrick. Of Javier making love to her in their bed. Of seeing the look on Lara's face as she was reunited with her husband. Sariah felt a spark inside of her and her vision changed. Her laying in bed with Javier, his face close to her very pregnant belly as their little one kicked inside of her. Her daughter playing with Luc and Lara's son in the gardens at Belrick. Her walking hand in hand with Javier at sunset, kissing him, and pressing his hand to her flat belly, letting him know that life was growing in her again.

Sariah opened her eyes with a gasp. The world seemed to be holding still, waiting for her to make her choice. Sariah brought the blade up, and in one stroke, took off Elliana's head in a blinding blue flash. "Justice is done for the ones you've wronged." The Crow smiled at Sariah and disappeared as Sariah collapsed, her world going dark.

Epilogue

Sariah felt the satin linens below her and smiled. They smelled of Javier. She reached for him, but found that he wasn't in bed with her. Frowning, she sat up, pulling the blanket over her breasts.

The door to their suite pushed open and two little girls ran in the room giggling. They jumped into bed with Sariah and snuggled up to her. "And just what do we think we're doing, young ladies?" Sariah said with mock disapproval. Then she reached down and tickled them, their bellies, their necks, their ribs, their feet, anywhere she could reach.

The girls wiggled all around the bed with giggles and false indignant shrieks of, "Mommy!" She showered them each with kisses as Javier came through the door carrying a tray.

"You three make a pretty picture! Is there room for one more?" A chorus of yeses made him smile, and he sat the tray down on the nightstand, jumping into bed across all three of them. This sent the girls into a new round of giggles before Javier chased them off. "Go see cook for your breakfast, and let me kiss your momma in peace."

The girls jumped off the bed with pretend shrieks of "Ew!" as they ran out of the room. Sariah waved a hand and the door shut behind them. A flick of her fingers, and it was locked.

Javier raised an eyebrow at her suggestively, and with a wave of his hand, all of the candles in the room lit up. He leaned down and stroked his hand across his wife's short hair before running it down her cheek and lower to cup her breast. He leaned down and kissed her passionately, as he had every morning since she chose him over her revenge.

Acknowledgements

Firstly, I need to thank my husband, for supporting me in all of the crazy things I do, and loving me unconditionally. You're the one I get to annoy most forever. I love you.

Next, I would like to thank my girls, for giving me all of the love, and keeping my imagination running wild. Without you guys, I'd have no need to daydream.

I would also like to thank my best friend, Liz, who kept pushing me to complete this novel so that they could read the whole thing. Without you, this book would never have come into reality. I love you! I'd like to thank my friend Bethany, who helped me to see that my book was valuable in the bookstore world.

I would also like to thank those family and friends who helped proofread and edit this novel: my Aunt Karin, and Kirsten. Thank you for all of your help and time.

Finally, to my partner in crime, and one of the best friends a girl could know, my sister, Sarah. You named Luna, and like Luna is for Sariah, you're always there for me. Thank you.

About the Author

Laura Henning is married with two young girls and three cats. She has a bad habit of scheduling herself to the gills, and escaping her schedule in fantasy books- of her own mind as well as other authors.

Laura writes fantasy and urban fantasy books, which feature strong women and lots of action. Check her out on Instagram @laurahenningauthor

Read more at instagram.com/laurahenningauthor.

www.ingramcontent.com/pod-product-compliance
Lightning Source LLC
Jackson TN
JSHW082156110325
80588JS00004B/6